W9-CJQ-430

Praise for the Outremer series:

"The praise that greeted Chaz Brenchley's *Tower of the King's Daughter* in hardback was considerable, with particular praise being lavished on the prose . . . here was a fantasy sequence to rival the most impressive in the genre . . . Atmosphere is . . . conjured with tremendous skill in this book, never, however, allowing it to swamp the adroit plotting . . . This is fantasy exactly as it should be: ambitious, highly coloured, and supremely confident in its grip on the reader's kingdom . . . From its first confident chapter . . . Brenchley's grasp of his colourful narrative never falters, and his descriptive powers are exemplary." —*Orbit*

"The intensity verges on horror at times . . . Compelling reading." —*Locus*

"Chaz Brenchley's striking new epic fantasy series [is] a revelation. The atmosphere is so well described you can almost taste it." —*Starburst*

"A refreshing (and necessary) change . . . The recipient of a British Fantasy Society award, Mr. Brenchley [has] a never less than skillful style and turn of phrase . . . Along the way there are all the adventures a discerning fantasy reader could wish for and Brenchley's concise, muscular prose makes the story flow, free of genre clichés . . . Recommended." —*SFX Magazine*

"Drama and spectacle to spare. Brenchley's prose is clear and vivid . . . His ability to integrate the magical and uncanny into his more grittily realistic portrait of life on the outposts of Empire grounds his fantasy in a wealth of believable detail . . . thorough and striking . . . captures with brutal verisimilitude the harshness of life within a despotic religious/military community . . . Brenchley the horror novelist and Brenchley the fantasist come together in perfect alignment . . . the kind of dark, painful power rarely seen in the literature of heroic fantasy." —*Cemetery Dance*

"As with all Brenchley's novels, the prose is beautifully crafted and a joy to read . . . I can't wait to see what happens next." —*Northern Review*

Also by Chaz Brenchley

The Books of Outremer:
THE DEVIL IN THE DUST
TOWER OF THE KING'S DAUGHTER
A DARK WAY TO GLORY
FEAST OF THE KING'S SHADOW
HAND OF THE KING'S EVIL
THE END OF ALL ROADS

Visit the series website at
www.outremer.co.uk

TOWER OF THE KING'S DAUGHTER

The Second Book of Outremer

CHAZ BRENCHLEY

ACE BOOKS, NEW YORK

TOWER OF THE KING'S DAUGHTER

An Ace Book / published by arrangement with
the author

PRINTING HISTORY
Orbit first edition / 1998
Orbit reprint edition / 2000
Ace mass-market edition / July 2003

Copyright © 1998 by Chaz Brenchley.
Cover art by John Howe.
Cover design by Rita Frangie.
Text design by Julie Rogers.

For information address: Orbit,
a division of Little, Brown and Company (UK),
Brettenham House, Lancaster Place, London WC2E 7EN.

ISBN: 0-441-01080-6

ACE®
Ace Books are published by The Berkley Publishing Group,
a division of Penguin Group (USA) Inc.,
375 Hudson Street, New York, New York 10014.
ACE and the "A" design
are trademarks belonging to Penguin Group (USA) Inc.

PRINTED IN THE UNITED STATES OF AMERICA

10 9 8 7 6 5 4 3 2 1

Best things come in big packages.
The start of something this big,
it has to be for Ian.

For they have wrongfully seized
   his fiefdoms,
At which we should surely
   grieve;
For this is where God was first
   served
And recognised as Lord.

—CRUSADER SONG,
ANON, C. 1143

ONE

The Heat of Judgement

THE SLAMMING OF the castle's gates at his back, at his naked back should have been the sound of doom, disaster. It should have been the echo of a lifetime's failure: betrayal of his father, betrayal of his God. He had come to the Sanctuary Land in chase of a dream, a legacy of faith; he had given his life in service to the Ransomers, and they had cast him out. He should have died instead; he should have wished to die.

He did wish to die, perhaps, in some secret inner place he could not look at. Perhaps he only raised his head to see the road that would take him there, the place where he could meet death and be grateful.

He raised his head and saw the road, and saw who stood there waiting; and the booming echo of the slamming gates, the doom and the betrayal were all shadows flung behind him as shadows should be, by the light ahead.

* * *

SIEUR ANTON HAD brought clothes out with him, tunic and breeches and soft boots, begged or bought from another knight's squire.

"Sieur, thank you . . ."

"Don't," the knight said. "Not yet. I lied to the court, Marron; you will find my discipline at least as stern as theirs, and no easier. If you can't practice obedience to me, I will have no use for you; and I won't keep you simply for your own sake."

"I can obey you, sieur," simply, honestly, from the heart, "and I will."

"We'll see. Here." Soft bread and an apple pressed into his hands, the good and the bad, and if this was Sieur Anton's discipline. Marron wanted more of it, a lifetime's more. "Eat, and listen. You are my squire, given and sworn; you can sleep with the other squires and the servants, or you can sleep in my room as you have before. Either way will cause you trouble, because of whom you serve. That choice I leave to you."

"Sieur, if I sleep with you—"

"In my room, Marron."

"Yes, sieur—may I pray with you also, at the hours?"

"I would insist on it. Is that your choice, then?"

"Please, sieur."

"Good. You will suffer for it, I warn you now; but that cannot be avoided."

Neither apparently was it going to be explained, but Marron wasn't worried. He thought squires and servants could teach him nothing now about suffering; he thought life itself had little more to show him.

"One last thing. There is to be a ceremony of sacrament in the stable yard, after the brothers have taken their supper. That will not be easy for you either, but regard it as the first test of your service: you must be there."

"Sieur, where you go . . ."

"Hmm. Within limits, I trust. I shall be there, but we cannot stand together. Stay it out, Marron, that is all. It is needful. Now eat. I am not accustomed to repeating my-self."

Nor was he likely accustomed to having his servants speak to him with their mouths full, which was why Mar-ron had been standing with his hands held rigidly at his sides. Only his nose was twitching with an ill discipline, alert as always to any scent of food after a fast, while his mouth ran wet and his words slurred.

"Yes, sieur. No, sieur . . ." *Whatever you like, sieur,* so long as Marron could tear and chew and swallow, bite and savour as though the wolf in his stomach were arbiter over his head also, and ruled his manners.

He heard the knight laughing, and didn't mind that now. Neither was he anxious about what might come this evening, despite Sieur Anton's warnings. He was brother no more; the Order had no direct authority over him now, only through the authority it had over his master—what authority Sieur Anton had elected to give it—and it was always careful in its dealings with the knights. What harm could be done him, if he stood through another rite? A ceremony of sacrament: that might mean anything. His own profession had been a sacrament; so was confession, and a man's last prayer before a priest, and any number of little rituals between. It was kind of Sieur Anton to be concerned, but not necessary . . .

SO HE THOUGHT, young and hungry as he was, young and forgetful. Until he stood in the yard among the other squires—who were already nudging and whispering, giving him dishonest words of welcome then crushing back to make an uncomfortable space for him to stand in—while Sieur Anton was drawn up among the knights, each of them shining in their white in the torchlight. One man in every ten held a torch, masters and knights and brothers drawn up in their ranks; so many shadows flick-ered and danced across his eyes it was hard to see anything clearly, but still Marron could see more than he liked or wanted.

The Order stood in its order around that mound of wood, the squires and other servants squeezed in where they could; the preceptor stepped forward from the line of masters and raised his hand for silence. Every eye was on him, and not Marron alone was holding his breath to hear.

"The night gone," the preceptor said, his voice harsh and carrying, "treachery near handed this fortress to the enemy. Only the God's grace protected us." *And me,* Marron thought rebelliously, but did not breathe. "Those who betrayed us were our own vassals, kept by our kindness, their lives within our gift. Which lives are now forfeit by our law, and may the God have mercy upon them, for we shall not."

That was all. The preceptor gestured and stepped back; a brother with an axe took his place in the light, breaking open the kegs that stood arrayed. He set the axe aside and lifted each keg one by one, pouring viscous oil over the heap of wood and tossing the empty kegs onto the pile.

It was the preceptor himself who took a torch and hurled it, setting the oiled wood ablaze.

Two burly brothers came out of the stables, through the only clear path in that crowded yard, dragging a small figure in white between them. One of the Sharai lads, Marron saw, his hands bound behind him.

"No . . ."

It came out as little more than a groan, inaudible in the sudden murmur of many voices. Marron drew breath to cry aloud, to push forward and shriek against this savagery; and was suddenly seized from behind, lost his breath in a startled gasp and twisted round to see Rudel standing there.

"Don't be a fool," the jongleur hissed in his ear. "You can't stop this. Watch, and remember . . ."

*   *   *

MARRON FOUGHT THE man's grip for a moment, uselessly, and then subsided. Rudel was right, he would only make more trouble for himself and perhaps for Sieur Anton too, and to no effect. Nothing he could do to stop the Sharai boy being picked up and swung between the two brothers, too numbed it seemed even to struggle; nothing to prevent his being thrown through the air and into the roaring flames.

Marron sobbed, but that too was lost, this time in the howling as the boy writhed and burned. The brothers went back to the stables, came out with another boy.

MUSTAR WAS THE fourth. Marron's eyes were not too dazzled by tears and firelight, his mind not too dazed to know his friend. Again he tried to twist free, and again Rudel held him still; and all he could do then was stiffen and stare, bear witness and swear a silent revenge.

At least Mustar struggled and cursed, before he was fed to the fire. Then he screamed, agony and despair, and that long dying cry seared itself into Marron's skull. *Remember,* Rudel had said, needlessly; this could never be forgotten, nor forgiven.

THERE WERE PERHAPS a dozen boys brought out from the stables, a dozen survivors of the night, though Marron had stopped counting before the boys stopped dying. Some might have been quite innocent; there had been fewer surely on the wall with ropes.

When the last of them was still, when only the flames were moving. the Ransomers were dismissed, by the preceptor's word. They filed back through the narrow way into the castle; Marron barely noticed that the jostling throng around him had dispersed also, until Rudel shook him gently back into himself.

"Remember that, lad, but don't dwell on it. This is a cruel country." *These things happen,* he was saying, as though they must, as though they always would. He sounded like Sieur Anton. Perhaps all men sounded that way after some years in this cursed-cruel country; perhaps he would himself. "Now, will you speak with me? Privately?"

Secretly, he meant; they were private already. Marron thought that he didn't want to hear any more secrets, he held too many as it was. He wanted to be new, reborn, he wanted to start again, Sieur Anton's squire and nothing more. "Sir, I ought to . . ." What ought he to do? He didn't know. Seek out the knight, he supposed, or else run to his quarters and find work there, sweep or tidy, polish Josette and see if Dard's edge were true yet after last night's exercise . . .

But there was no strength in his legs to carry him, no strength in his will to defy Rudel. It was so much easier simply to stand here where the heat of the fire tightened the skin on his brow, where the smell of charred meat was all that was left him of Mustar, one last reminder like a whisper from his spirit, *this they did to me* . . .

Standing meant listening: the jongleur assumed a consent he had not given. But listening was easy too, words were fugitive, he wouldn't have to remember them . . .

"Marron, you have been in the penitents' cells, yes? Today and yesterday?"

"Yes." Answering questions wasn't hard, he could do that and still think of Mustar, still watch for faces in the flames. All magic was light, it seemed, so all light should be magic. There should be signs, he wanted signs to show one young soul gone to paradise, if the Sharai knew the way to any such . . .

"You remember when we went down the steps that day and turned back, when we heard a man screaming?"

And went out and down the hill instead, and saw the missing stones and the bead at the man's throat, and so from there to here and so Mustar burned. "Yes."

"Do you know, did you learn where they are keeping that man? While you were down there?"

Broken hands and blood, all his bones showing, they have been kind to him. "Yes."

"Tell me where. Tell me all you can: where they hold him, how they treat him, how often he is—"

Seen? Visited? Treated? Marron could tell him a lot, perhaps, more than the man expected; but, "Tell me why," he said instead.

"Because I want to help him, get him out." A great confession but no great surprise, not now.

"That's heresy."

"Treason, I think; but yes, it's a capital offence," and they were talking about it in the light of an execution-pyre, and each turned his head towards the flames, as if to feel again the heat against the eye, the almost-pain of it this far away. "For both of us if you help me, if we are taken. Will you?"

The screaming of him, and the hands; Marron's thoughts were blurred, it was hard to remember that there was a difference, Jonson in the cell and Mustar in the fire. Both had screamed, both had had hands. The rope that bound Mustar's had burned through more quickly than his flesh; Marron had seen him stretch his arms out in the flames, and his hands were burning claws clutching at the light, and always would be.

Marron meant to say yes already, he thought he must; simply listening made him guilty, so why not? So much for being newborn or innocent, starting afresh; Sieur Anton would condemn him before the court himself, if ever he found out. Secrets and lies already, oaths as good as broken—*I can obey you, sieur, and I will,* but not in this—and him not two hours old yet in his new service . . .

First, though, "Tell me why," he demanded again. "Why risk so much, what is that man"—Jonson, but that surely was not his name, and Marron should have had no chance to hear it in any case—"what is he to you?"

Rudel smiled, spread his hands. "I am from Surayon," he said, "and so is he."

TWO

Where She is Sent

THE GIRLS HAD seen the light and heard the screams, but they'd known what was coming long since, after a day's hard labour among the wounded.

Blaise had brought their breakfast that morning, and seasoned it with news of armed parties riding out to scour the country. He'd been grim and bitter, his mouth twisting on the words, a fighting man forbidden to fight last night and unable even to ride this morning, held back by duty. Julianne had felt accused and hadn't resented it, unfair though it was; she knew that sense of being wasted, of being seen as useless. Too well she knew it already, and would she thought learn many finer nuances in her life to come.

Not today, though. She'd been determined on that. As soon as they'd eaten, she and Elisande had made their way to the infirmary dressed in her plainest gowns, those she could most easily sacrifice. Master Infirmarer had been in no position to turn the girls away; he had too many injured men on his hands. There were always more men wounded in a night battle, a wicked disproportion; more yet could be expected, brought back from Master Ricard's expedition; and the Order's strictures allowed that caring for the sick and injured was fit work for women, acceptable even to a Ransomer in time of need. The girls were guests, to be sure, and should not work — but they were needed. Two competent pairs of hands down below freed two men to stand guard above, lest the Sharai come again.

So yes, Julianne and Elisande had been permitted to help, if not made exactly welcome. The worst of the wounded had been given what crude treatment was possible last night, in a hurry and by lamplight; lesser injuries had received a quick binding and short shrift else. Now by day was the time for care and skill and patient examination, and while Master Infirmarer and his brethren occupied themselves so, Julianne and Elisande could go from cot to cot with water for wounded men to drink and more to ease the unwrapping of last night's bandages, to wash away the caked blood beneath. No one had cared or even noticed when they pushed their awkward veils aside, except for those few who had refused their aid altogether, who had turned their stiff heads on stiff necks and refused even to look upon them, far less suffer themselves to be touched by female hands.

As the hours had passed, Elisande particularly had not been content simply to ferry water and prepare the injured brothers for other men's ministrations. She had doctored minor wounds herself, applying salves and bandages, teaching Julianne to do the same. To her obvious frustration, she'd been forbidden to assist in the surgery, which took place in an inner room that was all lamplight and shadows, knives and hot irons and screaming. Elisande had tried to bully and then squirm her way in, calling that she had some knowledge of such treatments that might benefit them all, surgeons and patients alike; but that door was closed firmly against her.

When the noon bell sounded even work in the infirmary had slowed and the less grievously injured had knelt beside their cots, to whisper prayers in echo of the master's lead. Elisande had gestured with her head then, Julianne had nodded; the two of them had slipped outside and just walked for a while in the still shadowed air of the courts before going back to their chamber to shed their filthy clothes, wash the blood and stink from their skins and offer their exhaustion some rest.

Elisande had slept for an hour, Julianne not at all, only lying staring at the patterns of shadow on the ceiling, seeing pictures of the night gone by and the morning that had followed: battle and death, an army defiant or else simply philosophical in defeat, a hundred separate hurts in the men she had helped and no joy even for the healthy. She had not thought it would be like that.

There had been no survivors among the invading Sharai, not one. She had asked, once, only to be certain: were wounded prisoners taken elsewhere, some more secure place of treatment? The man she'd asked had laughed at her, and she'd read the truth in his laughter, in what he would not say. There were no prisoners, wounded or otherwise. A knife to the throat, perhaps, as she'd speculated on the wall, or a club to the skull to save blunting good steel: war without quarter. They called themselves the Ransomers, but it was the land they came to ransom, with their lives if necessary; they offered no ransom to the Sharai.

When Elisande woke, they'd dressed and eaten quickly and then gone back to the infirmary, taking a brief detour on the way just to look into the north ward, just to satisfy a curiosity barely spoken between them. All the bodies were gone, and brothers were swabbing blood from the flagstones; an hour's sunlight to dry them and there would be no trace remaining of all last night's death and terror. Elisande had murmured something under her breath, a last benediction for the Sharai fallen who would have no other rites said over them, and then both girls had turned and gone on their way.

＊   ＊   ＊

THE WOUNDED HAD overflowed the infirmary, filling two dormitories besides. The girls fetched food and water to them, changed dressings, spent a good deal of time only sitting by one cot or another, speaking to the men who lay there or simply listening while they rambled and drifted in and out of consciousness. More than once Julianne found herself holding a young man's hand, playing sister or mother as best she could as his injuries overcame him, as he slipped slowly into death, She'd have washed and prepared their bodies also, she had no fear of the dead; but that she was not allowed to do. The brothers had their own rituals, it seemed, which were private and not for female understanding.

Julianne also had her own private needs. Eventually she'd slipped away alone, and good fortune or some higher power had brought her shortly to the door of a small chapel. Like the great hall, this too had a gallery; she'd climbed the steps and knelt in the shadows above, not meaning to pray, only to be quiet for a while.

But her eyes had been distracted by unexpected colour and gleam. Lamps and candles had burned in the chapel below, showing how the walls were painted; everywhere she'd looked she'd seen images of the saints and their deaths, images too of the God's victory here and throughout the Sanctuary Land. The glory of Ascariel glimmered gold behind the altar, and the vessels that stood there were certainly silver where they were not gold.

Looking and looking, she'd seen at last that she was not after all alone; a man had been kneeling close beside a pillar, as far within its shadow as he could come. She'd been doubly glad then that she'd come up into the gallery.

She'd not been able to see him at all clearly; but even so there'd been something about him, his bare head and the way he held himself, his dark clothes that were none the less not the habit of a brother. She'd been fairly certain she could put a name to him.

Then another had come into the chapel. Again bareheaded, this time in a habit but again not a brother; him she'd been certain of.

He'd knelt beside the other man and touched his wrist, bringing a gasp, a jerk of the head, almost a shrinking away.

"Do you know me, child?"

"Yes, Magister Fulke." Only a whisper, but Julianne had heard it perfectly; there could be no secrets spoken before the God.

"Good. But you need not call me so; that title is re- served for the Order."

"Please? If I may . . . ?"

"Well, but you must answer me a question, then. Why did you forsake us? Brother?"

"I did not, Magister. I was, I was cast out . . ."

"No, tell me true. Why did you forsake us?"

Blaise had begun to weep, then. Marshal Fulke had waited, patient as the God Himself; it was Julianne who'd moved, to rise and slip away. There could be no secrets spoken before the God, but this history was not meant for her to hear, and she would not spy.

She'd slipped soft-footed down the stairs, and gone back to her work among the wounded. It was only later that it occurred to her to wonder quite why Marshal Fulke had so deliberately sought out her sergeant, what he might have offered the man in exchange for his story, or what further service he might demand.

INEVITABLY, SPENDING SO much time among the in- jured, both girls had heard all the news of the day: how, following the scouts, a small army—half the garrison— had ridden out to surprise the enemy; how it had been the captured stablelads who had let down ropes from the wall to give the raiders entry; how the surviving boys had been put to cruel question since.

How they had spoken of a new leader among the

Sharai, a man who sought to unite all the tribes against Outremer. Hasan, they said was his name.

How they were condemned, out of their own mouths convicted; how they were all to be put to death that night, as justice and the law demanded.

ABOUT MARRON NO brother spoke at all, nor would speak when they asked; except the one who cleared his throat and spat wetly onto the flags of the floor, rasped, "Treacher," and turned his head the other way. Marron was a worry, but not a great one. They'd seen him last night, free and fighting and then walking from the ward with d'Escrivey, very much like a squire at his master's side. That surely meant that he'd been reprieved, that he would be forgiven his act of rebellion in the village that even the strictures of the Rule hadn't stopped the brothers gossiping about; the girls had had the story from Blaise, who'd had it from a dozen different men in a dozen forms but little different one from another.

Julianne had been sure, at least, that Marron was reprieved. Or at least had tried to seem so, to herself as to her friend. Elisande had grunted, "So where is he, then? I want to look at his arm," and had asked again, and had again got no answer.

At close of day, in that little time of shadows after the sun had sunk below the castle wall but not yet to the horizons of the guards above, Elisande had taken Julianne by the elbow and tugged her discreetly out of the infirmary.

"What is it?"

"Before they start that bell ringing, and no one listens to us. Come on. Put your veil straight, and look demure . . ."

Through the castle to the kitchens; and from there down a narrow turning stair into darkness, into the hard bowels of the rock, one hand feeling for Elisande and the other for the wall when she could see neither, only a hand's span from her nose . . . Julianne had known what this place was, no need to ask. And before they reached bottom she'd known why Elisande had brought her here, and why she'd brought also a scrip filled with linen and ointments.

They'd come from darkness into light: a small chamber, an oil-lamp, two brothers on guard by another doorway. Not armed except with staves, but alert; and very surprised to see two women on the stair and firm of purpose.

"We have come to tend to Fra' Marron," Elisande had said, brandishing her scrip. "We understand he was hurt in the fighting last night; his arm will need dressing, at least . . ."

All so convincing, so likely, so legitimate; and all so wasted, because both guards had shaken their heads together, and one had said, "He is not here." Short of snatching up the lamp and pushing their way past the men to check every cell in that dark passage behind the men, there had been little the girls could do but nod and climb the stairs again. Elisande had tried a little more, one more time with the single simple question, "Can you tell me where he is?" and had received no more satisfaction than at any time this day. The man had shaken his head again, just as the great bell had thrummed its first calling strokes through the stone above their heads; he'd shaken it once more, emphatically, touched a finger to his lips and turned towards his brother. The two of them had knelt, casting their hoods over their heads but facing each other so that, almost knocking heads as they bowed, they'd entirely blocked the way through to the passage they guarded. No chance to slip by them; Elisande's eyes had spoken her frustration. Even so she'd lingered a little, squinting in what light there was, peering down the passage as though she thought she could see through dark and rock and all to find whom she sought there.

As they returned to their chamber Julianne had spoken her conviction again, that the boy was well or well enough. "Not in the infirmary and not in the cells, that brother wouldn't have lied to us, he wouldn't demean himself so. Marron's not badly hurt, then, and he's not badly in trouble . . ."

And others were, which was why Marron was a worry but not a great one. Others were death-doomed, irretrievable: their names not known and their faces hardly glimpsed and not remembered—only stable-boys, after all, and she'd seen so many through the years; why should she have made an effort with these lads, how could she have known?—but their trial a great weight on her regardless, and on Elisande also, a crushing weight they'd carried all the day and could not put down now.

AND SO THE day and the evening that had followed. Blaise had brought their evening meal himself—no spare hands to serve them, he'd said, that jongleur Rudel scrounging a meal with Blaise's men, and he'd never known such a thing happen in the Order, that guests should go unattended—and had delivered a fierce scolding for seasoning, once he'd learned why their gowns were smeared with dust and wetter, deeper stains.

Elisande had borne it snarling, Julianne with an unnatural patience—at least so Elisande had said afterwards, when they were alone, that her patience was unnatural; she'd managed a half-smile and a nod, "Yes, it was taught me,"—and at last he'd gone. To be with his men, he'd said, and left unspoken the reason why. Young men, some of them: were they fretful, cold with the thought of the thing to come, Julianne had wondered, as she was herself but would not say so, or not at least to him? Or did they want to watch? Young men could be fierce; and they were Elessan, all of them. A hard people, hard to themselves and harder still to others. The Sharai were their enemy and the God's also, branded so bone-deep, soul-deep. There would be little mercy in their hearts in the face of Sharai treachery.

Blaise might even want to watch himself, she'd

thought. Having missed the opportunity to fight. That tirade he'd unleashed on Elisande and herself had sounded more resentful than anything else. He was a warrior trained and ready, there'd been a battle, he'd had no part to play in it; and what had been his own clear charge he'd clearly failed at, to keep Julianne safe and safely distant from the fighting. Blood-letting cooled a fevered body; for a fevered spirit, someone else's blood might be enough.

SO THEY'D KNOWN it was coming, that glow of light reflected from the walls, fierce red on dull; and foolishly, stupidly, she'd thought she could simply turn her back to the screened windows and wait, see nothing and pretend that nothing was all she knew.

She hadn't thought about the screaming. Certainly she hadn't expected the cruelty of how it was made, a chain of single links: how one boy had died before the next was burned, and each one's screaming was the story of a life from bright sudden consciousness to exhausted end, and each brief silence after was the loss of life.

Some man must have made that decision, one at a time: the preceptor himself, most likely. For the cold satisfaction of his men, or else for the added suffering of the boys who must wait; or else for both. She'd tried to think of it as an affirmation, each boy declaring his death to the sky or to his god and not one being lost in another's agony; she'd tried and failed, it had been too much to ask of her. She'd only suffered, sobbed with each separate scream and each sudden silence, and her only victory had been that she had not screamed herself. Unless that had been her father's victory, and not hers at all . . .

AT LAST, AT long last there had been no more screaming, and the stretching silence had been washed over by a hissing whisper. When she'd wiped her wet face and sore eyes — on her veil, of course, and what else was it for, of what use was it if not for that? — and looked around, she'd seen Elisande standing silhouetted against the dim red shadows at the window.

Saying that prayer again, she'd guessed, the *khalat,* speaking the boys' souls to whatever paradise awaited them, if any. If there were any world beyond this, some- where less savage, if that was not just a lie fed to the ig- norant and unlucky to keep them subservient to their masters' unkind law. She doubted it herself; but in the end she'd done what little she could, she'd walked across to stand beside her friend and offer her own unspeaking respect to the ritual, in the hope that it might mean some- thing at least to Elisande, though it came too late to help herself and was far too small, far too late to help the dead.

Standing so, with folded hands and not a movement in her except her gulping throat and gasping breath, deter- minedly not closing her eyes to the fading light of the fire outside, she thought at first that it was only her blurred sight that made the light dance in the pattern of the screens across the window.

Then that it was a sudden flare from one of the lamps, shifting all the shadows to flickering confusion.

Then that it was an insect's wings battering the air too fast to see, and the body of it invisible in the intricacies of dark and light that pierced and shaped the screen.

She thought so, or hoped so in defiance of what she thought, what she expected from the first quick hint of strange, the catch of nothing at her eye. It was only when blur and dance and flicker stretched to a shimmering worm a finger's length and longer, a finger's width and narrowing like a taper, like an over-fine image of a fin- ger; only when she saw how it drew spangles of light to- gether to weave itself a body; only then did Julianne take breath and clamp her throat hard around a thin steel wire of a voice that she barely recognised as her own. "Djinni Khaldor. This is — an unexpected visitation," she said, though she wasn't even sure that it was true. After the

tensions and terrors of last night and the long weariness
that had been today, after the monstrousness of the fire
that guttered still in a courtyard too close, out of sight but
not out of hearing, she felt too exhausted to be surprised
by anything.

True for Elisande it was, though, so much at least.
That girl gasped and jerked her head around, needed a
moment of blinking to find the hover-and-spin aglitter,
the thread of distortion of light and air that was the djinni
this night; and then needed a moment more to stiffen herself to the task before she stepped deliberately between it
and Julianne.

"Had I been expected," the djinni said, and its voice
was as large and as quiet as before, seemingly quite un-
affected by the form it chose to take, "you would have
waited in vain."

"And to our loss, I am sure," Elisande said, though she
sounded as though she meant that not one jot. *Careful,*
Julianne thought, Julianne's fingers said against her
friend's wrist, just the lightest touch for such a solemn
message; *don't let your anger confuse your words. You
know these creatures, how subtle they are,* and Julianne
was still a nervous pupil, clumsy and uncertain. Even so
there was something she must say, something she had to
learn, though she wouldn't batter at the djinni with questions as her soul was crying to.

"Not so, but there would have been no purpose to my
coming. You would have known already what I sought."

"Even so. People like to be asked, sometimes," and
now suddenly Elisande had the voice exactly, as she had
used it before: respectful but not subservient, determined
to speak and treat as an equal without harbouring any
delusions that equal she was. "Neither could we have
gifted you that thing you seek, had you not come here to
collect it . . ."

"It lies not in your gift, Lisan of the Dead Waters; neither is it a thing to be collected, except that there is a
debt."

That meant it spoke to Julianne—impossible to tell with no face turning between them, no clues of body for even her high-trained eyes to read, and oh, how she resented its immunity—and it wished some service from her. Again, neither aspect of that was a surprise.

The only possible surprise lay in the answer that she gave; and again, perhaps, the only one surprised was Elisande.

"A debt unacknowledged," Julianne said slowly, "is no debt at all."

Now it was the turn of Elisande's fingers to speak to Julianne's, *careful, careful! You don't know these creatures, how powerful they are,* even as the djinni replied.

"That is true. Similarly, though, a debt acquired in ignorance is still a debt. It may be forgiven, but not ignored. And those who choose to trespass into a society they do not understand should not seek to deny the consequences of their choice."

Julianne nodded, bowed almost, the point confessed; then she turned her face deliberately towards the dying light beyond the windows and said, "I was wondering just now whether the Sharai were right in their beliefs, in the god they worship and their prospects of paradise hereafter. It occurs to me that though nothing mortal-bound can know, the djinn might have that knowledge."

"Daughter of the Shadow, the djinn are mortal also. Of a kind. Time will not touch us, but still we can be slain. And no, we do not know the gods, neither the truths behind their promises. All faith is hope, no more; I can offer you nothing else."

Not true, it had offered her kindness, and she valued that. Now there was a debt she did acknowledge; this must be what she had wanted; she thought, to have her own reason for saying yes. Why she should have wanted to, except for some curious sense of honour that the djinni itself seemed to recognise and respond to, she couldn't say. At any rate, she felt relief far more than anxiety as she said, "Tell me what you want, spirit, and I will do it if I can."

Elisande choked, spun round, laid the palm of her hand across Julianne's mouth too late "*No!* Djinni, she did not mean—Julianne, you *can't* . . ."

Julianne reached up, took her friend's hand in both of hers and held it calmly, almost patted it. "Yes," she affirmed. "I did mean it, and I will do it. A blind promise, I know, to a creature of guile and subtlety; none the less, I make it willingly. There is a debt." *Now.*

"Go where you are sent, Julianne de Rance, and marry where you must."

That at least, at last was unexpected. She bit down hard on any question, steadied her mind and said, "Well, I will; but—"

"I have not yet said where I will send you." It waited then, for a long, slow beat that echoed unbearably in Julianne's mind; and it was laughing as it went on, "Go to the Sharai, daughter of the Shadow."

More than unexpected, this was startling. Questions teemed on her tongue, and were swallowed with difficulty. There had to be a way to ask without asking; she was too muddled to find it, but Elisande not, it seemed. Elisande said, "That was the duty you laid on me, at our last meeting."

"It was."

"There must be a reason," enunciated oh so carefully, not to have it sound as if she were asking, "why the djinn would see Julianne and me both among the Sharai."

"There are many reasons, Lisan, and two that I will tell you. Human children take the care of their friends upon themselves; if I send Julianne into lands and among a people that she does not know, it seems to me likely that you will travel with her. She calls me subtle; I do not know if this be subtlety, but you have not gone alone."

"I do not wish to go to the Sharai."

"No, but I wish it, and others will be glad if you do.

You can tell the imams at Rhabat that the *khalat* was properly said for the dead in their time of dying."

"It was said. That is enough."

"For their god, perhaps, if god there be. For the comfort of their families and the satisfaction of their priests, not so. It should be known. Also, Julianne will find her father there."

Her *father*? Elisande's nails dug deep into her wrist; she gasped, wrenched her hand free and said, "I did, I did not know my father was there."

"He is, and he will be; and he will be in great danger. You can save him, though it might be better if you did not."

"Djinni . . ." This was too much for her; what it said made too much sense and no sense, it left her reeling. "I wish that you would tell me, straightly, what it is that you would have me do."

"I have told you that, three times now. Once more I will say it, but not here."

"At least tell me how to find them, then, where my road should take me . . ." That was a plea, desperate as it began, almost shouted; but she let it die, thinking that a demand for information was a question in all but name, and the djinni might treat it so, might assume another debt as fair exchange.

All it said, though, was, "Lisan can tell you that. She can show you, she is your road if she will be so. For now, fare well."

This time no thunderclap, no sparks; it dwindled only as it had grown, to a petty agitation of air and light, to an absence. She wondered briefly what a djinni's body was, how it was made or how many ways it could make itself, what more it could be. Only briefly, though.

My father . . .

She turned to Elisande and said, "Will you come?"

"I do not want to."

"You said that."

"I am not free, Julianne . . ."

"No more am I," she said. Duties weighed her down, promises conflicted; she had sworn obedience to her father, but for her father's sake she would break that oath, and any. "I am going. Alone, if I must."

"You cannot. You said yourself, you do not know the road; nor do you know the customs of the people, nor how to travel in the desert. You would die, long before you saw Rhabat."

"Even so. If my father is in peril . . ."

"We are all in peril." Elisande's fists were clenched, and her face also; Julianne could not read her thoughts. But, "Well," she said at last, "I must betray someone, it seems. Many people, perhaps, and disaster may come of it. But I cannot let you go alone. Besides, I might be less welcome here once you were gone. Doubly so, once for my own sake and once because of you. I do not want to find myself in one of those cells they are so fond of. So yes, if you must go, I will show you the way of it."

Julianne kissed her then, once for love and twice more formally, on each cheek, another promise sealed and this one not to break.

How they should leave — how to escape might be a better way of putting it — was another question, and she was out of the practice of asking questions tonight. Morning would be soon enough. Then she would have other questions too, she would try once again to learn just why Elisande had come here, and why she was so reluctant to move on. Two questions with one answer, most likely, a purpose not achieved; but what that purpose was, Julianne determined that she would learn. Tomorrow.

For now, she took herself to bed. Elisande aped her, undressing silently, putting out the lamps, lying down in the dark; but Julianne lay a long time with her eyes wide open, staring at things she could not see, the vaulted ceiling not truly one of them; and she didn't ask but she suspected that Elisande aped her in that also.

*   *   *

BOTH GIRLS SLEPT through the bell next morning, slept through the hour of service and could have slept later still. Julianne could have spent half the day in bed. Her conscience touched her with a sharp question, though—was she resting, or hiding?—and the answer had her up in short order.

She nudged Elisande out of bed also, sweetly smiling to rub the salt of her virtue in deeper; but they were both soon glad that she had. Julianne fetched in the cooling ewer of water that waited on the landing, left by a brother before the bell; they washed and dressed, and almost immediately heard footsteps on the stairs outside, a cough, a finger scratching at the curtain.

"Come."

Blaise it was who came, which Julianne knew already; his tread was unmistakable, heavy-booted against the soft shuffle of the brothers' sandals. This was the second morning running he'd come with a tray in his hands, bearing their breakfast; the second morning she'd seen him blushing, fighting to keep his eyes unfocused as if he trespassed somewhere sanctified, entering his lady's chamber before ever she'd deigned to leave it. *And he nearly did catch us in our beds,* she thought, *and what would he have done then, if I'd called him in? Died of shame, most like . . .*

"Blaise, good morning. Are you our servant once again?"

"My lady, I took this from the brother who was bringing it. I have a message for you. His grace the preceptor would welcome a visit from you this morning, if you are at leisure."

"As he knows perfectly well how much I am at leisure, I take it that's a summons. Can you tell me why?"

"No, my lady," he said stolidly, meaning, she thought, that he knew perfectly well and would not tell. Because he'd been ordered not to, or because it was not his place to do so; either one would fit.

"Did he mean immediately?" she asked, with a hint of

the plaintive in her throat and her eyes on the breakfast-tray. She *was* hungry, after a weary day and a wakeful night. Diplomacy said to hurry, but . . .

"Immediately you have breakfasted, I think, my lady.'

Of course, the preceptor was a diplomat too. She nodded, placated.

"Did he mean me as well?" Elisande asked.

"I could not say, my lady. He asked me to bring the message to the lady Julianne."

Which clearly meant *no* in Blaise's mind, but Julianne had a mind of her own, and was determined to assert it.

"Of course, you as well. You are my companion, my chaperone," with a wicked smile, *perhaps I need the protection of a chaperone, perhaps no girl is safe with His Grace the Preceptor* . . .

Elisande grinned back over her shoulder, as she took the tray from Blaise.

HE WAITED OUTSIDE the chamber while they ate; neither girl hurried. The bread was good and the honey sweet, the sheep's milk rich and nutty and the preceptor a busy man; he would neither waste half an hour of his time nor begrudge it to his guests.

When they were ready, Blaise led them to a part of the castle they had not visited before, unless Elisande's private wanderings had brought her here. It was all new to Julianne.

Another ward, another tower: but here the stone flags were covered with rushes, to mute the sound of Blaise's boots. A brother on watch opened the door to the preceptor's private apartments and bowed them in, unless he was averting his eyes from even veiled women; it was subtly done if so, and Julianne couldn't tell.

The room they came into was a fine, a classic example of what her father called costly austerity when he was feeling generous, religious hypocrisy when he was not. The furnishings were simple, but of that simplicity that cost dear: the chests and chairs were unadorned but of high quality, made from woods brought from the homelands, hundreds of miles at great expense. The rugs on the floor were plain, colours of earth and straw, colours of humility; they were knotted silk of a style that Julianne had seen rarely, traded from Sharai who had journeyed in the uttermost east. The walls had been washed a soft white and carried no decoration save a pair of woven hangings — Ascariel, they depicted, the golden city in light and darkness, and even in darkness it lit up the night — and the looped sign of the God, not jewelled or chased as she had seen done in Marasson, but beaten with great craft from a weight of solid gold.

The room was empty. The brother at the door bade them wait, and refresh themselves if they would; goblets of glass and silver stood on a chest, with a flask beside. Elisande sniffed it, and her eyebrows rose.

"Jereth," she murmured. "The Sharai make it, from herbs and berries. It's . . . uncommon, in Outremer."

In Marasson, also. Julianne had tasted it once, as a small child, just a sip from her father's glass. She remembered the flavour still.

Elisande lifted the flask and poured, two small measures; then she looked to Blaise, and her eyebrows asked the question.

"Thank you, no, my lady. I was not invited."

He stepped outside, and the brother closed the door.

Julianne took the goblet Elisande passed to her, bent over it, inhaled — and was briefly young again, excited by everything, thrilled to be taking treasure from her father's hand. She tossed her veil aside and sipped, and the taste was exact, a moment of sour herbs that twisted the mouth before sweet fruit soothed it. *Like medicine,* she'd said the first time, and her father had laughed at her; but she thought the same now. There was bitterness there, not quite disguised, and the memory of that lingered longer than the dulcet. As though the asperity were the purpose of it, and the sweetness only there as an allay. And yet the

balance of the two was unimpeachable, a touch more of
either would have done it irreparable harm. It was a drink
for adults, she decided, with a sigh inside; and yes, it
made her feel a child again.

"This is — exceptional," she said.

"I am glad." It was the preceptor's voice, soft, mel-
lifluent and at her back, where she had thought there was
only wall behind her.

She turned more sharply than she would have wished,
and saw how one of the hangings still billowed, where he
had come through a hidden door. A doorway, at least: not
a door, she would surely have heard the hinges. His sandals, on these rugs — that she could forgive herself for, if
he'd been trying to walk silently. Which she was sure of.
This man she thought did nothing without thought, without deliberate intent.

He stood before her now, only a long arm's reach
away and he had long arms; and a mild gaze, a benevo-
lent smile, silver hair and a bald crown, the God's own
tonsure given to a faithful servant. He was the image of a
peaceable religious, and she believed that image not at
all. And rightly. *This is the man who ordered all those
boys burned alive.* And stayed perhaps to see it done, or
sat in here and listened to their screaming . . . Or maybe
he'd been reading or praying or sleeping, maybe he'd
heard not a single cry of it, maybe he'd put it completely
out of his mind. It made not the slightest difference.

She reached to draw her veil over her face again, but
the preceptor forestalled her. "Please, not while we're
private. Primitive customs are for primitive people. We
have offered you poor entertainment these last days, I
fear," he went on, "and it's too late now to improve our
reputation in your eyes; but a gesture, at least, a touch of
how we'd sooner treat our guests . . ."

"You have lost no reputation with me, your grace," she
said.

"Meaning that we had none to lose?" His smile, his
voice, all his manner said that he was teasing; but oh, he

was sharp, he struck uncomfortably close. "Come, sit down; you worked yourselves to exhaustion yesterday on our behalf, at least you must rest today."

His gesture as well as his words included Elisande; she said, "May I not pour you some *jereth,* your grace?"

"We call it monks'-wine here, child," and the reproach was so gilded even Julianne was hardly aware of it, "I suppose because it is not—quite—forbidden by the Rule. But no, I thank you, I do not take it myself. Please, sit."

She did, they both did, close together on a settle. *Like children,* she thought again, with a twinge of irritation, *come to be disposed of by their father.*

Because that was what was happening here, she realised suddenly, even before the preceptor said it directly. He was making dispositions. It was implicit, twice implicit in what he'd said already. She really should wake up or he'd have her dancing to his delight, only that his voice lulled her so . . .

"There is no way," he said, "properly to thank you both for your labours yesterday, so I am cast already as an ungrateful host; and I regret, I deeply regret that I must add to my failures in that regard. But your father sent you to us, Lady Julianne, for your protection, to ensure your safety; and the attack on this castle two nights since has thrown that safety into severe question." He didn't say, he didn't need to say that it was her own actions that night that drew her into real danger; again, that was implicit. "I have been considering the situation since, and I am afraid that I have no choice in this. The Sharai may return in greater strength, to invest us or assault again; for your welfare, I must send you forth. I will detail a party to accompany you. The road is not perilous, but neither is it invulnerable, and your own men are no longer enough. There are traders here too, bound for Elessi; you can all travel together. The greater numbers, the greater safety."

Julianne nodded slowly. "How soon, your grace?"

"As soon as may be. Tomorrow, if you can be ready."

"Your grace, I can be ready today, if you wish it." *I'm ready now, I'd ride out as I am and never look back, never see or wish to see your pleasant face again except in nightmare . . .*

"All the better. Shall we say after the noon heat, then? If that will give you time enough to prepare? You could be some miles on your way before nightfall, and perhaps a day earlier in Elessi."

"Of course. I am sorry if we have caused you worry; your hospitality has been generosity itself."

"Not at all. Hospitality is the heart of the Rule; in serving you, we have served the God, which is all our purpose."

And did you serve the God last night, with your fire? She'd have preferred an easy answer to that question, something she could live with, a sigh and a sad shrug, a simple "no"; unfortunately, even without asking, she knew that he would say yes, and mean it.

The preceptor gave orders at the door: knights and troops to be detailed, the traders alerted. Then he returned to his guests, and they sat and drank and talked of other things. Her life in Marasson, a little of Elessi, though each time he turned the conversation that way she turned it back. When she arrived there would be soon enough to learn its ways. If ever she did arrive there . . .

He asked no questions of Elisande, which was some small relief. Julianne still had her own questions, but this was no place for her to ask and he no man to hear.

When their goblets were empty he offered to refill them, and she declined: pure politeness on each side, they both knew the interview was over.

She stood, so did he, so did Elisande. They made their formal farewells, he promised to see them on their way himself, she thanked him graciously for the courtesy; she adjusted her veil and turned towards the door, which was opened before she reached it, the brother there bowing deeply or else avoiding the poison of her gaze, as before. She swept past, Elisande at her back.

Blaise brought them back to their chamber, a watchful escort who made them both mute. As soon as they were alone, though, Elisande said, "Well. That makes it easier, I suppose."

Indeed, easier for their escape, to fulfil her promise to the djinni and embark on some blind adventure; but it would be no easier for Elisande to leave this place. The frustration and distress of that was laid clear and heavy in her voice, denying each one of her words.

THREE

The Corruption in the Blood

ALL NIGHT MARRON had been trying to sleep with a deadly secret, to pray with a heresy in his head.

I am from Surayon.

From Surayon and free, still free because Marron had not denounced him, and would not.

I am from Surayon, and so is he; and the bare announcement was so shocking, Marron hadn't even recoiled. Hadn't even stared, had only stood numbly while the words settled in his head. Even Jonson had not admitted so much; he'd had a little more care for his much-abused body, and a little less trust in a chance-met boy. Not so Rudel, who had betrayed them both, himself and Jonson, given them over into Marron's hands; and Marron's hands were not strong enough to hold them, and so all three would suffer, he was sure.

He had tried to sleep, and could not; had tried to pray, and could not. Then he had tried to hide it all from Sieur Anton, though very much doubting his ability to do that also.

. "Marron, don't mumble the prayers in future, they're not a lesson for impatient boys to babble through."

"No, sieur."

"You were restless all night, too. What kept you from sleeping?"

"Nothing, sieur, I don't know . . ."

The knight had sighed. "Marron, didn't I tell you not to lie to me? Show me your arm."

Well, there had been some truth in that at least, though his silence was a lie. The arm had been painful all night, if not as painful as his conscience. As he'd gazed at it this morning, as Sieur Anton had pushed back the sleeve to expose it, they'd both seen how it was swollen on either side of the stained bandage, how the tight skin shone; how beneath the skin darkly vivid and telltale streaks ran out to reach almost to his elbow, almost to his wrist. When he'd tried, he couldn't bend his fingers.

Sieur Anton's breath had hissed softly. "That's not good."

"No, sieur." It had been frightening, truly.

"It needs care, but not from me. I won't even unwrap it. Take it to Master Infirmarer, Marron, for his opinion. Right now, I think."

"Oh, please, sieur, no!" Being frightened had not seemed so bad, in comparison. "There are, there are so many others hurt, worse than I am . . ."

"Perhaps; but even so, someone with more skill than I should look at this. It's been denied the chance to heal too often, and some poison has got into it. Why do you not want to go to the infirmary?"

"Sieur, Master Infirmarer might not want to treat me. I am not a brother now." He had been cast out, in utter humiliation; he couldn't have borne that rejection again, so soon.

"He will treat my squire. I am sworn to the Ransomers still, if you are not. And they are sworn to serve all those who fight for the God, whether they are of the Order or not." And then, against Marron's stubborn silence,

"Would you rather lose the arm? That may happen yet, if we leave this."

"Sieur, will you, will you come with me?"

The knight, his master had laughed shortly. "No, I will not. You are not a child, Marron. I will order you to go, though, if that makes it easier for you. Remember, you have promised me your obedience."

"Yes, sieur."

Another laugh, more kindly in the face of his misery; and, "We can wash and dress first, though. And eat, I would not send you fasting to such a trial. Can you fetch a tray without spilling it, or shall I send another lad?"

"I can fetch it, sieur."

AND HAD DONE, had fetched it and carried it away again, had done all for his master that a squire should though it had cost agonies of pain, agonies of anxiety; and now at last, too soon was making slow steps towards the infirmary, cursing his arm and all its long history of mistreatment, cursing himself and everyone except Sieur Anton who'd caused the wound to start with.

Nearly there despite his dawdling, he turned a corner and found Rudel sitting in an embrasure with a small reed pipe in his mouth, moving his fingers over the holes but not blowing, making no sound at all.

"Marron, good morning." The greeting was cheerful enough, though the eyes were watchful.

No more so than Marron's. *I am from Surayon*, he'd said, and little more.

"I have to go to the infirmary. Sir." Still no easy *Rudel*. He never would have found that truly easy, with a man twice his age and many times his experience of the world; he might no longer be a brother here, but the lord God help him, he wanted some distance today.

"Yes, I thought you might," a casual smile hinting that there was no mystery at all in this meeting, only a little

thought, a little care and a willingness to wait. Also no
pretence that this was not deliberate. "How is the arm?"

"Not good, sir." Sieur Anton's words, because he
could think of none of his own.

"No? Show me."

Well, that was better than showing Master Infirmarer.
Marron eased back his sleeve, displayed his arm with its
distorted, miscoloured flesh.

No hiss of breath this time, and no anxiety on Rudel's
face as there had been on Sieur Anton's: only a thoughtful interest, a slow consideration, and then a finger lifted
to touch gently, first here and then there.

"Does this hurt? And this? How if I press, is that
worse . . . ?"

Marron bore it with nods and grunts for answer, trying
not to flinch even when that careful finger sent a surge of
pain all through his arm and on through every bone of
him, making him dizzy and shaky on his feet.

"Steady, lad." Rudel's strong hand gripped his shoulder, held him still until his head cleared. Then the jongleur's head lowered to the bandage, and Marron heard
him sniff deeply, once and then again.

"Sir?"

"You've a malaise in there, lad, it's been too long left
unhealing. And Master Infirmarer will do little enough
for it; he can't stop the sickness, only wait till it's stench-
ing bad and then cut it off. At the elbow maybe, at the
shoulder more like, if he waits."

Marron didn't question Rudel's judgement. Blindly
believing, his first impulse was to ask again for company.
"Sir, would you come and talk to him? He won't listen to
me, but . . ."

"No more to me, lad. I'm a jongleur, remember, and
he's a proud man. What do I know of men's bodies, or the
poisons that corrupt them? What could I possibly know,
that he does not? But in any case, there's no need. That's
what Master Infirmarer would do for you, he'd leave you
with a paddle or a stump. I can do better. Come with me."

He walked off along the passage, away from the infirmary; Marron hesitated only a moment before following, though he breathed doubt as much as hope. What indeed could a jongleur know, that the Master Infirmarer of the Society of Ransom did not?

I am from Surayon. There was only that, the ultimate declaration of sorcery, heresy and treason. It wasn't much, to build a hope upon.

But no, in honesty, that wasn't all. There was the man himself, and the confidence of him: last night the confidence to trust, this morning it seemed the confidence to heal. To diagnose, and then to heal — and Marron hadn't doubted the diagnosis, so why doubt him now?

Because he's a jongleur, because he's from Surayon, because he's the Order's enemy and my master's enemy and must be mine also . . .

But still Marron followed him to a small windowless chamber that stood dark and empty, a storeroom lacking stores. Rudel pushed the door to behind them; it grated along the floor and its hinges squeaked, and when it was closed there was no light at all.

"Now," his voice said in the shadows, "we need at least a glow to work by. Don't be scared, boy. You asked me once if I'd seen magic, do you remember? The true answer to that is, never in the dark . . ."

A soft-shining ball of light floated between them, above their heads. Marron glanced at it briefly, then gazed levelly at Rudel.

"Well," the jongleur said, "I see that you're not scared. Of course, you've seen the King's Eye, haven't you? No reason why you should be, then; but I've known men twice your age who pissed themselves when I conjured a little light, and then refused to admit it after. Refused to admit either part of it, the light or the piss . . ."

He'd seen more than the King's Eye, though that was enough and more, far more than this. He'd seen the preceptor call forth the sign of the God in flowing blue light every night before service, and set torches aflame with it after. And, more nearly, "Sir, I have seen this before."

"What?" Rudel was very still suddenly, and his little light burned brighter, burned hard into Marron's eyes.

"This light, sir. I have seen another man do this," and was not apologizing for it, standing squarely to the truth and glad for the chance of it, for the change.

"When have you—Wait." Rudel reached for his shoulder—*wrong shoulder*, but Marron wasn't going to say so, certainly wasn't going to show how much that fierce grip hurt him, even so high on his bad arm—and said, demanded, "You saw him, didn't you? You saw Redmond!"

"I don't know, sir," more truth, "but I saw the man in the cells. He wouldn't tell me his true name."

"And no more should I have done. Forget it, if you can," though he must have known that Marron could not. Any name would have been hard to lose; that one, not possible. "Only tell me how it happened, that you saw him. You must have caught him unawares, surely, if he made a light like this. He wouldn't have known to trust you . . ."

There were other questions there, how Rudel knew to trust Marron, and whether he was right; but all Marron said was, "Yes, sir," and then briefly the story of his last afternoon.

"So. Two from Surayon, and you have met them both now. And betrayed neither. That's your life forfeit, Marron, if not your soul."

"My soul too, sir," he said, stubbornly insistent. All his life he had known this, that the God condemned black heresy and all who harboured it. The death that came first, in the fire or otherwise, the justice of the Church was only a forerunner.

"I don't think so, lad. Truly, I don't. But never mind now, eh? You've given us your silence; I don't ask for your faith too. Let's see what I can do for you instead, shall we? Give me your hand."

The hurting one, he meant, the one that already looked swollen and discoloured as the arm above it was, worse than an hour ago. Marron held it out, though even so much movement was painful and only the pain said that it was still something of his, so stiff and awkward it felt, like a length of wood clumsily grafted onto living flesh. Rudel took the weight of it in one hand while his other unpicked the knot of the bandage and peeled that away, pulling sharply when it stuck to itself and to the open wound beneath. Marron let out a hissing whistle, the best he could manage for a scream; the jongleur apologized distractedly.

The arm looked very bad. Even the muted light of Rudel's magic couldn't hide the streaking in the flesh, even the pain that blurred Marron's eyes and made his head swim couldn't stop him seeing creamy yellow pus in the gaping wound. No balm, no horse-liniment would cure this now. Hot knives, he thought, were all his future held; and would Sieur Anton keep a one-armed squire?

Rudel's thumb stroked down all the length of his forearm, and left a numbing coolness where it touched. Again, the other hand, the other side; Marron sighed softly, as the pain receded.

Again, this time with all the fingers spread, spanning the open mouth of the wound. Rudel said, "My friend in the cell below could do this better."

Not with those hands, Marron thought, remembering. And opened his mouth to say so, and gasped instead; not with pain this time, nor the fear of it, but only with surprise as a warmth flowed from Rudel's fingers, flooding through his arm like water, soothing, cleansing.

He closed his eyes against the prick of tears, and turned his head aside. And condemned himself for cowardice, turned back, looked down deliberately to see how those damning streaks receded as he watched, how the skin of his arm paled from purple-red to pink.

"Sir, what are you—" No, that was foolish, he knew what; but, "How are you doing this?"

"We have a certain skill, with living flesh," Rudel said. "I cannot knit the wound together, time must do that, and your own strength of body; but I can drive the poison out, and subdue the pain of it for a while."

"Is it magic?"

"I suppose it is. Or knowledge, rather; but that's what magic is. An understanding of what lies under the surface of the world. I can see more clearly, or deeper than you do; my eyes are not defeated by the surface of a thing, when I choose to see beneath it. And what I can see, I can work upon."

All this time his hands were working, touching, stroking; more than Marron's arm was tingling now with the warmth that ran from the jongleur's fingers. All his body pulsed with it.

"There. That's as much as I can manage," and indeed Rudel was sweating, seeming to shiver as he released Marron's arm, as he stepped back and pushed his big hands through his damp hair.

"Sir, thank you . . ." Marron's turn now to touch that arm, in wonder at the lack of pain. The wound was there still, like a dark hole ripped unkindly and gaping red at the edges; but the sickly glint of pus had dried to a colourless crust, and the streaks that had warned of evil working within had reduced to a little redness, a little local swelling.

"Others could have done more. If you're careful, though, it should heal now. Come, let's put that bandage back. Fresh air would be better, but we don't want your master asking questions."

"No, sir," fervently. "Please, what am I to tell Sieur Anton? He told me to see the Master Infirmarer . . ."

"Lie to him, Marron. I'm sorry, but you must."

Marron nodded unhappily. It was a small deception next to the great secret that Rudel had burdened him with, but still it hung upon him, souring the wonder.

Sensing that, perhaps, Rudel said, "Marron, let me tell you something about Surayon."

"Sir, I don't want to—"

"If you are to help me—no, that's too fast, I won't assume it, but if I am to ask for your help, you have to know a little, at least. A little of the truth. There have been a great many lies told about us. Lies that justify what has been done to my friend below, and worse things done to others." Rudel settled himself on the floor, and gestured to Marron to do the same. He sank down cautiously against the opposite wall, cradling his arm against a pain that didn't come.

"When Outremer was won," Rudel began slowly, "when the Ekhed were overrun in the south and the Sharai driven back into the desert, it was the King's voice—the Duc de Charelles he was then, before he took the Kingship—it was his voice that divided up the land. His voice against the Church, largely. He had led the army, all the separate armies; he was overlord, he had kept the commanders focused on the great goal, Ascariel. Without him they would have broken apart long before, warred between themselves, seized what land they could and likely lost it all within a year or two as the Sharai tribes picked them off, one by one. A rotten fruit will fall to ruin. But de Charelles held them all together, with the great aid of his friend, the Duc d' Albéry.

"Then he seized Ascariel, and the Church Fathers claimed it for their own as soon as the news reached them. If they had been given the Holy City, they would have taken all Outremer."

"Would that have been so bad, sir?" It seemed to Marron that the Church Fathers had hegemony over the homelands, in despite of kings and courts. Pomp belonged to the princes, power to the priests. That was the way of things; even his uncle's lord, the Baron Thivers, deferred to the presbytery whenever his tenants looked to him for judgement. No one protested overmuch beyond a little ritual grumbling when a decision went against them. It worked, he thought; why worry?

"Imagine your preceptor and his like, ruling the Sanctuary Land as they rule this Order. It would have been catastrophe."

Marron thought about it briefly—and nodded. He'd seen little of Outremer yet, but he had seen Fra' Piet lead his troop against a heretic village, and he had seen the preceptor's justice just last night. This was not, after all, the homelands. He knew that many, perhaps most of the people in this country did not hold to the true faith, as the Order defined it; but the very ground here was still holy to them, as it was to the Church. They still insisted on their right to worship their gods in their way. How long would the preceptor have tolerated that? There had been massacres enough in the early years, before and after the fall of Ascariel; under the rule of the Order, which at this distance was the rule of the Church, there would be massacres still, and many of them. Barren villages, razed temples, deserted towns . . .

"De Charelles had been fighting the bishops all through the campaign, as much as he'd been fighting the Ekhed or the Sharai. There were plenty riding in his train, and they wanted to burn every unbeliever that they passed. He kept them in check until Ascariel, but even so much wasn't easy. Afterwards would have been impossible, if they had been ceded the authority they sought.

"Technically, though, they weren't there as emissaries of the Church Fathers, only as vassals of their temporal lords; so de Charelles summoned a conclave and divided up the territory, without inviting any of the bishops in. By the time the Fathers heard about it, they were far too late to react. The thing was done: de Charelles was King by acclamation, the states of Outremer were established and they none of them belonged to the Church."

Tallis and Elessi, the northernmost states, the head of the hammer—and Roq de Rançon on the northernmost border between the two: the pivot, the stronghold, the nail that gripped the head.

Below Tallis, Less Arvon; below that Ascariel the state, with Ascariel the city at its heart. Rudel was right, who held Ascariel held Outremer, their hand it was that gripped the hammer. The King's hand it was, and always had been.

Between those two, though, between Less Arvon and Ascariel lay a range of mountains, thrusting like an elbow towards the coast; and in those mountains lay hidden Surayon, the Folded Land, which must have been all but hidden even before it was Folded: buried in its valleys, a tiny state so unlike its sisters, so weak, a runt, a gesture . . .

"He had to placate the Fathers somehow, or they'd have been fomenting rebellion among the faithful just when he needed to look to his borders. He was King; he gave the dukedom of Ascariel to his son Raime, which was almost as good as giving it to the Church. A pious man, even then he listened to his priests more than to his father. Since then, with the King in seclusion—well. There are few Catari remaining in Ascariel, despite all the amnesties, and every temple follows your order of service. Other, older traditions have been denounced, and none would dare revive them.

"The King knew, I think, that this would happen; and he knew that there'd be trouble with Less Arvon. The Duke of Arvon was a fiery man then, and his son the Little Duke is worse. They give no credence to the Church, and little respect to Ascariel. That's why the King created Surayon, and gave the principality to the Duc d'Albéry: to act as a buffer between them, a cool head and a cool voice. Rank without strength, a man both sides could listen to without distrust.

"The Duc d'Albéry had been first squire, then friend, then counsellor to the Duc de Charelles. But de Charelles became the King and went immediately into his seclusion, without warning or explanation; d'Albéry became Princip of Surayon, which brings its own seclusion. Time passes, and men change.

"The Princip was always a curious man. More probing than prayerful, he has been called. Not good at taking things on faith, and always interested in what was new, always asking why. Which might be another reason the King gave him Surayon, to make an uncomfortable neighbour both north and south. Arvonians are great traditionalists, as the Ascari are religious; perhaps the King thought d'Albéry could be both a peacemaker between them and a thorn in their sides. It makes little sense to my eyes, but the King's mind is a mystery, and not only to me.

"The Princip might have been a bishop himself, if he hadn't been born to land and high position; he had the inclination as a child, he spent some years of his youth in a monastery. He might have been a Church Father himself by now, if it hadn't been for that questioning mind.

"It was that brought him to Outremer, I'm sure, more than loyalty to his friend or service to his God. Especially not service to the God. He made a good soldier, but he hated the war with a passion; he pushed for the amnesty at Conclave, and was first and most thorough in its implementation.

"So Surayon became a haven for displaced Catari, a place of refuge. First state to trade with the Sharai, too. And the Princip talked to all these people: believer, unbeliever or heretic, there were no questions asked at the borders but plenty in the palace. He brought in scholars and friends from the homelands to talk to them also. When the Fathers protested, flirting with heresy they called it, he brought in bishops and priests too — but they were mostly friends of his before they were ordained or acquired rank, and his habits of question are infectious. They were none of them blindly obedient to the commands of the Fathers, nor to the teachings of the Church.

"That was a long generation since. We are anathema to the Church now, and to our neighbours, north and south; but the Princip protects us, and we go on learning. We *are* heretics, Marron, by your Order's definition: you must understand that. We don't worship your God in your way. Neither any god of the Catari: we are heretics also to the devouts of the Sharai, of the Ekhed, of them all. But the Sharai treat us more kindly than our own people do. We share knowledge, we share trust, we share our children even; and so we can do such as you have seen this morning, some of us. Some can do a great deal more. It's not evil, it's only understanding; and that's Surayon, that's what we are. We will not shy from any question, so long as it leads us towards truth."

This was the man, Marron struggled to remind himself, who only ten minutes since was urging or ordering Marron to lie for his own protection. Truth must be a flexible concept, in Surayon as elsewhere.

But he thought Rudel was mostly speaking true here. What he'd said was not so different from what the priests said about Surayon, only that they thundered it as blasphemy. The bones at least were the same, though the living spirit they described could not have been more opposite.

And it didn't matter, anyway. True or false, neither image was real, not to Marron, not there in a room at the Roq that day. What was real was his arm, rotten with corruption an hour since, halfway to healthy now; what was real was the man Redmond who called himself Jonson, who lay in blood and filth with broken hands in the cells below; what was real was the ashes of a great fire, the burned bones of children.

Rudel was quiet now, seemingly waiting for him to speak. Marron hesitated, opened his mouth and found his lips unaccountably dry, had to pause to lick them before he tried again.

"You said," he began, knowing that he damned himself with every word he said and meant to say, "last night you said that you wanted to rescue your friend."

"Yes."

"How can I help?"

*   *   *

IT WASN'T DIFFICULT to collect black habits for disguise. Marron had been ready with excuses, with lies hot on his tongue, but there was no need; the vestry was so busy no one had time to ask questions. Men from several troops were all drawing fresh clothes at once; Marron simply picked three habits from a pile and walked out with them. Rudel lingered, talking to one of the brothers briefly before he followed, back to that convenient storeroom.

With habits thrown on over their other clothes and a spare thrust under Marron's girdle, giving him a shape he'd never owned, with hoods drawn up to hide their faces they walked through the castle, through the courts, through the kitchens quite unstayed.

There was still no guard at the head of the narrow stair, no interest from the brothers at work by the ovens. Marron held his breath a little as they slipped into the shadows of the stairwell, but this time no screams rose up to meet them. Fingers brushed the curve of rock on either side, soft boots made little noise on cautious feet beneath their habits; none the less Marron found himself longing for sandals. Treachers, he thought, should tread more softly than they knew.

At the last turning before the chamber below, just where a little fugitive lamplight made a visible shadow of Rudel, he stopped. One hand retreated inside the habit, slipping free of the sleeve altogether; Marron guessed it must be fumbling for something Rudel carried inside his everyday clothes.

After a minute, the empty sleeve filled and the hand reappeared. It held something clenched within the fingers now; something that began to glow, to pulse with light as Marron watched, to beat clear and blue with the steady rhythm of what might be Rudel's heartbeat, was far too slow and steady to be his own.

Rudel opened his hand, and it was a blue stone that lay there on his palm, an *ayar*-stone Marron thought, though he had to squint to see. Whether Rudel invested it with that light, or whether he used his skills simply to draw out the stone's own subtleties, Marron couldn't tell. A stone that shone, that was all he knew, something obviously far greater than a sign of faith.

A stone that fell, as Rudel tossed it; but it almost flew, it fell more slowly than it ought, as though the air were honey-thick around it. Struck a step and bounced, higher than a stone should; and the stone sang as it struck, unless it was the stone of the step that was singing.

It rose and fell, struck and bounced and sang again, a different note this time, high and bright and resonating sweetly with the first as it lingered. Marron felt a thrill in his bones at that music, he felt almost transparent in the pulsing light; it was an effort to remember that there were guards below if none above, that they must be alerted, wondering, suspicious. That this sudden, unexpected touch of wonder had made a nonsense of the creeping so quietly down this far . . .

He reached to touch Rudel's sleeve, an unspoken question. The older man raised an arm in response, *wait, and trust*; then, as the glowing stone vanished around the curve of the stair, leaving only its singing light behind as a guide, that same arm gestured slowly, *forward now*.

Marron followed Rudel, his nervousness overridden by the summoning music. Down the last steep steps and into the chamber below, and yes, there were the guards: two brothers standing rapt, entranced, their eyes wide and unblinking, gazing at the stone as it hung impossibly in the air, as the light of it flared and faded and flared again, as the music throbbed and echoed in that small space.

It wasn't only shock or wonder that held them so still. Their faces were quite vacant; it was as though their spirits had been snatched from them, leaving only coarse and empty flesh to occupy their habits as they stood. They seemed to notice nothing when Rudel walked casually between them, into the passage beyond. Marron stared at the stone, as they were staring; and he too felt the call of it, felt his own will drawn forth, draining his muscles and

his mind till he was lost almost in the beat and rhythm of
the light, of the song . . .

"Marron!" A hand gripped his neck, and shook him
gently. He startled, shuddering; turned his head to find
Rudel. There was a smile on the man's face but tension
beneath, some urgency in his voice as he whispered,
"Come, I need you to show me where my friend lies.
Close your eyes, if the *ayar* is too strong for you . . ."

"Yes, sir," uncertainly. He could close his eyes, but
what about his ears? The music called to him, as keenly
as the light. He pulled his hood lower over his face for
what small protection that could offer and took a step,
two difficult steps towards the passage.

And checked, turned, went back; fighting against the
summons of the stone, he walked tight-legged and determined to where the oil-lamp burned unregarded in its
niche, its gentle yellow light quite lost in the fierce glare
of blue.

Marron picked it up, gazing in at its pale flame, using
that as a shield against the pervasive, seductive pulse in
the room around him.

"Good lad," Rudel called, his voice soft, barely audi-
ble above the high wordless chant of the *ayar*-stone's
song. Marron didn't know why he was bothering to be
quiet still; he thought thunderclaps and lightning would
not call those men back from wherever their lost souls
wandered. "You're not as mazed as you seem, are you?"

Yes, I am, he thought, all but stumbling over the hem
of his habit as he tried to walk with his eyes still fixed in
the lamp's flame. The stone's song rang in his skull, a
chord constantly changing as if it sought, as if it reached
to find and draw him back into its spell again. He struggled to focus his swimming mind as his eyes were focused, feeling his way, glad when Rudel's big hand
closed on his sleeve and tugged him into the shadows of
the passage.

The light and music followed them, but less overpow-
eringly now; after a dozen paces he risked lifting his eyes

from the lamp and saw Rudel laughing at him. There was a kindness in the laughter, though, and something close to admiration in the nod that followed.

"Well done. And I'm sorry, I'd forgotten that you would be as vulnerable as they. It takes a strong mind to fight off the lure of an *ayar*-stone awoken."

"What of the penitents?" Marron asked in a whisper, his anxious eyes darting to the doors of the cells.

"There are none. They were all released yesterday: a special dispensation, by order of the preceptor. They were lucky; his need for men overruled the need for discipline."

It was true, the cells were empty. Or their doors were closed, at least; he didn't open any, to check inside.

Only at the end of the passage was the one door still bolted, speaking of its prisoner within. Marron reached for the bolt with his free hand, forgetful for a moment, remembering his injury only when Rudel forestalled him with a touch.

"I told you to be careful with that arm."

"It doesn't hurt, sir." *Not any more.*

"Even so, you should rest it. And keep it hidden for a few days, if you can. Don't let your master see how much improved it is. Now, the stone will hold those men till I release them and they'll remember nothing, they'll only be surprised how quickly the morning has passed them by; but someone else may come, so fast as we can, lad, though I fear that'll not be fast . . ."

Rudel worked the bolt as he spoke, easing it back from its bracket. He pulled the door open and grunted in surprise, facing a black blankness.

"What . . . ?"

"It's just a curtain, sir."

"Oh." Rudel pushed through, with Marron following. The cell was in darkness, no witchlight from the prisoner today; Marron raised the lamp high, and the flickering glow showed them all the walls of the cell, lined with the instruments of question.

Again, Rudel grunted. "Where—?"

"Over there, sir." Just a pile of rags, it was hard to see that there was a man among them. Rudel muttered something under his breath, which might have been a curse or a spell; when he touched the lamp it flared far brighter, an unnatural white light driving sharp-edged shadows around the cell.

Then the big man moved, crossing the cell in quick strides to fall on his knees beside the stirring prisoner.

"Redmond." No hiding the name now, no point to it; Marron was as committed, as guilty as he. "Redmond, how bad—?"

The man on the mattress pushed himself up slowly onto one elbow, with a clink of chain. The rags fell away, answer enough; Marron heard Rudel's breath hiss from his mouth, matching the prisoner's own harsh, effortful breathing.

"You, is it? And my little friend." His voice was weaker than yesterday, even; Marron put the lamp down, making shadows dance, and poured water into the goblet that had been set again just out of reach.

Rudel took the goblet, and held it for the man to drink; shaking, Redmond spilt as much as he swallowed. Then, "This is foolish, Rudel," he said.

"No. This is necessary. What, should I leave you to the tender brethren's care? Should I stroll contentedly about my business overhead, and give never a thought to all your pains? Or to your future?"

"I have no future. Which being true, the more reason why you should not risk yourself. Nor strangers, who don't know what they chance," with a glance across at Marron.

"He knows enough. Enough to choose. Young men were always idiots. Remember? But you have as much future as any of us, Redmond."

"Or as little," dryly snorted.

"That, too. If we're not here, though, they can do us little harm."

"And how will you remove us, shall we just walk out through the gate?"

"Better than that, we can ride. You and I, in brothers' garb. A party leaves this afternoon for Elessi. A mixed party, knights and brothers and private men-at-arms, to guard a pair of girls. The Shadow's daughter, and her companion. Had you heard?"

"I heard she was on her way. Not here."

"Well, here she is; and sent away now, since the Sharai raided two nights since."

"Did they?" That struck home, it seemed, far sharper than the other news. "Hasan?"

"It's said so, yes."

"Well. He failed, I presume."

"This time. Thanks to Marron."

"Indeed?" Another glance, and this time the hint of a smile to follow, in so far as his twisted mouth could manage that. "But this is politics, and young Marron is impatient. I am sorry, Rudel, you were explaining your plan, I think?"

"That's it. This party is put together hurriedly; the talk earlier was that it would leave tomorrow. Now it is today. There will be a deal of confusion; it will not be hard for you and I to hide ourselves among them. Then we ride out, we slip away at first camp, and no one here knows that you have gone; not till tomorrow at least, and I will leave something that should confound them for a day or two longer."

"A simulacrum. Good. Rudel, that is an attractively simple plan."

"But?"

"But I cannot walk."

"Ah. Your feet, is it?"

"As my hands are. Neither can I ride."

"Well, I can do something for those. For the moment . . ."

"Not for a day's ride, Rudel. Nor even half a day. Nor for the flight after that. I am dead, boy, I have accepted that and so should you. The best kindness you could do me now would be to help me cheat their questioners."

"*No!* It is not, it cannot be that bleak . . ." Rudel thought scowlingly; Marron watched him, watched the prisoner, watched the door. And took a moment's pleasure, though only a moment's, to hear Rudel called "boy."

Then, "We will still make the attempt," Rudel declared. "I can help you out of here, to a place of hiding. Then, this girl is Julianne de Rance, she must have baggage; she must have a baggage-wagon. So will the knights, those lordlings are fussy about their dress. Or there are traders travelling with the escort, wagons again. One way or another, we will find a way to move you. In a box, if need be."

"You're a fool, Rudel. Better to leave me, I'm quite prepared to die."

"I'm not prepared to let you."

"Stupid. It will happen; it will be here if you leave me, it may yet be here if you try to take me. Then like as not it would be you too, and you must not risk yourself."

"I'll be careful," Rudel promised, laughing. Fluent liars they were, Marron thought, these men from Surayon.

"Sir," he murmured, too soft for either man to hear. Tried again more loudly, more boldly. "Sir . . ."

"Yes, Marron?"

"Someone will see us and ask questions, if we carry him through the kitchens."

"We won't need to carry him. As with your arm, so with his feet; I can heal somewhat, and hide the pain a while."

"Yes, sir," because he'd known that already, he only wanted to have the man about it.

"Ah. You think I should stop arguing with my stubborn friend here and do what good I can, is that right?"

Of course it was right, and of course he could not say

so directly, except by a fierce flush. "There is, there is danger, sir, as long as we are here. You said so . . ."

"The questioners came early today," the man Redmond said from his pallet. "That's why I'm so weak. I couldn't light a firefly just now, Marron. But they won't be back till tomorrow, and no one else visits me. They probably won't be back," correcting himself swiftly. "Even so, the boy's right. Set on, Rudel. Don't worry with the most of me, just work on my feet. The rest I can bear."

For how long was a question Marron dared not ask aloud, and neither he thought did Rudel. The man looked in no condition to be stowed in a box or hidden on a baggage-wagon; but men could endure much, when death was the alternative. Even a man who screamed so much where it could do no harm to scream, might bear the same pain in silence where that might save his life.

Rudel pulled the rags away from Redmond's body. The ankles were shackled as well as the wrists, Marron saw. That would stop prisoners reaching the water with their feet, he supposed; then he saw the feet themselves, and thought the shackles quite unnecessary.

Cruel boots, that man must have been wearing. He wondered what even Rudel's magic could do, against crushed and twisted bones and mangled flesh. *Not much*, had to be the answer. It hadn't healed his own wound, after all, only sapped the poison. If there were poison in those feet, it was the least of all the harm done to them.

Even so, Rudel took them into his lap, held them in soothing, smoothing hands and began to croon under his breath. The fierce light dimmed, letting dull yellow lamp-light fill the cell again. All Rudel's focus, Marron realised, all his attention was on his work; there was nothing to spare now for better seeing, and no need to see more than he had already.

Marron let his eyes drift around the walls, trying at first to make out what each separate instrument was for and how it worked. Learning too much, understanding too well—*there, that wooden box with the wedges, that must be the boot that wrecked those feet. One at a time, too, that's worse. Take it apart, build it afresh around each foot in turn. Let the man see, show him how it works. Then adjust to fit. Adjust the foot, that is. With those wedges, driven home by hammering, look, there's the hammer . . .*

Enough of that, very quickly. He slipped over to the curtain and beyond it, to stand with the door half-shut and his head peering around, watching the passage.

Watching the end of the passage, if he was honest; where blue light still beat to the rhythm of Rudel's blood, from where music still sounded, thin at this distance but still distinct, still striking home. The stone at least was not weakened by Rudel's distraction. Perhaps its power was inherent, then, and not endowed . . .

HOW LONG HE stood there, he had no idea. Time was impossible of judgment anyway, here where they were buried so far from sunlight; and he lost the touch of his own body, even, knowing nothing but the pulsing call, the song's high summons until there was again a hand on his shoulder, shaking him, jerking him back into himself.

"Marron," Rudel said softly, "I can use your help now."

"I was," *I was caught by the stone again, not so strong as you named me after all,* "I was watching, in case anyone came . . ." He could lie too, why not?

"I know." *I know what you were doing,* Rudel's smile said, *or what was being done to you.*

Marron went back into the cell at Rudel's heels to find Redmond sitting up on his mattress, gaunt and pale still but looking better by far than he had, when? When Marron left the cell: ten minutes ago, an hour ago, whenever.

"We need to make a simulacrum," Rudel said, "something to confuse whoever comes, so that for a day or two they think they still have Redmond in their chains. I can do this; but first I must open those shackles, without breaking them. I can do that too, but it will take time. What I want you to do, Marron, is collect whatever you can find in the cell here that could be man-shaped, or any part of a man. Metal or wood or rag, it doesn't matter; I can cloak the truth of it, but I need something to work on. Pretend you're making a poppet, for your sister to play with. It needn't look real, or anything close to real. Man-size, that's all that counts. You know how children pretend."

"Er, yes, sir . . ."

He'd never had a sister, but Aldo did; they'd made toys for her, figures scratched together from twigs and straw that had delighted her past reason.

This was different, though, hugely so. He looked around, trying not to see purposes now but only shape; and still felt stupid, expected the men's laughter as he reached for giant tongs that were hanging on one wall.

A brazier stood below them. Heated, they could tear a man's flesh from his bones; Redmond might know that too well, by the fresh bubbled scars on his chest. But never mind knowing. They were an arm's length or longer, and jointed; they might make a pair of legs for a foolish figure.

There were wooden staves for arms, so much was easy, and a great iron ball so heavy he could barely lift it, that could be a head. A body to join them all together, that was not so simple; he gazed, thought, finally scooped up a double armful of the rags that made Redmond's bedding and his clothing both. He laid out the largest, heaped the rest atop it and sat down to knot them all together.

A glance across as he worked showed that neither man was watching. Rudel had wrapped both hands around one of the shackles that held Redmond's wrists; Marron thought he was staring at it, staring through his own fingers at the crude iron ring. Except that his eyes were closed, he could be seeing nothing. It was Redmond who was staring, at the top of his friend's head. Could these men see into each other's skulls, to read their thoughts?

Marron turned back to his own task, something he could do and was determined to do well. *At least let them not laugh, not that . . .*

KNOTS AND TWISTS of rag: he bound the tongs to the loose body he'd tied together, and then each of the two staves that were to be its arms. The iron ball was harder, he couldn't see how to fix that to the rest so that even a child could pretend the figure was whole: *this poppet's been beheaded*, he thought, and swallowed a tight little giggle.

And shook the stupidity out of his head, and looked around again; and saw rope, a thin coil of it in one corner. Fetched that and set about weaving a simple net, looking up only when a metallic click snatched at his attention.

That shackle was open, he saw, though he couldn't see or guess how. Locked or riveted, either way it should have resisted the force of a man's hands, and Rudel hadn't even been trying to force it.

Magic, he thought, without even a shiver of wonder any more, and turned back to his weaving and knotting.

WHEN HE WAS done, he wrapped the net around the ball—*hair and a beard*, he thought, stupid again, close to giggling again—and tied all the ends to the rag body of his grotesque poppet. He couldn't play with it, he couldn't so much as make it sit up, the iron ball was far too heavy; but lying down as it was, it looked—well, actually it looked ridiculous and nothing remotely like a man, but he'd done what had been asked of him. That, at least . . .

There had been other sounds from the corner where the pallet lay, where the men were: clicks and rattles, murmuring voices. When he looked, he saw that Redmond was free at last of his chains. More, he was moving with Rudel's help, struggling slowly to his feet.

That should not be possible, even on this most impossible of days. The man's feet were still wrenched far from human shape; Marron ached in sympathy, just looking. He couldn't imagine the crippling agony of such ruin, far less the agony of standing on them.

But Redmond was standing, and showing no pain. He did lean on Rudel's arm, but Marron thought that was only for balance, for support against a dizzying weakness.

"Good," Rudel said to him. "How does it feel?"

"It doesn't feel at all," said softly, said almost with a chuckle.

"Well, you'll suffer for that later; but it should see you out of here now, and on your own feet. Now, Marron. Good," again, as his eyes ran over Marron's creation where it lay on the floor. "That's perfect. Can you lift it over onto the mattress?"

"Yes, sir." Or not lift, exactly, but lift and drag, slowly, with great care against the fragility of the knots. One stave-arm did slip free of its bindings; Marron flushed, muttered, gathered it up and forced it further into the mess of rags, tied it in more tightly.

"Marron, I said to rest that arm, remember?"

"Sir, you said to make a man-sized poppet for you." *Remember?*—but he wasn't up to insolence of that degree. Not yet.

"All right. But be careful. If it bleeds again, it could poison again. Now come here and take my place, help to keep Redmond on his feet."

NOT A HEAVY task, that: the man was lighter than the poppet without its head or felt so, bird-hollow bones and no flesh.

"Your arm?" Redmond asked, and there was more

strength in his voice than anywhere in his body, and his voice was thread-thin and empty.

"A wound, sir," and Marron shook back his sleeve to show the bandage; he had seen so much of this man's pain, he owed that much at least. "It won't heal . . ."

"It's not been given a chance to heal," Rudel grunted from where he hunched across the figure on the mattress, looping shackles over staves and tongs as though they were wrists and ankles, as though the slack iron gripped tightly. "Torn open, ripped open again and again, at least once deliberately, not to let it heal."

"You, uh, he, uh, Rudel has made it better, though . . ."

"For the moment. Like Redmond, you will pay later; and both of you deserve it. How could you let this happen to you, old fool?"

"Some busy steward knew me. Can you credit it? Forty years on, I was playing trader with wagon and ribbons and no beard to my chin and still the idiot stands there stammering, 'The Red Earl, Redmond of Corbonne, oh, sir, call out your guard . . .' What could I do?"

"You could have killed them all," Rudel murmured, in a tone that denied his own words, *of course you couldn't*.

Marron believed both, that the old man was capable of it but never would. Marron, frankly, knew himself to be gaping. Redmond of Corbonne? The Red Earl, the hero of the great war declared heretic, renegade ten years later, one of the few Surayonnaise anathematised by name and known by name even back in the homelands—the Red Earl, this patchwork starveling creature?

Marron held a legend in his arms and did not, could not believe it.

Which Redmond knew, could clearly read on his face. The dull eyes glittered for a moment, as he whispered, "Never mind, lad. All dreams die. Now watch, this might amuse you. Don't be scared . . ."

He nodded towards Rudel and the figure; Marron wrenched his head that way, though not his giddy thoughts, not yet. This was the Red Earl: a master, a monster in battle, who had ridden his horse knee-deep in blood through the streets of Ascariel, who had shielded the King himself from the spear of the High Imam on the steps of the great temple and then hewn the Imam's head from his shoulders; a great and heretical monster fit to frighten children with, who had been corrupted by his overlord in the Folded Land, who had with his own hands killed every last true priest trapped in that unhappy land when the evil Princip closed it off from the world by his wicked charms . . .

Scared? Why would he be scared, who had seen so much magic done today and other days? Marron frowned, and watched more closely what Rudel was doing.

Rudel was kneeling with the figure, that absurd poppet in his arms like an overgrown child or a sick companion. He had the great head of the thing cradled against his neck, somehow holding the weight of that iron ball between shoulder and chin; he was whispering to it, while his hands stroked all over, wooden arms and body of rags and the long metal legs of it.

As Marron watched, he spat onto the rough iron and rope of its head; and then he let it go, he pulled himself away and stood up.

The figure stayed sitting as he had left it, a mockery in chains. The head should have fallen then, the whole thing should have toppled over and torn itself apart, and did not. It sat like a man, leaning its weight on one arm; and when it did move it tried to stand, it tried to follow Rudel.

And was stopped by its shackles, which should have fallen from its limbs and did not, though they had no flesh to cleave to.

Marron gasped. Only Redmond's grip on his arm kept him from stepping back, only the Red Earl's whisper of a chuckle stopped him from pulling free and running. *See? I knew you'd be scared*, the chuckle said. Marron shuddered and stood firm.

"Well?" That was Rudel, and the question was aimed at him.

"Sir, you said, you said it was to fool whoever came. It does not," his voice dried, so that he had to cough and lick his lips and try again, "it does not look like the Earl Redmond to me . . ." Nor like any living thing, human or otherwise.

"No. Not yet, and not to you. Neither will it. But bring him close, Marron, help him over here."

The last thing Marron wanted to do was to get any closer to that animated thing, where it was standing hunched over, at the limits of its chains and pulling. But Rudel's eyes were on him, and the echo of the Red Earl's chuckle was in his head yet; he forced his reluctant feet forward, while a cold rank sweat prickled all his skin.

Closer and closer, slower and slower but closer still, almost to touching distance; if it weren't for the shackles, the thing could reach and touch him. Not that, but Redmond did reach out and touch it, lightly on what should have been its elbow; then he drew his hand back, spat on his fingers and reached to touch again.

"Now," Rudel said softly.

And now the thing changed, or seemed to. Marron could still see tongs and staves, but he could see also a shimmer around them, a glassy transparent flesh. The soft and greasy padding of its body acquired hard ridges of ribs and a glimmer of skin, though that was all seeming, it was rags yet. Rags and illusion. Even the head, that impossible weight balanced on what could not possibly hold it, even that cold iron had the image of a face across its net of rope, hints of hair and beard. And yes, that might be Redmond's face, if anyone's . . .

But it wasn't, not anyone's at all; this was a thin and useless magic, it couldn't fool a blind man in the dark. Marron opened his mouth to say so, if more politely, and was forestalled.

"You see what you expect to see, Marron lad," Rudel told him. "You made it, you know what it is. You see a hint of the charm, but only a hint because your mind knows what lies beneath. Everyone sees what they expect to see. The guards, the questioners expect to see Redmond, and they will. For a while, they will. Even when they apply their instruments, they'll see and hear what they expect, because nothing else is possible to them. They *know* they have him here, they know they burn and mutilate a man; and so they will.

"Now. Two brothers came down here; I don't believe anyone was watching, but still three should not walk out together. You go up first, Marron. Give me that spare habit, go back to the storeroom and leave yours there, and then be about your duties. And thank you."

"Yes, sir. Er, what happens next?"

"For you? Nothing. You are your master's squire, nothing more than that. Say nothing, try to remember nothing. Pray for us, perhaps, if you do pray, if you must. Otherwise, I hope that the next you know is gossip in the servants' hall, when at last they notice that one or other of us is missing. There will be a deal of disruption in the castle after that, and I suppose they will think to track along the road to Elessi, but I don't believe they'll find us once we're gone."

"Earl Redmond won't go far, sir, not on his feet . . ." Even with two days' grace, say. Mounted men would catch them in a spare hour, Marron thought.

"No; but if we can't run, we can hide. The men of Surayon are well-practised in evasion, Marron." *We have hidden our whole country, remember?*

REALLY MARRON DIDN'T want to leave, he felt he was being cut out of the story half-told. Rudel was right, though; he shouldn't linger with the men like a conspirator. Let them go, let them get away, forget he was ever a part of their escape. Otherwise it might be himself taking a turn in this cell, facing the questioners, naked and afraid. He thought he would do more than scream; he thought he would betray them all, if any one of those instruments were used on him.

He kept his head low and held his breath as he sidled through the kitchens, but no man showed any interest. As far as he could tell, he wasn't seen either going into the storeroom as a monk or coming out as a squire; and as a squire, again he attracted no notice at all until he reached Sieur Anton's chamber.

Where he was greeted with a bellow of righteous fury, "Where in all the hells on this earth have you been, Marron?"

"Sieur, you sent me to the infirmary." Quite true, he did.

"That was hours ago!"

"Yes, sieur. There are many men there, hurt worse than me . . ." Also true, and equally as deceptive; and then quickly, before the knight asked a question he couldn't misdirect, he said, "Have you been looking for something, sir?"

The travelling-chest stood open and half-empty, with heaps of clothing scattered across the bed and the floor.

"Yes, I've been looking for you. Pack for me, Marron. For us both."

"Sieur?"

"The lady Julianne rides to Elessi today—"

"Yes, sieur."

"You knew?"

"Gossip, sieur. Among the squires."

"I thought you'd been to the infirmary? Well, ne'er mind. Word moves faster than the wind, in this place. Did the gossip say who escorts her?"

"Her own men, sieur," repeating Rudel's words while his mind raced, "and a troop of brothers, and knights beside . . . ?"

"Knights and their squires," Sieur Anton said briskly. "Pack; then run down to the stables. It will be a dreadful scrimmage, especially with the lack of stable-boys to help. Every knight's man will be out to see his master's

needs are serviced, first and best. Be sure that you suc-
ceed. I shall want one of the destriers, Alembert I think,
ready an hour after prayers; and you will need a mule.
There will be a wagon for the chest. If you can't carry it
alone — and don't, don't even try — ask another squire to
help you. That's all."

"Yes, sieur. Uh, should I pack the mail shirt, or—?"

"Don't be a fool, Marron. This isn't a jaunting-party. I
shall wear the mail."

FOUR

A Snare in Shadow and Sun

JULIANNE HAD COME one last time to the midday prayers, and had insisted that Elisande come too: "We've got to look good. Virtuous young women, obedient to the God, the Church and our parents." That had won her no more than a snort, but she'd gone on determinedly, "We don't want to give them any reason to doubt us, anything that would make them watch more carefully than they will in any case."

"They will in any case," Elisande had iterated. "No matter how pure and good we seem to be. They're delivering the young baron's wife, the countess-to-be; you'll have his men about you and all these sworn brothers, all of them with the scent of Sharai blood hot in their nostrils still; what else are they going to be but watchful? That's what they're *for*. Going to service today won't make them any less so."

"Well, it might," Julianne had said, knowing the weakness of her own arguments but convinced none the less that she was right, that any small allaying gesture would help. She still didn't see how they would ever slip away; there she must rely on Elisande, who was smilingly relaxed about it, *not a worry, don't trouble yourself, they'll all be looking the wrong way as we pass. You wouldn't believe how many wrong ways there are, that a man could be looking . . .*

"Please, Elisande?" Julianne had said at last. "Maybe it's unnecessary—"

"Absolutely it's unnecessary," from her friend, which was when she knew that she had won.

"—But please? Because I ask it, if you can't see any better reason? Because I think I ought to go, and I don't want to go alone . . . ?"

That was insistence, cloaked by diplomacy; and at that appeal, Elisande had finally subsided with a nod.

SO THEY HAD come, and had found Blaise also in the gallery, already on his knees with his bare head bowed; he'd looked as though he had been there some time, as though he had come to pray privately before ever the bell had called the brothers and their visitors to worship.

Elisande had stretched out a hand to brush imaginary dust from his shoulders, *see how long this good man's been at his prayers?*

A nudge, a stern glare that had threatened to dissolve into a giggle; Julianne had grabbed her friend's shoulder, gripped it tightly, tried to pretend that she was simply pushing Elisande into her place. And had failed utterly, to judge by the sparkling grin she received in return; and had given up, and bitten down on the back of her own hand hard enough to leave white marks behind, until the resurgent giggles subsided. And then had wanted to take Elisande's hand, simply to do the same to her; but that deceiving girl had been already kneeling at the balustrade, as pious-seeming as Blaise himself, *this is what you wanted, isn't it?*, and there had been nothing Julianne could do but join her.

*   *   *

AFTERWARDS, BLAISE STOOD when they stood, and stepped aside to let them leave first. Seeing his cap gripped tightly in his hands, thinking how many of the brothers and knights below had knelt and prayed with their hoods thrown back, she wondered vaguely what had come of Master Fulke's great mission; she'd heard no more of it, since that first thundering sermon.

Well, thundering sermons had that effect more often than not, especially on young and bullish men. A surge in the soul, an answering cry, a fire that burned for a night—and then the cool bleak light of morning, the drudgeries of duty and the fire burned down to ash. Preaching rarely lasted. Even the famous sermons that had ultimately led to all of this, the great call to arms in the homelands a lifetime since, even those had been only the key that opened the gate to let the people loose. According to her father, at least. Too many younger sons landless, ambitious and bored, he'd said: they'd seized the priests' sermons for their own excuse, as a chance for rewards far greater than the God's content. Not fine words that had kept them marching and fighting through scorch and freeze, disaster, starvation and disease.

Hot enthusiasm had faded, perhaps, or else was being turned to cold and careful plans; or had been forgotten altogether, perhaps, with the Sharai raiding and the countryside to scour, herself to be escorted safely on. An order such as the Ransomers needed an enemy; perhaps that had been Fulke's true mission, to give them unity and purpose, and this sudden rising of the old enemy had driven out any need of a new. Surayon might be safe for another generation, if the Sharai came back . . .

"Not so long a rest as we had thought, sergeant," she said. "I trust your men are not too disappointed?" The castle likely offered little in the way of recreation, but more at least of comfort than the dusty road. If she knew soldiers, they'd have been glad of that.

"My men have not been resting, my lady," he answered, with a touch almost of outrage in his voice, as though she had offered interference and insult both. "I have had them drilling with the brothers, every day since we arrived."

"Of course you have." If he wanted an apology, he could look for it in her tone; she would not give him the words. But if she thought she knew soldiers, she should remember that they had sergeants too. In this case a sergeant who was blatantly disappointed, who would have liked to respond to Master Fulke's call and go riding against the heretics of the Folded Land; who would be doubly disappointed—if she knew sergeants, if she knew Blaise at all—that he'd had no chance either to fight against the Sharai. "Well, at least they'll see Elessi sooner than we expected yesterday. We'll all be glad of that," she said, sowing more seeds of deception.

"Yes, my lady. Shall I send someone to help you with your packing?"

"No need for that. Elisande and I have seen to it." Blaise had been shocked from the first day, that she'd brought no female servants with her. There'd been women along the way, happy to do her laundry for the sake of a few small coins, but it had still offended his sense of what was right. He'd been constantly anxious, she thought, that she might ask some unsuitable service of his men. She'd almost yielded to the temptation a time or two, just for the pleasure of seeing his face. "I'm sure the brothers will bring my chests down, when the wagon is ready for them."

One of her chests was actually a little lighter than it should be. The gowns she and Elisande wore yesterday had been given to the village women to be washed, and were not yet returned. It was no great loss; they'd have been spotted still, most likely; it took the hand of a mistress launderer to wash blood from linen without leaving a stain. And she had gowns enough and to spare. Let the village girls have the good of them, if they could find an occasion to wear such things or a market to sell them in.

*   *   *

SHE AND ELISANDE went back to the guest chamber one last time, where they found the usual light midday meal set out for them. After they'd eaten they rested, or Julianne did, or at least she lay down and pretended. Elisande stood at the window, stiff and silent; facing her failure, Julianne thought, still without knowing where the failure lay. For herself, she was preoccupied with what lay ahead. The desert, the Sharai, her father: all daunting, and such a veil of confusion obscuring the journey and the point of it. Her father in danger, and she could save him, the djinni had said—*though it might be better if you did not*, it had said that also—but that foretelling had been granted her only as an inducement, encouragement to go. It was not the purpose. *Marry where you must*—but it was the Baron Imber she must marry, and she would not find him among the Sharai.

She didn't understand, she could make no sense of it; but she would go, for her father's sake, as much to defy as to obey the djinni. If she, if they could slip away from their escort unnoticed, and evade the search that must follow. They'd stand a better chance on horseback, Merissa's speed would serve Julianne well; but she couldn't outpace even the heavy destriers of the knights if she were double-loaded, and they had no mount for Elisande. Besides, taking a horse from the lines would make the escape far more difficult, well-nigh impossible. No, best to go afoot, cover what ground they could and then hide up, hide and hope. Elisande knew the hills and the ways of the hills, that was to their advantage. And it would be hard territory for trackers, worse with the dust in the wind. They had a chance, at least. Perhaps the djinni would watch over them, it was so keen to see them on their way . . .

SO SHE LAY, and pondered, and had little rest; then a brother came, hunched and puffing heavily from the stairs, to say that the wagon was ready for their baggage, and the litter was ready for themselves—*your gracious presences* he said, but *the baggage of your bodies* he meant or seemed to mean, from the way he kept his hood up and his face down, avoiding the corruption of any exchange of eyes—and the preceptor himself was there to bid them farewell, and would they please hurry?

Not that he said that last either, but it was very much implicit in his bowing and ushering motions.

On the landing outside another brother waited to help with the chests; again he hid his face, but he was a scrawny figure of a man, she thought he had been leaning against the wall for support the moment before she emerged. Well, let him struggle with the weight of her goods, it would be fit retribution for his prejudice . . .

Down the stair and across the court with Elisande, down the long narrow ramp to the stable-yard; and here indeed was the preceptor as promised, and the much-cursed palanquin with her faithful bearers standing by, and remembering the steep and terrifying drop to the plain she was glad to see them there.

"Your grace, this is kind of you, when you must have so much else on your mind."

"Nothing supersedes the proper courtesies to guests, Lady Julianne. I would allow nothing to do so in any case, when they have been so thoughtful and generous as yourself."

Proper courtesies indeed; all this was second nature to them both. As they exchanged good wishes with gently mannered tongues, her eyes above her veil were busy surveying all the activity in the cobbled yard: the traders who were taking advantage of the escort to accompany her to Elessi, as they thought; that escort itself, brothers and knights and their squires, their horses and their baggage-train. Chaos it could have been, in Marasson it would have been; here it was disciplined chaos at least, noisy but organised.

At last the formalities of her leave-taking were satisfied, on both sides. She curtseyed one final time to the preceptor, he bowed and handed her into the palanquin; Elisande followed with a minimal curtsey of her own, and pulled the curtain down at her back.

The noise flowed up around them, horses and men passing, heading towards the gate; Julianne heard d'Escrivey suddenly bellow above the clamour, sounding at the very end of his patience.

"Marron! Where have you been skulking?"

"Sieur," into that sudden silence that always falls around a furious man in public, "a brother asked me to help carry the ladies' baggage . . ."

"Indeed? And did I not ask you, command you even, to give that arm *rest*? Are you stupid, as well as wilful . . . ?"

Any further exchange was lost to her, in a sudden rattle of hooves. The boy Marron was never out of trouble, it seemed. Those brothers must have grabbed him as he passed; he was too young, too new to his role as squire to refuse politely, even despite his wounded arm. Well, he'd learn. Under d'Escrivey's scathing tongue, doubtless he'd learn quickly.

The litter jerked and lifted; Julianne settled back against the cushions, finding herself glad that those two were in the escort. The knight was a knowing charmer, the boy an innocent one; she enjoyed the company of both.

Then she remembered she'd have little enough time to enjoy that company, and might have sunk into anxiety again except that Elisande beside her picked up a flask, uncorked it, sloshed, sniffed and unexpectedly beamed.

"Surely not?"

"Yes, indeed. A parting gift, from the preceptor who will miss you so very much. But this really is kind of him."

No, not that; merely practised. She'd have done as much herself. She was extremely glad, though, that he had done it.

"My lady," Elisande at her most graciously sub-

servient, "may I pour you a morsel of monks'-wine, as
we know it here?"

"Are there goblets?"

"There are. Two."

"Then yes, thank you. And will you join me?"

"Lady, I will, by your esteemed favour."

AS THE CURTAINS masked the drop itself, the *jereth*
helped to mask her fear of it; but only somewhat, and
only from herself. The litter rocked and swayed, they
struggled to keep their goblets level, not to spill the precious little that tipped and ran within the bowls; and as
the curtains swung away sometimes from the litter's side
to remind her of the fall, how far it was, how little held
her back, so Elisande's laughter and the bittersweet taste
on her lips and tongue were still not always enough,
sometimes it all peeled back to leave her naked.

Before they'd reached bottom Elisande had an arm
round her shoulders, tighter than friendship, and was saying, "What is it, Julianne, why are you so afraid?"

"Afraid? I'm not afraid, don't be stupid, I don't know
what you mean . . ."

"Of course not; but why?"

A sigh, and "Give me some more *jereth*, and I'll tell
you."

"Finish what you have first, your hand is shaking. I'll
not have you spilling this, you don't appreciate how rare
it is."

Not so. She appreciated how rare it tasted, and more:
the power of it to draw her mind down to this simple act
of sip and swallow, how the flavour of it filled her and
possessed her so that for long moments from the first
sharp touch on the tongue to the slow fading sweetness in
the throat there was nothing else, nothing that mattered,
only this. Now there was rare indeed, anything that could
make her forget herself, her father, this foul descent . . .

She swallowed obediently, and felt the hot gold-and-green of it all the way down to her stomach. Elisande allowed her a dribble more, which she only gazed into: blood-dark it was and flecked with darkness, the colours of the herbs long lost in the berries' juices.

Then, "I fell from a roof, once," she said shortly, to Elisande's expectant silence. "High places, long drops— they've scared me ever since. Nothing feels solid, when you can see what lies beneath."

After a moment, Elisande laughed. "Don't go to the Sharai, Julianne. They won't welcome you, not if that's your idea of a story told."

"I don't like to talk about it." Nor to remember the falling in the dark, how she hadn't screamed even then, how she'd bitten her tongue so deep to stop it; how the stars had spun about her, each of them wanting to watch her downcoming.

And after, how she'd never climbed again: how she'd tunnelled rather, how she'd become a creature of streams and cellars, turning her back on the light and air of the high walls and the rooftops. That especially, she didn't like to talk or think about.

Elisande sighed. "Well, come to the Sharai, then, Julianne. No towers, no roofs. No heights, except at Rhabat; and you must go there, but you needn't climb, except inside. Just don't look out of the windows. And if they can't teach you to be comfortable up high, perhaps they'll teach you how to be comfortable inside a tale, whether it's your own or someone else's. Then I'll ask you what you were doing on the roof, who you were with and who you were chasing, or who was chasing you."

"I won't tell you. I'm sorry, but—Elisande, I've never even told my *father* . . ."

For a moment, the other girl's eyebrows said she was impressed, as she was supposed to be; then she lost it, her face stiffening suddenly. "Julianne, I've never told my father anything important, not since I was a child. No one does, do they? No one should, at any rate. Fathers are for hiding things from. Friends are for sharing with, at least the stories after."

Julianne shook her head; she'd never had that kind of friend. *Nor that kind of father*, she thought, surprising herself with just a hint of regret. Daughter of the King's Shadow was a role, a position for which her father had made the rules and she'd grown into them like a well-trained sapling, bending to order and yielding as much fruit as she could bear. She'd never thought of keeping secrets from her father, until she had to do it; ever since it had been a burden of guilt to her, a silent betrayal and an extra reason for obedience thereafter.

ON LEVEL GROUND at last, where dusty track merged with dusty plain, Elisande recorked the flask of *jereth* just as they heard hooves, a single horse cantering up to the palanquin, slowing down.

"A secret," Elisande said. "Practise with your sergeant, pretend he's your father; he stands in his place, does he not?"

He had before, when they were on the road to the Roq; now she thought not. She thought that whoever commanded the contingent of Ransomers commanded the caravan, which meant he commanded her and Blaise also.

"My lady?"

"Yes, sergeant."

"I have spoken with Master Sharrol. He believes we might make eight miles today, if we pushed on till dark; but there is a convenient village at six miles' distance, where you can be decently housed and the men may camp. There is water and perhaps a little forage for the cattle also. He believes we should stop when we arrive there, and I agree with him."

"Master Sharrol commands, does he?"

"Yes, my lady," with reproach in his voice, as though she should have known that. "He is deputy weapons master to Master Ricard."

Which meant a lot, clearly, to Blaise, and carried some little of the same weight with her. Everyone who knew the history of Outremer knew the name of Ricard; no guarantee that his deputy would be an equal man to him, but at least a likelihood that he would be of the same type. A certainty, surely, that he would be more than fit to see a caravan such as this safe to its destination. Alas . . .

"Very well. Thank you," and she didn't even pretend to give her own consent to the arrangement. Let them think, oh, *please* let them think that she was content to have all ordered for her, no hint of rebellion, not a trace, not a question of it in their self-contented minds . . .

THE DUST ROSE and the sun sank, in the world outside their curtains; Julianne felt cocooned in swathing softness but no, not safe, not that. She was not. She had to break out of this and fly, like any imago: that was the opposite of safe.

"How will we ever—?"

"We will. Trust me. I have some craft in moving quietly, unseen."

So in truth did she herself, though city streets and palaces were her habitat. Out there, she'd follow Elisande's lead. For that at least she could be grateful, that she didn't have to go alone . . .

Unexpectedly, the gentle swaying of the palanquin was stayed; after a moment, the bearers set it down. Elisande knelt forward and peered through the gauze, then shook her head.

"Wherever it is we're stopping for the night, this isn't it. Just a pass. But no one's moving . . ."

Julianne nudged her aside, to look herself. A wide pass or a narrow valley: hills rose on either side. The traders with their ox-wagons were all at the rear; as the dust-cloud cleared she saw Blaise's men on foot ahead of her, and beyond them a column of black and white on horseback, brothers and knights. There was confusion at the head of the column, but she couldn't see what had caused it. Not trouble, she thought, not an ambush. She couldn't imagine what else would halt them, though. Not the djinni again, surely; other traffic, perhaps, causing an obstruction if the road narrowed further?

Here was a rider, neither black nor white, headed back towards them: Blaise again, coming to report.

"My lady?" He sounded hoarse, more from excitement than dust, she thought.

"Yes, sergeant. Is there a problem?"

"A messenger, my lady. An Elessan, from the Baron Imber's party . . ."

Startlement robbed her of breath; she took a moment to steady herself, glad of Elisande's sudden grip on her arm, before she said, "What party?" *What baron?* she wanted to ask also, but could not.

"They are only a few miles from here, my lady, on their way to fetch you. This man was riding ahead, to warn the castle of their coming; Master Sharrol is sending him back, to say that we are on the road already. We will meet them at the village where we intended to halt."

That made sense; men on horseback might reach the Roq before nightfall, but this slow caravan could not. There was no point, in any case, in returning, except to greet her promised husband—*or his uncle*, it might very well be the other Baron Imber, insisting on all the proprieties—in more suitable surroundings than a military encampment . . .

It was only her father's rigorous training that allowed her even so much judgement. For the rest, her mind was a whirl of muddled emotion. In all her anxieties, all her darkest imaginings, she had never anticipated this. She'd not forgotten but had allowed herself to overlook the messages sent to Elessi by her father and the preceptor both. They might miscarry, they would surely be delayed; the count would be in no hurry to send for her, knowing her safe in Roq de Rançon . . .

But she'd been wrong, it seemed, three times over; or

else she'd simply been hopeful, where no real hope existed. Deluding herself, pretending like a child that bad things, the worst thing simply would not happen . . .

Well, it had happened. One Baron Imber, or very likely the other, would be waiting for her an hour's travel down the road. Where did that leave their secret intentions, how could they possibly hope to slip away now?

"It changes nothing," Elisande murmured, her words no more use than her hand that stroked Julianne's arm, trying to soothe away the tensions that made her tremble, trying and failing. "There will be more men, that's all. Tripping over each other, challenging, arguing, jumping at shadows . . ."

Julianne nodded, grateful for her friend's effort, but she believed none of it. This was disaster, this was the end of her promise to the djinni. It meant her father's lethal danger, though she didn't know how; and it meant her own life taken from her, forced into a pattern of others' deciding. *Marry where you must*, she remembered bitterly, and could have laughed except that she felt so empty. Hollow, nothing left even to rattle and ring inside her, to make her body sound.

WELL, LET IT be, then. Others had worse lives—*and shorter*, flames and cries in the night and both died slowly, slower still in her memory—and she was well trained for this, for her loss of joy. She didn't need even contentment; she could be ruthless with herself, as she must.

She stilled her trembling by a conscious effort of will; she sat cool and upright on her cushions, swaying only as the litter swayed as the bearers picked it up, as the column moved ahead.

"Julianne, are you—Are you thirsty?" Elisande asked after a while, meaning something else altogether. "There is still some *jereth* left," *and it's good for more than thirst*, her voice was saying.

"No, keep what remains. We'll keep it for my husband," and here was a wonder, she could say even that without bitterness, without any feeling at all. "It will make a fitting greeting, don't you think? A betrothal-cup, a drink of something rare," *and if it's his uncle meets us we'll keep it yet, I think . . .*

"The Baron Imber," Elisande said thoughtfully, "is being given something more rare than *jereth*. I only hope he knows its true value."

And she followed that with a kiss on the cheek, sudden and impulsive; Julianne smiled at her, said nothing and felt nothing, or persuaded herself so.

THERE WAS A lulling, a soothing in the motion of the litter; it took her back to the days of her smallness, when nurses were big and rocked her against their shoulders, or set her in a rocking cradle.

Her father was enormous then, those times he came to see her. He would swoop without warning, throw her in the air and make her squeal. He was enormous still, she thought; and still he threw her about with little warning beyond what she had known all her life, that this was what he did. This time, she thought, she would not squeal. Neither would she scream, nor sulk. She would run away, if she could; the djinni, she thought, was bigger even than her father, and so could throw her further.

If it were not frustrated, if the dead weight of the Baron Imber, either one, did not hold her heavy at his side . . .

LULLED, SOOTHED, SHE could almost lose herself in dreaming despite the prick of such thoughts; time flowed by her and she was little aware of it, with Elisande silent at her side.

At last, though, the palanquin was set down again, and this time there were buildings all about them, simple huts of sun-baked mud. And here was Blaise again, dismounted now, saying, "My lady, this is the best shelter we can find for you. There is a bed at least, and I have men drawing water."

"Thank you, sergeant." She stepped out, with Elisande at her back; looked around, saw groups of peasants standing, staring. Wondered which had been displaced to give her this roof for the night, and did not ask. Said only, "Where is the baron's party?"

"Just ahead, to the east of the village. Master Sharrol has said that we will camp to the west. The baron will visit you, I am sure, when you have refreshed yourself."

Yes. She was sure of that, too. And with men watching the road both east and west she thought they would be more than lucky, they must needs be blessed if they were to escape tonight.

"Will you bring up my luggage, please, sergeant? We should change our dress before the baron calls, I had sooner not meet him in my dust."

"Of course, my lady. It may take a little time."

She nodded. The more time the better; she was in no hurry to face this meeting, whichever Baron Imber it might be.

THE HUT WAS bare indeed, four rough walls of mud bricks and a roof of matting overlaid with mud, all of it cracked and gaping under the hard sun's weight; she really didn't trust that roof at all. Rain must fall sometime in this godforsaken country, else why the dried-up river beds? When it did, she thought this hut and all this village would, must melt away in a run of filthy water.

It wouldn't be tonight, she was clear on that; but she could see skylight through the glimmering cracks, and she was not clear at all that the roof's own weight of dust and dryness might not drag it down atop her as she slept . . .

Only that she hoped not to be sleeping, of course, she

hoped to be slipping secretly away from Blaise and the baron both. She gave her hopes no credence, no stamp of reality; no true vision, they were nothing to be clung to, only wisps and vapours in her mind's eye. But still, it was a simple choice. She could try escape, or she could lie here like a good girl and have the roof fall in on her, now and forever after . . .

There was one small window in the hut, set in the wall opposite the doorway, letting in light enough to lift the gloom of shadows if not her own gloom: light enough to show the simple bed, a straw pallet on a timber frame that was probably an expression of great wealth in such a place as this. Lacking anything else to look at, she looked out of the window and saw how the ground dropped away to another of those winding dust-trap gullies that would be a running river in its season, if that season ever came again. Beyond was a gentler slope flecked green and yellow, the villagers' starveling gardens.

Footsteps and a grunt at the doorway, which might or might not have been asking permission to enter: when she turned around they were coming in already, two men carrying her biggest chest. It had taken no time at all, she thought, regretfully. Then the men set their load down and straightened slowly, black habit and white tunic, and she recognised first one and then the other.

Not a man, the one in white, little more than a boy: "Marron," she said, "should you not be serving your master?"

"He has ridden ahead with some of the other knights, my lady. He left me no orders . . ."

So the squire had made himself useful, helping the brother hump her chest along. Both parts of that were strange, she thought. Marron had helped with the loading also, back at the castle, and had been berated for it. And why was it a brother at the other end, when Blaise would presumably have given orders to his own men to see to her comfort?

She found an answer, part of an answer, simply by

looking. The brother had his hood up and the rim of it
hanging low across his face; but he forgot to keep his
head down as he stretched and grunted, easing his back as
though the weight of the chest had been too great for him
comfortably to bear. Light fell in to deny the hood's shadows, she saw nose and mouth and an unlikely beard, the
glitter of immodest eyes, and—

"You!" Elisande gasped beside her.

"I indeed," he agreed, bowing to her; and then he
turned and walked out of the hut, and only then did Julianne manage to see through the habit to the true man beneath. No brother he, that was Rudel the jongleur . . .

Elisande had been quicker, and as ever she was
quicker also to confront. Julianne would have thought
about it, wondered, sought the chance to ask a private
question later; true to her father's teaching, *never act in
haste, never show impatience or surprise.* Elisande
lacked such a father, so much was clear: she was straight
out after Rudel, through the doorway before his shadow
had cleared it.

Julianne followed, to find the two of them still moving
away from her. Rudel had remembered his guise and was
walking like a brother, specifically like one of those
brothers who would not look at women; he crabbed along
the roadway, his head twisted awry and his shoulders
turned to his small companion. Who stalked at his side
like an angry bird, her hands matching her voice, gesture
and tone both stabbing, accusing.

". . . following me, is that it? Creeping at my tail, first
in one shape, now another? This is *ridiculous*!"

"If it were true, it would be." At least his voice wasn't
cringing, as his body was. He sounded almost as angry as
she did, though very much more under control. Julianne
gazed about, as casual-seeming as she could, and saw no
man close enough to overhear. Anyone might be lurking
in this building or that, though, or following close behind. There was no swifter way to declare that you had
something to hide, than by twisting to look over your

shoulder; she wouldn't do that. Elisande might be careless enough to give herself away—herself and the jongleur: they both had their secrets, manifestly, and it seemed that each knew the other's—but Julianne at least would be more cautious.

"Oh, and is it not true?" Elisande hissed now, loud enough for half the village to hear if it were listening. "I was there, and so were you; I am here, and behold . . ."

"You overvalue yourself," Rudel replied: deliberately soft, Julianne thought, an obvious rebuke that could only make Elisande the angrier. "I had a reason to go to the Roq, and I have a reason to join this party, and you are neither of them."

Elisande seethed, but at least she did it silently, giving Julianne her chance to catch up. She slipped her arm through her friend's, trying to disguise the sharp grip she took of the smaller girl's elbow, the little warning shake she gave it; then, loudly, she said, "Brother, thank you for bringing my chest. Elisande, will you come and help me? We must find fit dress to greet the baron when he comes, and I fear the gowns will need a good beating before we can wear them, this road has been so dusty . . ."

That earned her such a glare, she had to swallow a bubble of laughter for diplomacy's sake. Rudel bowed to her, and moved away; and now she could look back, turning Elisande as she did so. She saw no danger, no eavesdropper: only Marron walking off in the distance with another brother, too far distant to have heard anything.

Elisande fell stiffly into step beside her, still twitching with fury. Julianne wanted to learn what it was that lay between those two, how they knew each other and what their secrets were; very badly she wanted it, but this was not the time to ask.

She steered her friend quietly back into the hut, and lifted the lid of the chest. Blinked a little to see how crushed her dresses were, she hadn't thought herself so bad a packer; but the road had been rough and no doubt the men had been careless, tossing and bumping the chest as they heaved it on and off the wagon. She sighed and stooped, lifted out the topmost robe and gave it a rough shake, said, "You should wear this, the colour will suit you admirably . . ."

AN HOUR LATER they had washed, more or less, in cool and cooling water; they had stood like peasants behind the hut, draping their chosen dresses across dry thorn-bushes and beating them with twigs till the swirling breeze carried no more dust away than it brought with it; they had come in coughing, gritty, laughing at their own foolishness, having to wash again.

Now they sat, washed and dressed and veiled with virtue, primly side by side on the bed, leaving the chest for their awaited visitor the baron; now they heard voices, footfalls, heavy men in heavy boots approaching, and for once Julianne couldn't tell at all what her friend was thinking but for herself she was thinking dread, cold and darkly private thoughts.

Shadow in the doorway, a tall man stooping low, call-ing before he entered: "My lady Julianne?"

Both girls stood; she replied, "Come in, sir. I am Ju-lianne de Rance. This is my companion, the lady Elisande."

Gracefully, he turned that stoop under the lintel into a low bow. "Karel auf Karlheim, my lady, ladies both. Cousin to the baron-heir."

Ah, was that how they managed it, then, how they drew the difference? The baron, and the baron-heir? That still was not to say which one led this reception-party, but all knowledge was useful. "You are welcome, sir." Which he was, she decided, as he straightened—cautiously, wary of the roof not a hand's-breadth above his head—and the light fell full on his face. A cheerful young man he seemed, which was one characteristic she had defi-nitely not learned to expect of an Elessan. Neither in re-pute nor in her experience did they smile overmuch, but this Karel was grinning widely, relaxed and easy as he gazed about him.

At first his eyebrow spoke his thoughts, quirking humorously; then, "My lady, there are some few of us come to make our bows to you, and Master Sharrol too; I think perhaps this is too small a court. Forgive the discourtesy, but if you would honour us by stepping outside . . . ?"

"Too late." A growling voice and another shadow made another man: one who stood a full hand shorter, who did not need to duck this doorway, though his shoulders were broad enough that almost he had to sidle through it.

The jaunty Karel lost his smile in a moment, or put it aside, rather; stiffened and set his face and voice to duty, named the newcomer to her like a sentry cut from stone: "My lady, the Baron Imber von und zu Karlheim, brother-heir to the Count of Elessi."

This much she knew, they had met before; though whatever else her father had made of her she had been a child still, and like a child what she had seen most of, what she best remembered was the scar like a livid red rope, like a living scarlet worm that hung on his cheek with its head buried behind his ear and its tail winding down into his beard. His head was shaved, and his eyes seemed too small in his face, too small for the mass of him generally.

Like Karel, he wore formal robes as if this were indeed a court; unlike Karel, his strong fingers plucked at them to lift the hems above the mud floor. That much she saw as she fell into a full and courtly curtsey, heedless of her own dress that had seemed apt before and did not now, seemed almost an insult to his sense of what was fit for this meeting.

Her heart sank with her, that it was this baron and not the other; she hoped she was schooled enough to hide her feelings as she rose again.

"My lord baron, you do us honour . . ."

"I do my duty," he interrupted her, his voice as heavy

and insistent as his body. He gazed scowlingly about him, and no, she could not ask him to sit on the chest as she had meant to; but she had no time to think of any other arrangement, because a third man appeared in the doorway and Karel named him too, almost a repetition and a great surprise.

"Lady Julianne, the Baron Imber von und zu Karlheim, son and heir to the Count of Elessi."

What, *both* the barons? Automatically she hid her startlement beneath the practice of good manners, flowing down into another curtsey, perhaps a little deeper this time and held a little longer, as befitted a woman greeting her promised husband, a future subject greeting her future lord.

He was no more than a shadow to her yet, a name without a frame, a figure glimpsed half-hidden behind his uncle's bulk in that ill-built, ill-lit and increasingly cramped hut. As she rose, keeping her eyes submissively lowered against her rebellious curiosity, she let one brief prayer flicker across her mind, that he would be made more in his cousin's mould, less in his uncle's.

He spoke her name and more, he said, "Lady Julianne, this is a kindness from the God, that we meet even an hour sooner than I had looked and hoped for." His voice was neither the cousin's nor the uncle's, younger and huskier than the one, less abrasive than the other; she lifted her head and saw that his face also was entirely his own. He stood taller than his uncle, an inch or two shorter than his cousin. The last of the sunlight touched him where he stood in the doorway, making his blond hair shine, and his soft short beard. She knew his age, of course, from her father: he was twenty years old, a son come late to his parents after many daughters. His smile still held the shyness of a boy's.

For a moment they held each other's gaze. In all her wondering, her imagining of this encounter, she had never expected to feel a thrill course through her, a physical jolt that made her nearly cry aloud; but it was there and there it was, it happened, and she could have wept for the wonder of it. She could have knelt and gabbled her gratitude to the God and her father both for their mutual care of her, this gift quite unforeseen.

She gasped behind her veil, reached desperately for some politeness to return to him—and was granted no time to find it, because his uncle the elder Baron Imber shifted impatiently and rasped, "This is ridiculous. Out, all, why do we exchange courtesies in a hovel? A sty?"

He chivvied them with great waving motions of his arms, as though they were a gaggle of geese or servants, and lost his own dignity in doing so. Elisande clutched suddenly at Julianne's arm, and her face and her fingers between them said, *this shouldn't be funny. I know what this means to you and I shouldn't even be close to laughing, but oh . . .*

Except that Elisande didn't know, she appeared not to have registered any least little part of the epiphany that had swept through Julianne like a summer fire on a mountain, unpredictable and deadly. It scorched her still, quiescent but hot yet; confusion clouded her, as ash might fill the sky from that burning mountain. And yes, it was ridiculous, as all this scene was ridiculous, and like her friend she should have been fighting laughter, and was not. All she fought was the desire, the need, the hunger to look at him again; she was dizzy with it, and she would not.

His uncle gave her the excuse she needed, a reason to resist the haunting question, *is he looking at me yet, looking again, is he strong like me, can I be stronger?* His uncle, she thought, had probably been in a temper all the long ride from Elessi, at having to collect what should have been delivered; certainly he was in a stiff fury now, and directing it at the man in a master's robe who stood outside.

Used as she was to the subtleties of Marasson, where even the slaves dealt in soft words and hidden meanings, this was fascinating; it held her eyes, her ears and almost her attention, almost drowned the intense and crucial murmur, *is he watching, what is he seeing, do I give myself away?*

She thought this might be a feature now, from here to the end of her days: an ever-seeking after his attention, never satisfied by constant awareness that she had it all already.

She thought she might not mind that, proved it so.

". . . I'll send to my camp, and have the lady's tent erected there," Baron Imber, the wrong Baron Imber was saying, not bothering even to lower his voice, while every muscle of his body shouted outrage. "She will be mother to the heirs of Elessi, if the God grants her grace; how could you think to house her in a pit?"

"Better quarters in a village than a tent in the Order's camp," Master Sharrol replied smoothly, with no hint of offence taken. "My brothers have forgone the company of women, baron; some would feel themselves forsworn, to have one sleep among them."

"But not if she sleeps in shit, to save their precious sensibilities? How if she came to harm in the night, how then, would they not be forsworn then also? What of your oaths to safeguard and protect?"

"The Order will be watching the village all night, baron."

"You'll watch an empty village. I'll take the girl into my own custody, sir, where I can be sure of her."

"No, my lord baron."

That last came not from Master Sharrol, it came from Julianne: surprised her nearly with the speed and the force of it, never mind the impertinence. He spun around, glaring; she dragged in a hard breath and tried to palliate her refusal, too late. "Forgive me, sir, but my father sent me into the care of the Ransomers, and their preceptor set me in Master Sharrol's shadow. It is still for him to make disposition of me, unless he choose to relinquish me formally tonight?"

She said it soft as soap, and still saw the barb sink

home. Master Sharrol twitched, even, before he replied. "The morning will be soon enough, I think. We have already made our dispositions, as you say. Believe me, baron, the lady Julianne will be quite adequately guarded, if not quite bedded down in the comforts to which she is accustomed."

Julianne thanked him, rewarded him with a gentle laugh. "I am a soldier's daughter, sir, though it is a long time since my father went to war with a sword in his hand." It would not hurt, she thought, to remind them not only of her father's past, but his current position also. *Think on that, and quarrel no more*, she was saying, as she said, "I find no hardship in sleeping more roughly than I am used to; I can enjoy it, with my friends around me. Certainly I anticipate no danger," *except from him, that lingering tall boy I will not look at, I'll have him look at me and look and look . . .*

"You'll do as you're told, girl."

"And as I have said, my lord baron, my father told me to put myself in the hands of the Society of Ransom. Where I lie still, until they give me up."

"Yes, your father," and here it was at her back, that young man's hoarseness that might sharpen or blur further, depending on mood and moment; and still she would not look, not yet, not quite, though she blessed him for the interruption. "How did it come that your father left you to make your way alone to Roq de Rançon? We had heard him more careful than that."

"The King summoned him, my lord baron," *my* lord baron she wanted to say, and did not — quite — dare. Besides, the man should declare himself first, and with more than his bright eyes in a dim room. What colour were they? Green, she thought, but light played games in shadow, and her mind had been greatly shadowed when he came.

"Even so, a delay of a few days to see his daughter safe; the King would not have begrudged him, surely . . . ?"

And now she did turn suddenly, to let him see that her

laughter was teasing only, no malice in the world; and his eyes were green or grey, the sun was behind him and she couldn't be sure, but she said, "I know nothing of the King's grudges, sir, but the King's summons I do know," though in all honesty this was the first time she had seen it. She would not tell him that. "When the world tears open, a fool would not speak to it of delay."

"My lady?"

"I saw the wind rip the road apart," and she would show Elisande how she could tell a story, when she chose to, "and the sun's light burn in the gulf it made, as though all we see and touch were tissue laid over liquid gold. The horses were terrified," and her bearers too, the only time those solid, laughing men had let her down; not set her down but dropped her, and cowered wailing in the dust, and she had been terrified herself also, though she would not say that either. "There was no voice, but my father listened to it; and then he spoke to my sergeant," quickly, roughly, making plans for her without wasting the time it would take to explain them to her. "He calmed his mount," with an old soldier's exemplary horsemanship that she could never match though he had taught her all her life to ride, "and left his baggage with us, left us there; he rode into that flaming light, and it sealed itself behind him and was gone, with not a sign remaining," except the chaos of their party that had taken an hour to recover.

"Say it plainly, girl," from the other Baron Imber, the uncle of her man.

"My lord, that is as plain as I can make it. The King opened a strange path that day, and my father took it. I know no more than that."

One thing else she did know, as the younger baron, her own Imber reached to touch her for the first time, laying his hand lightly on her shoulder like a token and a promise both: that it would be hard, much harder now to run away tonight, although she must.

FIVE

Speaking True

THE ORDER'S DISCIPLINE was its greatest strength, Marron had heard that and heard it. He had seen it for himself two nights since, when the Sharai attacked the castle: it was discipline in battle that had driven the invaders back, not his sounding the alarm. He could have called forth as many men and seen them slaughtered, if their obedience and training had been weaker or less ingrained.

But that selfsame discipline was a danger also, it made the Order dangerous to itself. That he saw tonight, when he saw how easy it was for two strangers to hide themselves among the brothers. Dress a man in a habit, and it was the habit that men saw. An unknown face meant only a man from another troop, it raised no questions where several troops travelled together; a man with his hood thrown over his face was a modest man or a man at prayer, to be made way for or stepped around. One brother might have ridden all day beside Rudel and never asked a question. In fact Rudel had moved around, a little time here and a little there, a lot on his own beside the

wagons, giving no man the chance; but chances were that
he could have sat in state on my lady's chest all the way
and still no man would have challenged him.

And if one man, two men—two Surayonnaise, yet,
one a prisoner fleeing and one whose face had been seen
and seen around the castle in other dress than this—if
two men in a small party could sit over a fire apart and
never be approached, then so could two dozen, more. If
Marron were Sharai, he'd have his women weave black
cloth and sew habits by the hundred . . .

But Sharai he was not, nor brother now. Squire, yes,
and already a traitor to his master as to his God, holding
secrets that broke every oath he'd ever made; and he tried
not to stare at Rudel's fire as he saw to Sieur Anton's
horse and his meal and his errands, and he tried not even
to remember what he knew, and he failed of course at
every turn.

Failed also to feel guilty. Regretful he felt, and anxious, but guilty not. It was no just way to treat a man,
what Redmond had been put to in that cell; whatever the
laws said or the priests taught, the place had stunk of
wrongness and this rescue was a virtue.

Marron was to have no further hand in it. "Forget us
now," Rudel had told him, after Marron had freed Redmond from his cramping nest among the lady's gowns
and helped him to the camp. That had been a nervous
walk for both of them, but again no one had questioned
it. A squire lending an arm to an ailing brother: not a
common sight, perhaps, but nothing disturbing.

"Forget us now," Rudel had said, striking sparks to
light his solitary little fire. "See to your master's needs,
and your own. We'll be away once the camp is settled;
nobody will see us leave or miss us once we're gone."

"Which way will you go, sir?"

"Down that dry gully, I think, that runs by the village.
I can mask men's eyes, so that they do not see us; but
those banks run high, they'll give us extra cover. It's not
your concern, though, lad. We're grateful for your help,"

and a grunt of agreement from the exhausted, trembling Redmond, "more than grateful, but your part is over now. Let us go, and see to your own content."

Well, he would, or he would try to, but not he thought until this night was over. His duties were finished for the evening; Sieur Anton had eaten, had watched Marron eat, and had then walked over to the Elessans' camp.

"No," he had said, "you may not come with me. The young baron was a companion of my brother's for a time. I am — shall we say uncertain of my reception? I will not cower in the camp here, though, and avoid them. They will think what they will think, but I had rather let them see my face and think it. I doubt much will be said, if I am there and in my white. The elder baron may have a few rough words for me, but he is rough with everyone."

"Sieur, I should —"

"You should *not*. Amuse yourself, Marron; play with the other boys if they will have you, but don't play at dice with the sergeant's men, or you'll lose every penny in your purse and your purse besides."

"Sieur, I have none."

"No? Oh — no, of course not. Here," and a small leather pouch had flown into the air between them, giving him no choice but to snatch at it one-handed.

He didn't dare throw it back, but tried to give it. "I wasn't begging, sieur . . ."

"I know. That's why you have it. Don't be difficult, Marron. It's a knight's duty to see to his squire's wants, and a boy in camp wants money. Gamble if you like that, but only with my confrères' lads, they won't strip you unless you're stupid; and visit the traders first, let them have the best of it. A sword you have, but you could use a good knife to match it. Don't wear Dard, by the way. No one will touch it here."

And so he was gone. The purse-strings were knotted, but loosely; Marron picked them apart, worked the mouth wide and slipped a finger in. Eyes and finger both told him there was mixed silver and copper in there, thin coins with nipped and broken edges, fit wealth for a young squire's purse but not a knight's. Sieur Anton had been ready for this.

ONE CAMP THEY might call it, but in truth it was three. Outermost were the brothers' cooking-fires and their horse-lines, and the hard ground between where they would lie in their habits, in their troops, and sleep sword to hand till they must rise for prayer or guard or other duty in the night. Then came the knights with their tents and chests and servants—though Sieur Anton had no tent, only a blanket-roll and another for Marron to spread at his master's feet—and lastly, closest to the village, the traders had set their wagons in a circle and a bright fire to burn at the heart of it, invitation to all.

The dour brothers were poverty-sworn, the knights wealthy but well-equipped already; the villagers, the natives would have little to spare. But *the habit makes the man*, one of his uncle's sayings and too true he thought to be funny; the habit had near broken Marron in its efforts to make a brother of him. Any business was better than none, he supposed; and likely the traders lit their fire in any case, whatever company it brought them.

Fire, and food: he could smell what he hadn't smelled in weeks, hot meats roasting over an open flame. He'd eaten just, but Sieur Anton's notion of a necessary supper was little improvement on the Order's, only hard bread and harder cheese. Marron's nose would have drawn him closer even if he hadn't had money in his hand and his master's injunction at his back to push him on. There was a gap like a gateway left between two of the wagons; Marron walked through into the fire's welcome.

AND WAS GREETED by a gust of laughter that made him check, until he realised that it wasn't aimed at him. He wasn't the first to have been summoned by light and smells, far from it; there was a cluster of young men and boys dressed as he was and standing with their backs to him, all their attention focused on something he couldn't see. Squires from the knights' camp: some he knew by sight, a few by name, though none by any gesture of kindness. Sieur Anton's warning had proved true thus far, that the master he served might bring him enemies through no fault of his own, but would certainly bring him no friends.

He moved forward less eagerly, stretching to peer over the press of heads and shoulders. A sudden shrill scream- ing sound was followed by another ripple of laughter and movement, nudging elbows and a brief surge; he was still too far back to make out what so amused them. One of the taller lads glanced round at him, though; recognition fetched another laugh, a short bark with no hint of wel- come in it. A hand gripped his tunic, rough enough to jerk his arm — aching once more after the weight of the lady's chest with Redmond in it — and hard enough to make him yelp.

Again the same laugh, and, "Here, make room, boys. D'Escrivey's monkey has sniffed his brother out . . ."

Blushing, struggling, trying hopelessly to protect his arm in the jostle, Marron was pushed through the crowd; his eyes were smarting when they thrust him out into clear space again, which only made him blush the more. He cupped his elbow in his other hand, trying to look as though he only crossed his arms, and blinked rapidly to clear his gaze.

"Don't cry, little monkey," a voice advised him, cru- elly cheerful. "See, your brother's here . . ."

What Marron saw was a boy his own size, his own age, one of those few he could put a name to. Lucan this was, squire to Sieur Merival, but far from the dignity of his service now; he was choked with laughter, painfully doubled over, and he seemed to have a small black cat on his leg.

No, not a cat. It turned its head; Marron saw a little

wrinkled face, almost human and inconsolably sad. Its mouth opened and it screamed again, provoking a chorus of laughter and further advice. "Greet your brother, Marron, he greets you. Has he been watching you with your master, pretty monkey?"

Marron was only confused by that last, until he saw how the animal's paws—like hands they were, tiny but fully formed, fingers not claws—were clenched in Lucan's breeches, how its hindquarters worked against the cloth. Then he understood. He had seen dogs act so in their excitement, until they were kicked away.

No one kicked this creature, but a man's hand reached over and plucked it up; a man's voice said, "Enough. There's meat over yonder, if you lads are hungry and have a copper or two to pay for it . . . ?"

If they were hungry? They were young, all, and had probably not fed so much better than Marron; their masters might be less abstemious than his, but were likely less generous also. At any rate, their sudden rush away said that they were hungry, and that they had coppers to pay. Marron was left alone this side of the fire, alone with the man and his creature.

The man was a trader, that much was clear: the rich fabrics of his clothing said so, as did their condition, faded and patched, stained and ingrained with the dust and the sweat of the road. His creature perched on his shoulder, chittering and playing with a leash that was knotted one end around its neck and the other around its owner's belt.

"No appetite, boy, or no coins?"

Marron lacked neither, only the others' urgency and any desire for their company. Besides, curiosity was burning a question in his throat. "Sir, what—what *is* that?"

"Haven't you seen a monkey before?"

He had not. He had heard the word, as he had heard of gryphons and oliphants and harpies; he thought he had seen a picture in a bestiary at the abbey, but this looked nothing like that.

"Well," the man said, "now that howling pack has dispersed, perhaps he'll be a little calmer. Sit yourself here, and take him."

Sitting was awkward, trying neither to jar his arm nor to make a show of it; the effort drew a grunt from him, though no more. The man placed the monkey in his lap, but it leaped instantly onto his shoulder. Warm fur he felt, then sharp little fingers gripping his ear; its face peered at him, liquid eyes and sorrow and so very like a brother, he thought, all in black and only its suffering face to show. He felt more twinship than kinship, far more than the brotherhood the boys had mocked him with, and he was very aware of the purse clutched still in his hand. If the man had suggested a price, he'd have given it all, right then.

If he'd given it all or any of it, he'd have had Sieur Anton to face later. "I gave you money for a knife, boy, and you bought a *monkey* . . . ?" It didn't bear thinking about, but he'd have done it anyway.

"His name is Caspius," the man said, reading Marron's thoughts on his face, which couldn't have been difficult, "and he is not for sale. Don't waste your breath in asking."

"No, sir."

"And mine is Almet; and yours is—?"

"Oh, Marron . . ." absently, as he offered the monkey a finger to clutch at like a baby, except that the skin on its palms was quite dry.

"Marron. And you serve a knight called d'Escrivey, did they say?"

They had said so, he remembered, though not straightly. *Where a trader gleans, there are no secrets worth the picking after.*

"Anton d'Escrivey, would that be?"

"Sieur Anton," he replied sharply, instant defence of

his master's honour; then, "Yes, sir," quietly, turning his eyes to the monkey again.

"Well, he was sure to surface, sooner or later. A man like that can't stay buried, he's too good to lose. Here, boy, that monk's taken a fancy to you; and you to him, I can see that. Keep a hold of this, would you?" He untied the monkey's leash from his belt and looped the end around Marron's wrist, his bad wrist, but did it so light-fingered that there was no pain, only a moment's surprise that the man had noticed and remembered and cared enough to be careful.

The trader Almet walked out of the circle of firelight, and was gone; the monkey Caspius screamed its anxiety at the dark, and tried to scamper after. Marron drew it back by the leash, as gently as he could manage, and soothed and stroked and tickled until the agitated little creature quieted, relaxed, at last curled itself contentedly cat-like in his lap, clutching at his hand with all four paws.

Marron's purse lay on the ground beside him. He didn't remember setting it down; he must have done that quite unthinkingly, playing with the monkey.

And Almet must have seen it. Indeed, Almet had prob-ably seen through the leather and counted every coin in it. *If a trader refuses to sell to you, watch your purse.* One of his uncle's more sour sayings; Marron grinned at him-self, at his own folly. Of course the monkey was for sale. This was part of the bargaining. Leave the boy alone, let him fall absolutely in love with the creature; he'll pay more, he'll pay anything . . .

Only he wouldn't, not now. The trader had misread him, for a wonder, had not known enough. In that first moment, yes; but the immediate bond had proved too fragile, it had been snapped by what came after. Caspius was only a monkey now, worth a smile and a stroke but no more. The surge of sympathy had been lost; Marron didn't wear the habit of a brother any longer and had no brothers among them, or none that loved him. He served another master now, and burned to learn his story.

WHEN ALMET CAME back, he brought a wooden platter piled high with steaming hacks of meat, and a bunch of grapes in his other hand.

"Would you rather feed yourself, lad, or the monk? I doubt you can do both one-handed."

Indeed. Caspius was already capering from knee to shoulder, shrilling for food; Marron held the leash out mutely. Almet took it with no sign of disappointment or surprise, only a grin and, "That hungry, huh?"

"Uh, no, sir." *Yes, sir*, but he was having doubts suddenly, how far that purse would run. He must buy a knife, and a good one; best to curb his appetite, and be sure.

"Meaning yes, sir, but you want to save your coppers? Eat, boy, you did me a favour. Gossip carries value, more than a mouthful of meat is worth."

MORE THAN A mouthful of meat was what Marron took, in the end; more than a handful, a bellyful. And then licked fat and juices from his fingers, wiped them on dusty grass and took Caspius back, and did feed him grapes till the little monkey fell asleep.

As though that were a sign, *time for business*, Almet said, "That's not a thin purse, Marron, for a squire sent off to play. Your master cares more for you than for your clothes, seemingly?"

Marron blushed in the darkness, though he thought Almet was poorly placed to criticise anyone's dress. "These clothes were begged for me, sir; I wore . . . another style, two days ago."

Almet laughed. "I guessed it, lad. I was joking. But for a boy taken up, as you must have been, who I'd guess had no coin of his own — and only two days ago, was it?

Those others are quick, then, to make mock of you — I still say that's a kind purse to play with."

Sieur Anton is generous, he wanted to say, *and those others are liars*; but this was swamp, all swamp about him, and he was uncertain of his path. So, "There's no gold in it," that was response enough.

"Even so. Come, Marron, what did he send you for? Not a monkey, so much is obvious; I really wouldn't sell you Caspius, if it meant the wrath of your master on your head. So what, then?"

"Sir," with a sweet sigh of relief because he took no pleasure in these games, nor did he play them well, "do you have knives?"

"Do I have knives? I'm bound for Elessi, and the bóy asks if I have knives?"

"They might make all their own . . ."

"True, they might; but they do not. And just as well, for their own health and mine also. They have craft in Elessi, and no art. A good blade needs more than strength, it needs some beauty. Wait one short minute, Squire Marron, and I'll show you such knives as will make your heart weep for longing . . ."

AND SO HE might have done, but that he knew already the weight of Marron's purse. He fetched out no jewelled hafts, and no chased steel; a rack of plain daggers and poniards he brought, old and new and all of them well-made, sturdy in the grip and needle-sharp.

Marron knew that, for he tried them all. Only one he tried twice, though, only one he came back to for a second look. That was the oldest in the rack, its ivory handle cracked and streaked with use.

"A fine knife once, and a fine blade still," Almet murmured, at his side. "These others are its inferiors, only that the grip is as you see it, past repair. I should replace it, but a knife is a whole thing, and never so good patched. I wouldn't have said this, lad, but stay with that one, if you stay with me. There are other men here who would have knives to show . . ."

"No. This is for me," *if we can agree* he should have said, his uncle would have, he did not. "How much do you want for it?"

"No more than you can afford, boy. I'll not rob you. I can't sell it for the blade's worth, so throw that purse over and let's see. It needs a good sword to match it, mind," as he tipped coins into his palm and fingered through them.

"I have a sword."

"A good one?"

Two: one good enough, one startling. He could simply have nodded the question away, but he thought he owed the trader more; was sure of it when he saw what coins Almet kept, and what he put back in the purse. Cracked handle or not, the knife was a bargain at that price.

"Sieur Anton gave it me, it was his brother's . . ."

Almet stiffened, his eyes widened for a moment; then, "You should probably not boast of that, lad. Oh, I know, you did not mean to boast; but it were better not said at all, for your master's sake and your own."

Marron looked down, petted the sleeping monkey in his lap, then lifted his head again with sudden determination. "Sir? Can you tell me the truth, about Sieur Anton and his brother?"

"Marron, anyone who knows Outremer can tell you the story that Outremer knows. Whether it's the truth, that's for the God to judge. Do you truly not know the story?"

"I am new-come here, sir. I only know what my master has told me, and he tells it harshly against himself."

"So does everyone. This is a harsh country."

"Please, sir?"

"Well. You should know the facts, at least, and they are quickly told. They were close brothers, Anton and Charol, they loved each other better than many brothers do, when there's only one estate to share between them. But there came a day when both of them went missing;

their father sent his men to search, and they found
Charol's body, killed with a single stroke, and his sword
gone. His brother, too. Duke Raime put word out to find
Anton, to have him answer to this; but when he was discovered, he had already sworn himself to the Ransomers.
He admitted his brother's death, but his life belonged to
the Order and could not be forfeited. Rumour says that
Charol caught Anton with a boy, and Anton killed him to
keep that dishonour secret. It's only rumour, but if ever
he denied it, I've not heard. That'll be why your friends
are so unfriendly; Sieur Anton's squire must be Sieur
Anton's boy."

And it seemed he left a question hanging, *tell me the
truth of that?* Whatever Marron owed him, though, he
owed him not so much. Not even a denial. Whatever
passed between his master and himself was private to
them, and not for roadside gossip.

So he said nothing, and at last Almet asked, "Where is
your master tonight, then? If I'd known I rode with Anton
d'Escrivey, I'd have sought a glimpse of him before
this."

"He's gone to the Elessan camp," Marron answered
shortly.

"Has he, though? He's a bold man; he'll find few
friends there, I fancy. Or anywhere, even so far from his
home estate. The name d'Escrivey carries a heavy weight
these days; his kind will forgive much, but not this. I'll be
interested to see how well he bears it."

"You will find, sir, that he bears it very well," and
Marron was spilling the shrieking monkey and up on his
feet and the knife was there in his hand, his fingers
clenched about that cracked haft almost hard enough to
crack it further. The blade glittered in the light, but all the
movement on it was the fire's dance.

"Ah. Your pardon, lad; you are sworn to him, of
course. I spoke unthinkingly."

"You spoke with your heart, I think, sir."

"Aye, that I did—but don't make a quarrel of it, boy.

I have asked pardon; and you're half my size," and he stood himself to prove it, bending as he did to scoop the monkey up onto his shoulder, "and hurt besides. I won't fight a one-handed child. Nor would your master want you to fight me."

That was true enough. The noise across the fire was ebbing, people were turning to stare; Marron took a deep breath, turned the knife in his hand and thrust it into his belt.

"That's better. How bad is your arm? There are people here with some skill at mending wounds."

"Thank you, sir, it has been treated already." Treated and treated, and mistreated too; it was aching badly now.

"Fair enough. Don't go cold on me, lad, for a careless thought; I'm a careless man. I've seen most things, and most people in these lands. It's curiosity keeps me moving. I admit it, I'm curious to see your Sieur Anton; is that so bad?"

Marron hesitated, then shrugged awkwardly, one-shouldered. "No. I suppose not."

"Good. We recover some ground, at least. How were you hurt?"

Another hesitation, then the twitch of a smile, and, "Sieur Anton cut me, at sword-practice."

"Did he, though? I should have guessed it."

"Sir?"

"You have all the signs, lad, of a boy cut by his master. Even to trying to hide the hurt of it. Now come, there's money yet in this purse of yours," and he stooped again, retrieved it from where it lay forgotten on the thin grass, tossed it to Marron. "Will you spend it with me? I have other goods that might interest a youngster."

"No. Another night, perhaps," but Marron was remembering that there was more than a trader's wagon to interest him just now. "I think I'll walk for a while."

"As you wish. Don't go seeking your master with the Elessans, though. Leave that meeting for cooler heads."

The trader turned away, caressing his monkey as he

went; Marron nodded a belated thanks for his wisdom, felt a moment's pang for the loss of the monkey — so easy a relationship, defined by grapes and affection; that sadness an illusion, only the natural falls of its face, no more — and looked for the nearest way out of the circle of wagons.

THE KNIGHTS' CAMP was deserted, save for a few servants gathered around the last of the cooking-fires. Sieur Anton would find most of his confrères also visiting the Elessans, Marron guessed, and doubtless glad of new faces, old friends to talk with. He paused briefly to check that no one had disturbed his master's things — and his own, his one thing, the sword Dard; his fingers touched its haft lightly, *I've a brother-blade for you now* — and again at the horse-lines, to be sure that their mounts were settled and content.

Glad to have no other duties there, he hurried on to where the brothers were camped, and saw before he came to it that Rudel's little fire had been scuffed out, and that the two men were gone.

That was good, that was truly all he needed; but in itself it was only information, not reassurance. And he knew which way they meant to go, and he had nothing else to occupy his mind. There was no reason why he shouldn't wander back towards the village, a young squire at a loose end with his master elsewhere and neither friends nor chores to claim his time . . .

He tried to walk slowly in the starlight, not to be obviously seeking. Back past the horses and the knights' comfortable camp, past the traders' circle and the laughter of young men at play; before he reached the village, he found the dry and sunken watercourse.

Stars were brighter or more fierce, here in the Sanctuary Land; they seemed bigger somehow, as the moon did also. Though it lay a tall man's height below where he stood, Marron could see clearly how the absent river's bed was crazed, silt baked hard under the sun and only softened by the overlay of a season's dust. The banks were steep, and tangled with thorn and scrub which cast their own confusing shadows down. A man would have to stand where he was, right on the edge, to see clearly if anyone moved along it.

Marron himself could see no movement, but the watercourse turned and twisted sharply, following the lie of the land. There was security in that, too; no one could watch more than a short stretch. Similarly, though, no one in the gully would see a watcher on the bank until they were close, too close, coming round a sudden corner to be caught . . .

Rudel might need him after all, he thought, to strike ahead and warn of trouble waiting. He stepped out faster, finding a track that ran straighter than the watercourse but touched its bank often enough that he shouldn't miss the two men. They ought not to be so far ahead; Redmond would be stiff and slow, still carrying the pains of the cell on broken feet, despite Rudel's healing magic. Marron's arm told him the truth of that.

He scanned the track as far as he could see, and made out no figures on it; whenever he was close enough he peered down into the gully, forward and back, and saw no one.

He strained his ears as well as his eyes, as he came below the quiet of the village. The rowdiness of the traders' circle was behind him; was that the murmur of male voices ahead, or only the low whisper of a breeze in the bushes?

Voices, or the sound of a spring welling up in the watercourse, undefeated by the summer sun?

Voices it was, he was sure. He left the path to follow the bank and there they were, two black robes and two paler faces gazing up, gazing directly at him.

For a moment the picture of them seemed to smudge somewhere behind his eyes, a mist falling inside his head, a tingling touch that stilled him where he stood;

then there was a sough of breath released and Rudel's voice rising to greet him, more exasperated than pleased despite his good intentions.

"Marron. What are you doing here?"

"Sir, I came to see you safe away. I thought there might be guards on the bank, up ahead . . ."

"If there are guards," the soft voice came back to him, "we can deal with them. We can walk straight past, and they'll never know that we were here. The trouble that we face now, there *is* someone ahead of us; but not guards and not on the bank, down here in the gully . . ."

"Who is it?" meaning really, *how can you tell?*

"That I can't say, I cannot read so much; but two, and not moving."

"I could go and see, sir."

"You could. I shouldn't let you, but — well, you do have a knack for making yourself convenient, Marron. When you're not making a stupid nuisance of yourself. Can you act the innocent squire?"

"Yes, sir." *Been doing that all day. And will do, all my service still to come . . .*

"Go, then. Quiet as you can, but don't creep. And don't peer, and don't come directly back . . ."

MARRON STROLLED THE bank like any boy excused to idleness, and it wasn't he who crouched and tried to hide in darkness. Scrub shadows fell confusingly across the river's bed, and it was hard to see without staring, but he spotted them at last, two thin figures hunched under a thorn-bush —

Or thought he did. He blinked and squinted sidelong, trying to be certain of them; and the longer he gazed the harder it was to see clearly, to find clothes or faces among those shifting, blurring shadows.

It was making him dizzy, so much wasted effort, as it seemed to him suddenly, trying to outstare a thorn. There was no one there, it was only a trick of the dark; and oh, he was giddy with it, he needed to sit down . . .

AND DID, AND laid his head on his good arm where it folded itself across his knees, and when he closed his eyes the prickling in his skin died away and his mind steadied, a little. Though it was still hard to find any one thought that didn't slip and dissolve when he touched it except for that one strong, forceful shout of a thought, *nobody there, there wasn't anybody there, only the light and the shadows and the earth beneath* . . .

And so he sat, and didn't move again until some harsh whisper cut through the web of bafflement that held him. The ground was suddenly solid again and his mind was clear and he had seen them, two of them, local lads by their dress, simple robes and lengths of dirty cloth wound around their heads . . .

He stood up, cautiously for his arm's sake and the more so for fear of that dizziness returning; and heard the low sounds of voices in the gully, tight with a barely leashed anger, and one of them was a full-grown man's for sure and he rather thought Rudel's.

So he went to see, moving slow and shy and wary. There were four people standing in the watercourse below him now, two in black robes and two in dusty dun. Rudel and Redmond, yes, and that pair of lads—except that no village lad would outface armed brothers as one of them was doing, standing hands on hips and glaring, hissing, spitting in a whisper.

No lad at all, indeed. That was the lady Elisande, under those coarse rags; and the other, when he rubbed his eyes and squinnied, the other was the lady Julianne, with her long hair coiled up and hidden beneath the turban that she wore.

". . . Why should I tell you?"

"Not tell. Ask, I said."

"Worse. You of all men, what right have you to order my comings and goings?"

"We will discuss my rights later," Rudel said, and it was a wonder to Marron that he kept his voice so quiet, so much passion was in it. "For now, we will *all* leave this place, and we will do so together."

"Before we do," Julianne said, cold and clear and with an edge like a diamond, "may I know who my companions are? Truly? You are something else than a jongleur, Rudel, and I think neither one of you is a Ransomer."

"Later," he said again, with a gesture of sheer impatience. That might not have been enough for Julianne, by the way she stiffened; but he turned away from her, glanced up and said, "Marron, are you still fuddled?"

"No, sir," though the truth was, *yes, sir, all this fuddles me.*

"Good. This is farewell, then; take our thanks, and go back to—"

Back to your camp, back to your master, back to your life, but none of that was said. Redmond tugged urgently at Rudel's sleeve, Rudel's head jerked around, Elisande gasped and twisted, all three of them reacting to something Marron could neither see nor hear; but whatever sense it was that warned them, this time it came too late.

"Who's that?" The voice beat at them from the dark, from the far side of the gully. "You there, boy . . ."

Marron froze; his white tunic betrayed him and betrayed them all, making an easy target of him under these bright stars. Now he could see his challengers, three men emerging from the night in disguising black, brothers on patrol. They strode to the gully's rim, still fixed on him but no chance that they would not see the others down below.

Unless he ran, unless he drew them off . . .

He spun around and leaped away, winning a bellowing shout that was echoed on this side of the watercourse. Some man unseen among the huts of the village above him: twisting his head to look back as he ran, he cursed himself. If those three were to follow him, of course they must cross the gully; of course they would do it here where they were closest, before another of its sudden turns could force them further back. So there they were, stood right on the edge now and not staring after him but down into its shadows. At Rudel and Redmond and the ladies; and all Marron had done was bring more trouble to them.

He saw that, he saw another party of men come from the village, and then he felt his foot snagged by a thorn and he saw the world tumble.

Instinct thrust his hands out, both his hands, to catch his weight as he hit ground; a moment after the jar of contact, he felt the leaping pain released in his arm as that thrice-cursed wound split open yet again.

For the space of two breaths — one gasp, and one sob — he lay still; and through all the shouting and the throbbing and the blurring shock of his fall he heard one voice clear, Rudel's: "Go on, go on! I can hold these, we can turn back but you go . . . !"

And then he was up again with a thrust and a stagger and a yelp of pain as he used, as he had to use that damned arm to get himself moving; and the three men on the gully's bank were not so much climbing or leaping down, more slipping and sliding and in their minds as much as their bodies so, he thought, seeing how their heads rolled and their limbs hung slackly. Dizzy and cut loose he thought they were, seeing nothing, caught in a brutal maze . . .

No time to wonder at it, though. Nor to worry about the others in the gully, whether that mazement would be enough to see them away and free or else back in camp but undetected, if that was what Rudel had meant. The patrol from the village was coming after him; they either hadn't noticed what was happening below them, or else they weren't concerned. They wore dark tunics, but not the brothers' black.

And Marron wore white and was easy, too easy to

spot; and was slow, too slow after that fall, not destined to escape.

So he drew his knife and waved it high above his head, glanced back again and cried them on, "This way! They went this way . . ." and plunged forward headlong, trying to seem hound and not hare.

There were lights beyond the village, tents and bright fires burning; more men, many more men gathering and gazing at the noise, starting to run. That must be the Elessans' camp. He picked a path between that and the gully, trying to come not too close to either.

It was a race, but not for him to win: only to see who caught him first, the men who followed or those who came down to intercept. A hand snatched at his shoulder, missed its grip and grabbed again, sending another jarring pain down his arm to wake his wound to fire; he gasped, stumbled, almost fell. Turned his eyes upward to the bearded face of the man who had run him down, who was barely breathing hard despite the chase, and panted, "Sir, sir, they went that way," gesturing onward with his knife.

"Who did? I saw no one. Who are you?"

"Marron, sir, squire to Sieur Anton d'Escrivey." That checked the man's scowling disbelief, at least for a moment, though by the way his face changed it had not made him Marron's friend. Marron went on urgently, "There were men here, Sharai perhaps, I do not know; they wore Catari dress. I came on them back there, below the village, and they drew knives on me. I think I wounded one, see . . ."

He showed the man his knife, with blood clearly on the blade; the man grunted, and peered ahead into the dark.

"How many?"

"Three that I saw, sir . . ."

Another grunt, and then a gesture that brought his own men closer. Those from the camp had reached them also, big men, all bearded, all suspicious.

"Catari, three, the boy says. Sneak assassins, Sharai, by the sound of them. One is bleeding, perhaps."

Blood was dripping from Marron's fingers, but he kept that arm down at his side and hoped, prayed almost that no one would notice in the dark.

"Three Sharai? Why is the boy not dead?"

"They fled, sir. Not from me, I think," in swift response to their scornful laughter, *three Sharai assassins to run from one bare-chinned boy? We think not . . .* "Perhaps they heard you coming, sir?"

"Perhaps they did. Well, we will pursue, you will go to the camp," and he was passed from that man's strong and painful grip to another's, "with Barad to escort you, to have your own hurt dressed. There is blood on your sleeve."

"Yes, sir," and a cut in the fabric also, though he'd made that himself as he ran. Anyone looking closely would see that the cut did not match the wound, that the wound bled independently, that there was still a blood-soaked bandage between the two to prove it. That didn't really matter, as he'd made no claims about it—"no, sir, I was hurt before, the Catari's knife didn't cut me"—but he hoped to keep anyone from seeing so much. Blood on his clothes and a fresh bandage, he hoped that would be enough even when the searchers returned with no Sharai.

They might of course return with the ladies, or with Rudel and Redmond, or with both; that was out of Marron's hands.

His escort was a tough Elessi of middle years keeping a watchful grip on his good arm, making little pretence of assistance. Lord, but they were a suspicious people . . .

In through the circle of watch-fires that contained the camp, to where the tents were ordered in neat lines: a suspicious and disciplined people. Marron sagged a little against his escort's hold, though not with any fixed purpose in mind. The man's hand tightened in response, still more guard than help.

Then, for the second time tonight, the same question flung at him from the dark, and with almost the same exasperated tone: "Marron, what are you doing here?"

The voice this time was Sieur Anton's. So was the shadow, the walk, the body that stood before them: making no challenge, but obstructing the way so that Marron's escort had perforce to stand still, and Marron also. It was a precise gambit perfectly executed, and again was all Sieur Anton.

"You know this boy, sieur?"

"Indeed. He is mine own."

"Your name, sieur?"

"Anton d'Escrivey, of the Knights Ransomers. What has happened, why is my squire bleeding?"

The man's fingers slipped from Marron's arm, his tongue stumbled and slipped on his words; he said, "The boy surprised men in the village, sieur, Sieur Anton . . . He says he saw them off, we are searching now . . . By your leave, sieur . . ."

A bow and a sharp turn, and he was off without waiting for Sieur Anton's casual wave of dismissal. Marron thought he saw the man make a surreptitious sign as he all but ran away from them, the sign of the God but as the peasants, as the superstitious used it, a ward to fend off evil.

"You will become used to that," Sieur Anton said, sounding a little weary, a little amused, nothing more. "Now, Marron. Men?"

"Catari, sieur. Three of them, they might have been Sharai . . ."

"They might have been local here, and of the faith. People do live in this village, though they seem to have melted tonight."

"Yes, sieur, but these carried knives drawn. Before they saw me, even . . ." He regretted the lie bitterly, but it must be complete, one story told to all and stood by regardless of who came to challenge it.

"Ah. Hence all the fuss, I take it," because fuss there

was and spreading through the camp now, single men and squads of men hurrying east and west. "You there!"

"Sieur?" A young sergeant stiffened, almost saluted; it seemed that Sieur Anton had more reputations than one.

"Has anyone thought to check on the safety of the ladies?"

It was an order, politely disguised; this time the sergeant did salute. "I will do so immediately, sieur."

"Good. Take some men," *just in case. This might be a feint to draw us out, to draw our eyes away . . .*

Marron flinched. Those men would find no Sharai, no threat—and no ladies either. They'd scour the village, rouse every camp, search the night by torchlight. Two girls afoot could neither flee nor hide from so many men.

Nor could Marron do anything more to aid them; they must face their own reckoning, as he must his.

The sergeant hurried off, leaving Sieur Anton frowning at his back. "I ought to go myself," he murmured. "But the Elessans wouldn't welcome me, unless it came to a fight. And as usual, someone has to see to you, Marron. Are you always going to be this much trouble?"

"Sieur, I can see to myself . . ."

"I don't think so. Did they cut your arm, these men of yours?"

"No, sieur." Here at least he couldn't lie, not even by misdirection.

"The old hurt once more, is it? Come with me, then. Even Elessans must travel with a surgeon, for all that they value their scars so much. He won't make it pretty, but I fear that arm never will be pretty now. We'll have it stitched again, at any rate, if it's clean enough within. I am tired of seeing blood on your sleeve."

STITCHED IT WAS, after it had been bathed with something caustic, a liquid that burned on first touch and burned hotter as it bit deeper. The surgeon was a sour man who scorned Marron's first startled gasp and sneered at the trickling tears that came after; as he threaded his needle with coarse gut, he tossed over a pad of foul-smelling leather. "Bite on that, puppy, if you can't hush your yelping. I've no patience with the weak."

Sieur Anton took it from him, though, with a brief shake of the head. "You don't need a gag, lad. Here, give me your hand—no, the other, fool. Hold onto mine, that's right, and squeeze when you must. As tight as you need to, you can't hurt me . . ."

By the time the stitching was done, Marron had his face buried in Sieur Anton's shoulder and his teeth clenched in the knight's clothing, a gag after all. He'd not made a sound, though, nor moved his wounded arm from the surgeon's table; he thought he deserved credit for that, till he opened his wet eyes and saw how the surgeon's free hand still clamped his wrist, Sieur Anton's his elbow. Marron hadn't felt their weight at all, for feeling the fine silver fire of the needle bite and flow around the duller burning of his weeping wound.

When it had been bandaged one more time, and this time strapped tightly to his chest at Sieur Anton's insistence so that he could neither move nor use it, the two of them headed back towards their own camp. Marron at least yearned for his blanket-roll and sleep without dreaming, a black hand to ease pain and anxiety both, some short relief from this long night's work.

"Can you walk, or must I carry you again?"

"Of course I can walk, sieur! Or you must leave me, if I can't . . ."

"Of course."

And he could walk: though before long his incompetent feet were stumbling, misled by his deceived and stupid eyes, and it was or it seemed to be only Sieur Anton's hand laid on his neck that kept him upright. So light a touch and so much strength to be taken from it, there was magic in this, surely . . . ?

Lights and men moved about them in the dark, voices called, low and harsh and guttural. Three times they were challenged by patrols with weapons drawn; the third time was among the huts of the village, and the man who called them to a halt was that same young sergeant Sieur Anton had sent to check on the ladies' welfare.

"Oh—beg pardon, Sieur Anton, but . . ."

"Not at all, you do right; you should let no one walk these streets untested. I take it the ladies are safe and unharmed?"

"Sleeping soundly, sieur—at least, I hope so. One woke when I went in to check on them, and she's a tongue like a blistering hogweed."

Sieur Anton laughed. "May she be blessed with a complaisant husband, then. But do your work quietly, sergeant, to save yourself further abuse. The lady Julianne is no Elessan yet, and she may have more strictures saved up for you if you disturb her sleep again."

"My men are sworn to silence, sieur," and he himself was speaking in a mutter, standing close. Sieur Anton laughed again, but softly, before he steered Marron on with a touch more pressure from that hand at his nape.

Marron didn't at all understand the sergeant. How could he think the lady Julianne had sworn at him, when the lady Julianne—Marron knew—was not in that hut or anywhere near the village now?

Unless she and her companion had after all not fled. He didn't know where or why they wanted to go, but the danger of discovery might have driven them back. Though he thought he'd heard Rudel cry the opposite, that the ladies leave while he and Redmond stayed . . .

There still wasn't anything he could do, to learn the truth or affect it. Neither did there seem a need, for tonight at least. His body only felt the heavier, with one anxiety lifted from him. He was half-asleep already when they came to their encampment, and Sieur Anton's hand was actively propelling him along.

Not for the first time, what was proper was quite reversed between them; squire stood idle, dazed by weariness, while his master unrolled his bedding for him and advised him at least to take his boots off before he went to sleep.

Marron only blinked.

"Oh, for mercy's sake . . . Sit down, then, boy. Easy now, don't jolt that arm . . ."

And the master pulled off the squire's boots, unbuckled his belt, set it aside and saw the lad rolled into his blanket and drifting into sleep, though he grumbled under his breath all the while.

THAT WAS THE first thing Marron remembered in the morning, the low monotone that had seen him off to sleep: ". . . and how I am to haul my own boots off I am not entirely clear, this is what I keep a boy for, or I thought so. Marron, infant, how can you be so *young* . . . ?"

The monotone, and then the kiss. That was the second thing Marron remembered, a touch of dry lips and the brush of stubble, second and last before the welcome topple into nothing.

He thought about that briefly, before the other events of the night came back to him. There was confusion then and fear for himself and others, too many possible consequences; he opened his eyes and sat up with a jerk, too fast, waking his throbbing, stinging arm to fierce life.

Sieur Anton's place was empty, his blanket thrown aside. Marron struggled to his feet and gazed about him, saw the camp a flurry of squires and servants packing up and thought he'd best do the same, though his mouth was dry and his stomach grumbled with hunger.

HE WAS STRUGGLING to roll his master's blanket one-handed when he heard his name called. His master's voice: he looked up to see Sieur Anton striding urgently towards him, with a deep frown on his face.

"Marron, leave that. You are sent for. Come."

"Sieur, where—?"

"The baron wishes to speak with you. Make haste."

Sieur Anton had already turned away; Marron hurried to catch up to him. Had he thought his mouth dry before? Not so; now it was dust-dry, desert-dry, and all his fear was for himself.

For a minute, it seemed he was to be told no more. But Sieur Anton slowed his pace briefly, glanced down and said, "The Elessans found no trace of your Catari, boy, either last night or this morning when they looked again. Nor could the dogs find any trail of blood beyond your own. The baron will question you; be sure you do not lie to him. He has a truth-speaker with him.'

His voice was cold, heavy with suspicion, striking a chill deep into Marron's bones. Worse almost than his news, and that was fearful enough.

It was a shorter walk than Marron expected or hoped for, not half so far as the Elessans' camp. At the near edge of the village, a group of men was standing; just as Marron spotted them, Sieur Anton paused.

"Here. Drink a mouthful of this."

He held out a flask; Marron took it with gratitude, tipped it to his mouth and choked violently. Not water, some fiery spirit that coursed through him, burning.

"The lady Julianne and her companion have vanished," Sieur Anton told him softly. "You will be questioned vigorously. Be prepared; and, Marron, *tell the truth*!"

No more then: only a hand on his shoulder, driving him forward, that might look to others as though it were a guard against his fleeing, that in truth — he hoped — was meant to encourage, to reassure. He could find no other reassurance.

Certainly there was none in the men's faces that greeted him, nor in the one woman's. The half-dozen men, dressed in costly, sombre austerity, gazed at him as though he were a felon convicted already, brought for sentence. One stood slightly forward, shaven-headed, scarred and scowling, gripping his sword's hilt as though he would willingly carry out that sentence himself. Perhaps he would.

The woman stood to the side, with them but not of them, not allowed so much licence; and she was the surprise here, and the cause of Marron's most dread. She was robed as a Catari, bronze-skinned and black-haired as a Catari, but her face was unveiled; her face was terrible. He thought at first that she was diseased, a leper or worse. Coming closer, he saw that the stains disfiguring her cheeks and jaw were made of man, an intricate pattern of tattoo; and the mark on her brow, that was man's work also, the sign of the God set there with a hot iron, branded bone-deep. All her skin was puckered around it and her eyes were sunk beneath, glimmers of blue in pits of shadow.

Her face was terrible, but it was not her face that scared him so. It was her calling. He had heard tales of Catari truth-speakers. They had a magic, the stories said, to cry a lie whenever they heard one; and he could not, he dared not tell truth here.

"This is the boy?"

"Yes, my lord." Sieur Anton nudged Marron down onto his knees, with a discreet hand under his arm to help against the jolt of it.

"Very well. You, boy, you will tell us exactly what you know of last night's events."

"Yes, sir. Sieur. My lord." Did he mean now, this moment? Apparently he did; no one else spoke or moved, at any rate, so Marron took a breath and began. He told his tale again, his spur-of-the-moment invention that seemed less and less plausible each time he repeated it, that had had men running and shouting in the darkness but was only a ghost in daylight. Wise like any grown boy in the ways of lying—lessons learned hard, under his uncle's rod—he added nothing and altered nothing, though he could surely have made a more convincing story of it if he'd been free to think again.

Unrevised, it was a tale soon told, and greeted in si-

lence. By their faces, when he dared to look, not one of
these men had believed a word of it. And rightly so — but
no, he had to forget the truth and focus on the lie; if he
didn't believe himself, how could he make anyone else
believe him? He didn't so much as glance towards the
truth-speaker, for fear of seeing his lie writ as large as her
life upon that dreadful skin.

Kneeling, waiting for the next demand, he heard instead a sharp hoarse scream come from the village, followed by a low eerie wail that sounded barely human,
those few moments before it was cut off. Marron shuddered; no man else reacted, except for a hint of displea-
sure that twisted the baron's mouth, contempt for the
weakness of the one who screamed.

"My nephew's bride," the baron said at last, "has run
away in the night. Do you know aught of that?"

"Nothing, my lord."

"Strange. You cry an invisible enemy, what time the
girl disappears; you throw all into confusion, and you
wish us to believe there was no collusion between you?"

"My lord, the lady Julianne was seen and spoken to by
your own man, a half-hour after I was attacked . . ."

That dissembling protest won him a glare from the
baron and a cuff from Sieur Anton behind him, hard
enough to make his skull sing. Punishment or warning,
don't try this man too far.

"That man had a conversation with moppets," the
baron growled, "with rags and ropes, it seems. Are you
some man's moppet also, boy? My woman here will try
the truth of you. Imber, you stay. Your honour is entan-
gled here, and it stains my soul to watch this."

The tall young man behind him nodded a blond head
slowly, though *mine also* was written on his face. Another at his side — taller yet, and darker — touched his
arm, *I'll stay with you.*

Marron watched the elder baron leave with others in
his train, the younger remain and his friend also, and
cared nothing for any of that. All he cared for was the rus-

tle of the woman's skirts beside him, drawing near; the
touch of her hand on the nape of his neck, cold and hard
her fingers and so unlike his master's last night. Chill
doom, he thought they spelled. They would pick truth
from the strings of his body as a jongleur picked a tune
from the strings of his mandora, and there would be no
more mercy in these young men when they heard it than
there had been in their senior when he demanded it.

Moppets, he'd said. Moppets were children's toys, but
they were also—*rags and ropes*—the tools that Rudel
used to make his simulacra, poppets he'd called them, his
devil-dolls that sat and moved and he said looked like the
people they pretended to be. Perhaps they talked so too,
or seemed to . . .

Marron was making more sense of this morning's
news, slowly, slowly, and just when he didn't want to,
when he needed to stay bewildered. Rudel and Redmond
must have gone to the ladies' lodging and set their poppets there to fool the guard; which meant that yes, truly,
the ladies were gone. And he could say all that, he could
be forced to, betray himself and the ladies and the two
men too and so die, uselessly, too late . . .

Cold and hard her fingers, cold and hard her grip; she
laid her other hand atop his head, pressing down. His
mind spun, as though he were dizzy-drunk and sick with
it. He closed his eyes, but that was worse: colours he had
no name for oozed and pulsed behind his eyes, spread
and shrank and left lingering shadows in their wake.

Even so, it was an effort to force his eyes to open
again, a greater effort to make them focus on a pebble on
the ground before him, to see at least one thing clearly
and cling to that.

It would have been a greater effort still, an impossible
effort to focus his mind also on her voice, on the questions she thrust at him in a limpid, liquid, lilting, lisping
voice where even the words seemed to change shape inside his head. He heard them, yes, he knew they were
there; but he could not listen to them, nor keep his

thoughts even a beat ahead of his voice as it slurred in answer.

"Marron, do you hear?"

"Yes."

"Do you lie, ever?"

"Yes."

"Will you lie to me?"

"No."

He heard himself and was conscious of what he'd said, but always that little too late. Whatever this was that she did to him, however it was done it bore out all the stories that he'd heard. She could ask him anything and he'd tell her true, he couldn't help himself.

"Did you see three men, strangers, outside the village last night?"

"Yes," he said, he heard himself reply; and was briefly amazed until he caught his own thought a moment later, a picture-memory of three men indeed and all of them strange to him, not of his troop, the patrol of brothers sliding down into the gully.

"Were they Catari men?"

"I don't know." Well, and that was true too, he hadn't been close enough. It was most unlikely, there were no Catari brethren: he could say that, he could assert it, he could swear it, even, but he couldn't know for certain about these. There should be no Surayonnaise either in the Order's robes, but two had stood in that same gully last night.

"What of the blood on your knife, did you cut your own arm to claim the blood Catari?"

"No." No, he hadn't cut his arm, he hadn't needed to; only slid the blade up his sleeve and smeared it with what oozed freshly from his much-abused flesh. He'd been proud of that, pleased with himself even in the heart-pounding frenzy of the chase.

"Did the lady Julianne ask you to aid her escape?"

"No." She'd said not a word to him.

"Did her companion do so?"

"No." She neither, only worked her dirty little spell in his mind to muddle him as this woman was now, leading his thoughts in a slow dance, invading what should be private beyond any spying . . .

"Do you know where they are gone?"

"No."

"Ask him if he truly fought last night, if he truly wounded any man."

But that was not her subtle voice, invested with her magic. It was a man's, blunt and brutal; and like a great stone heaved into a still pool it shattered what spell the woman had woven, what bound Marron's tongue to her quest. She gasped, and he felt a tearing pain as she lifted her hands suddenly from his head and neck. He toppled sideways as if there were nothing now to hold him upright, hit the ground hard and lay there retching, curling up around his roiling stomach as his mind plunged sickeningly toward a spinning darkness.

Dimly, distantly he heard the man again, "Ask him!"

"I cannot, now," she said above him, and she too sounded sick and hurt, her voice no liquid binding now, only a stammering stranger. "See him, he could not speak again. You have broken it."

"Enough." That was Sieur Anton, no question of it, one word was plenty; and these were Sieur Anton's hands on his shoulders, lifting him gently back onto his knees, holding him steady, drawing him back from that dreadful abyss. "He has answered enough. He spoke the truth."

"Perhaps. I would have liked more." That was another, not the first man to speak. "My lady Julianne is missing—"

"—And this boy knows nothing of it, he said as much. Or do you doubt your woman's talents?"

"No, only her wisdom in the questioning. But you are right, Sieur Anton; my disappointment makes me harsher than I like. Is the boy unwell?"

"I do not know. He is hurt and frightened, shocked . . ."

"He will recover." That was the woman again. "We are both hurt. None should speak, save I alone. He needs rest."

"As ever; which, as ever, he may not have. Set your men to searching, my lord baron, call out your dogs to find your lady's trail; I will see to my squire."

His arms shifted, ready to lift. Marron squirmed, wriggled, almost fought to push his master from him. "No, sieur, let me be . . ."

Startled perhaps by this unexpected rebellion, Sieur Anton made no further move. Marron reached his one free hand blindly back towards the knight, gripped his sleeve and pulled himself cautiously, wobblingly to his feet. Swallowed against his rising bile, and squinted into the light until his eyes found the young Baron Imber.

"My lord," he said falteringly, "I am sorry, but I do not know where your lady is gone."

"Easy, lad. I believe you, though my uncle may not."

"Then let me help you search, let me show . . ."

"There is no need," the baron said, with the hint of a smile in his voice; and Sieur Anton rising beside him said, "No, Marron. A one-armed boy would be of little use, even on muleback, and you have nothing more to prove. Come, make your bow to the baron," and his hand on Marron's neck did that for him, bending him low to his stomach's great danger, "and let be. You would likely fall from your mule in any case, and lose yourself also. We will go back to the camp, and then to the Roq again; it is decided. This party goes no further, until the ladies are discovered."

"Sieur . . ."

"No, Marron. Obedience, Marron. Yes? God's truth, I wonder how you have lived so long . . ."

THE SICKNESS PASSED, though not the dizzy memory of it; the walk back to camp helped, as did his fumbling efforts to pack his master's goods, though Sieur Anton did

more to help than his rank properly required. They were
ready to ride before the other knights; in the delay, Marron said, "Sieur, someone should check that the ladies'
baggage has been collected from the village."

"No doubt someone has. It is hardly my responsibility,
nor yours."

"No, sieur, but everyone might think thus. Whose responsibility is it, with her ladyship's companion missing
also?"

"I do not know. Do you want me to run and find out?"

"No, sieur. Let me go. One look is all it needs, and the
walk would help my head. I feel better, walking . . ."

"Oh, go, then. But don't linger, I won't wait. You
could find yourself with a longer walk than you fancy."

"No, sieur," pretending that meant, *no, I won't linger*,
when they both knew that in truth it meant, *no, sieur, you
wouldn't leave me to walk.*

HE DIDN'T HURRY, neither his legs nor his belly would
allow it; and so much was true, that walking was better
than being still.

The traders' circle was broken, the oxen harnessed and
the wagons drawn up in line. The village beyond was
empty, as it had been almost since their arrival. Of the
faith the people might be; trusting they were not.

Then he came around a corner to find the headman's
hut, where the ladies should have slept the night. He was
genuinely looking to see if their baggage had been forgotten, in case Redmond had sought to hide once more
within that awkward chest; he thought he might perhaps
find Rudel here.

Instead, he found the young sergeant who had reported
speaking with the lady Julianne last night.

He found the man naked and spread-eagled, crucified
across the doorway to the hut: his arms high and his legs
wide, wrists and ankles nailed to the wooden frame. He

was gagged with a belt, perhaps his own; Marron remembered that wailing cry so quickly silenced.

Marron took the baggage on faith, along with Redmond's absence and Rudel's. He wanted only to turn and walk away, but the man's eyes held him, wide and white and agonised.

His body was all blood; it ran down his arms and down his chest and legs, it pooled around his feet, too much to soak the dust and disappear.

I spoke to her, his eyes said, *I did* . . .

Marron nodded.

The man's ankles had been shattered by the dull metal spikes driven through them—iron tent-pegs, Marron thought, perhaps—so that he sagged against those that pinned his wrists and screamed behind his gag, screamed all but silently; and arched upward to put his weight on broken feet and screamed again, sagged again until he could neither bear the pain of that nor breathe, and so he arched again.

Help me, his eyes demanded, *this is too much, too cruel* . . .

Marron's hand moved to his belt, where his knife lay couched. His fingers gripped the hilt; the man's eyes focused on them, with unbearable intensity.

Slowly, slowly Marron uncurled his fingers, moved his hand away and shook his head. He couldn't speak, he couldn't possibly explain; but he had to be so careful. He'd been incredibly lucky this morning—and *yes, incredibly lucky*, he didn't believe in so much luck and he wished he could see into that woman's mind, because he thought the truth-speaker had deliberately helped him lie—but he daren't risk any more questions, not so much as a single further doubt. He'd have been seen for sure, coming into the deserted village alone. Let the Elessans only return to find a body with a knife-wound to the heart where they had left a man alive to suffer for his fault, and Redmond's life and Rudel's were forfeit again, as was Marron's own.

So he turned and walked away, trading one stranger's life for three he valued more, if little more.

SIX

Where She Must

THERE WERE LESSONS in humiliation, lessons and lessons; Julianne thought she might never now be free of learning this.

THE NIGHT HAD been all breathless adventure at first, deliberately so: wings over time to make a child of her once more, those days and nights she'd slipped off with unsuitable friends to scout the rooftops of Marasson, later the cellars and sewers. So long as she focused on that and played the irresponsible girl again, she could do this and enjoy it, almost. So long as she kept a fierce grip on herself, her trembling fingers, her torn and treacherous mind . . .

Taking almost nothing with them—the flask of *jereth* and a blanket each, knives and food and water, silver and gold and little else; Elisande told her that all her clothes would be useless, so why carry the weight? They could go dirty till they found something clean—they had dressed to confuse, to look like boys from any distance, and slipped out of the hut by the window at the back. There was no guard at their door, Julianne had insisted on that. With friends to the east and friends to the west, she'd said, with men watching to the north and the south and the village deserted, she needed no further protection; she would not be treated like a prisoner, she'd said, to be guarded night and day. Besides, she was entitled to some privacy, she'd said, rustling her skirts in a way intended—and successfully so—to make her auditors blush.

So, no man at the door. But there would be men none the less in the streets, or rather the single street and the few alleys that made this hamlet; they were likely compromising their agreement by watching the door from a distance, men at every corner.

Out of the window they'd gone, then, she and Elisande; a quick scramble over the sill and a drop to ground and then a low-bending shuffle, almost a crawl sometimes as they'd used their hands to find their way through stones and scrub till they came to the dry river bed.

More scrub and thorns on the steep bank down; Elisande had tried to run through them, slipped and fell and rolled to the bottom with a muted squawk. Julianne, ever practical, had sat down and slid like a child, lying flat to let the bushes pass above her and laughing breathlessly, silently in the moon-made shadows.

Laughter that had died quickly, with a touch and a motion of Elisande's hand, a whisper no louder than a breeze: "There are men in the gully. Be still."

Still she'd been, a moment of chill terror before she'd remembered who and what she was: no child but daughter of the King's Shadow, and what was there, who was there here that she should fear? To be discovered and detained would be a concern certainly, an inconvenience, a problem; with her father's life at risk—*if* she could trust the djinni, and she must—it was a problem she would strive to avoid. But not from fear, no . . .

She'd turned her face to Elisande, shaped words on a gentle breath of air. "I don't hear them."

Elisande had shaken her head, *neither do I*, or else, *that doesn't matter*, perhaps both. "Two," she'd murmured. "They were coming; now they've stopped."

"Guards?" Julianne had asked, pointlessly: how could Elisande know, and what else could the men be?

But she'd asked anyway, and, "No. Not guards. I don't know, they mask themselves . . . Hush, here comes another, on the bank . . ."

Her tugging hand had drawn Julianne down, deep into the shadows beneath the scrub; and so Marron had found them and then seemed to lose them again, but the men had come along the gully regardless and Elisande had gasped softly, and then risen up to meet them.

And one had been Rudel and the other was apparently called Redmond, a name that resonated through this land's history but must, surely must be coincidence because he'd been old and weak and shuffling, no kind of legend.

Hard words there'd been, between her friend and the jongleur—though that style was no more the truth than the brother's robes he wore that night; she'd challenged him on that, and not been satisfied—and then there'd been the guards finding them and falling slackly unconscious before they could do more than cry an alarm; and that had been Rudel's work somehow and he'd done his own shouting then, to set them running as Marron had run already.

EVEN THEN, SHE hadn't wanted to flee. But there'd been more than her pride at stake suddenly, more even than her pride and her father's life. Whoever Rudel and Redmond really were, they'd brought another element to the night's adventure, a sense of greater danger which Elisande at least had recognised. Whoever Elisande really was, to know them well enough to curse them as she had . . .

So when Elisande's hand had snagged hers and tugged, she'd run with her friend along the gully. At least the blanket-roll roped to her back had been light and the peasant's robe easy to run in, though they'd kicked up choking clouds of dust and her boots had kept catching in cracks in the mud below the dust, so that she'd stumbled often and nearly fallen more than once.

For a while they'd run with the sounds of pursuit in their ears, though not pursuit of them. The twists and turns of the absent river's bed had led them away from that, away from the village and the Elessans' camp both; only once had Elisande pulled her urgently to a halt and then whispered a warning, guards ahead on the gully's bank. For a minute they'd stood still, silent except for her own panting breath and her friend's, irritatingly easier to her ears; then Elisande had gestured her on again at a slow walk. She could see the men who watched, standing shadowed against the stars; somehow, despite the bright sky, the men had not seen them.

Once past, they'd jogged on again until she'd simply had to rest, jerking at Elisande's arm to tell her so; she hadn't had the breath to say it. Her friend had nodded, gestured her to sit and crouched beside her, patient for a little while. Then she'd murmured, "We should get out of this gully anyway, it's leading us off our path. We need to head more northerly."

They'd clambered up the bank and found themselves in a wide bare valley, high dry hills all around them. Elisande had picked the direction, north and east, and set the pace, a slow walk at first that Julianne could match with comfort.

THEY'D FOUND THE road again, and crossed it: "I wish this were the other side of the gully," Elisande had murmured. "This is how they'll come, looking for us. But we had to come back to it; north and around, it's further but that's the only safe way from here. I'd never get you through the mountains, not on foot and in high summer."

There was an unspoken implication there, that alone she might have taken the mountain route and survived it. Julianne had been resentful, briefly—*sorry to hold you back, Elisande*—before she'd remembered that she owed the other girl a greater debt than this. If a little condescension was all the levy that her friend demanded, then she was getting guide and companion at a cheap cost indeed.

Besides, Elisande was probably right on both counts. She was hardy and experienced, very likely she could cross a mountain range afoot; Julianne was certain that she herself could not. She'd been having trouble enough in all honesty simply keeping up on the flat, now that the sight of the road had spurred Elisande to set a faster pace, a rapid walk that broke almost into a jog wherever the ground sloped even marginally downhill.

It was the sky, she'd thought, that wore her down. More than the thought of what she left, all she was running away from—a reluctant promise and a dreaded life, all thrown into question and confusion by her first meeting with that man, young man, tall man, heart-stealing thief of a man from whom she was also running away, though it rived her to do it—or the anticipation of what she ran towards, a mystery that might prove a monstrous betrayal if the djinni were false: more than all of that, it had been the sheer weight of sky that had dragged at her muscles and starved her of breath. So broad, so cold a canopy, the stars like chill candles and mind-sickeningly far away; her head had been bowed, she'd only watched her feet but still she'd felt it, still she'd hauled the great compass of it with every weary, aching step she took.

The hills had been no help. Black shadows or grey-glittering slopes of rock, either way they'd held themselves apart, they'd left it all to her. Elisande, too. She was wise, she was skilful, she had the knack to walk be-

neath the sky and not be touched by it; she was mean, she
was selfish, she'd chosen to let her friend, her poor suffering bewildered friend drag all this weight alone . . .

Well, no further. She was going to sit, she had sat; the
sky could drape itself about her like a robe, like a tent
fallen in on itself, it could do as it willed but she would
carry it no further, nor follow clever, cruel Elisande . . .

"Julianne—Oh, I'm so sorry. You're exhausted, I
should have seen it sooner. You're right, we must rest.
Not here, though. We must find some kind of shelter; if
they search this way, we'll need a place to lie unseen. See
that next hill, can you make it just to there? The night lies
about distance, it's not as far as it looks. And you've done
really well, it'll be dawn in a couple of hours and we've
gone all night, that's excellent. Far better than I expected.
So come on now, on your feet and just this last little
stretch, we'll play beetles and find some rock to hide behind, some shadow to lie-up in. Here, take a sip of this
first, it's the *jereth*. That'll put some fire in your blood.
Water when we get there, yes? You'll never have tasted
better, but you have to earn it first . . ."

AND SHE HAD earned it, with the sharp sweet flavours
of *jereth* in her mouth to speak to her of the world as it
was, no weary fantasies to mock her now. She'd known
herself to be only a tired girl trying to lose herself in a
harsh and mocking world, seeking to hide from the one
man who had ever drawn her, whose voice and face
sucked at her like a lodestone; and the sky was the sky
and the night the night, convenient darkness that would
prove too short, and nothing more than that.

And no, that hill had not been closer than it seemed, it
had been further away, it was Elisande who lied; and
every step had been an effort even with her friend's
strong arm to lean on, and when at last they'd reached it
and found the broken well and the path up and the little
cave where the path ended, she'd felt no curiosity, none

of Elisande's piqued interest, only relief that it was there
and it was empty and she could lie down now, which she
had done and had then done nothing more.

SHE WOKE RELUCTANTLY and late, to the feather-touch
of sun on her face and the far weightier touch of memory
on her mind, its physical proof on her body. She lay still
because every muscle felt stiff and sore and cruelly
overused; she didn't open her eyes because even her eye-
lids were too much for her this morning, if morning it still
was.

Sun about her, stone beneath her, a hard bed but it
would do; there were noises also, distantly the knocking
of rock on rock, but that could wait.

She let her thoughts run back, to see again everything
that she'd done yesterday, everything that had happened
to her and around her. Leaving the castle and meeting the
Barons Imber, elder and younger both; leaving the village
and meeting Rudel and Redmond in the gully, in disguise; leaving them—and leaving Imber, but she wasn't,
she *wasn't* going to dwell on that, on him, on his face and
manners and charm and the touch of him in her head and
heart where she'd thought no man would ever touch
her—and making that long trek through the night with
Elisande, which had brought her here . . .

And where was here, exactly? Her eyes opened without permission, without any intent on her part; she saw a
blaze of light and turned her head away, grunting at the
effort of even so little movement, the stab of pain in her
neck.

She saw light and shadow, no more than that; blinked,
squinted against the dazzle and saw rock walls, a shelf of
rock, a few small things on the floor and no more than
that.

Sitting up took an age, against the aching stiffness in
her body. She thought she could feel every bone in her
spine creaking in protest. She tossed aside the second

blanket that covered her, which Elisande must have laid
there when she rose, and then looked around again. A
small cave, with only one thing more to be seen in it, the
sign of the God Divided hewn into the wall. She tried to
see that as an omen, but couldn't make it work. Wasn't
she turning, running away from all that that implied?

No Elisande. That sound of stacking rocks some way
away, below, assumed a new importance. So did standing
up.

Had it ever been so hard? Well, yes. Once, twice,
often. After she fell, that long slow silence down and
down: after that, stirring a muscle, setting a foot outside
her bed had been a dreadful thing, impossible. The sense
of panic, the incoherent rush of terror — like a rush of air,
and the gilded ceiling of her room darkening, spinning,
rising up to greet her — had taken weeks to pass. Or not
to pass, to be taken and closed away, locked in ever
smaller, further places in her mind till it was lost, not forgotten but hidden even from herself.

And there had been other times, of course, times when
she was ill or hurt or sore from a tumble off a horse, more
sore than this; of *course* she'd felt worse than this, her
legs had been more rebellious against her will and balance harder to find. And she was not a child any more,
nor was she an invalid, and she still had her pride, she refused to let Elisande see her so weak. Nothing but a
night's march, after all, and there would be men hunting
for them ahorseback, this was no time to play the girl . . .

So she stood up. And cracked her head against the roof
of the cave, and swore; and rubbed angrily at the sore
spot on her skull, and made it hurt the worse. And saw the
length of cloth that had made last night's turban lying on
the floor beside her blankets, and stooped to pick it up
and wrap it round her head again, and was still wrapping
and tucking as she walked almost doubled over out of the
cave's mouth —

And reeled, straightened with a gasp that was nearly,
nearly a scream, and staggered back against the face of

the cliff, her hands grasping at stone behind her as her head spun and she screwed her eyes tight shut against the sun and the wide view of hills and the long, long drop that she'd come so close to stepping over.

She hadn't seen it last night, what with the dark and her numbing exhaustion and Elisande on that side of her, holding her arm tight and talking, talking. She'd known that they climbed, of course, but she hadn't realised just how high nor how steep the path had been, how there'd been nothing on the other side of Elisande.

Steady now, steady . . .

She stood braced against the cliff, feeling for the solidity of rock, trying to borrow a little. She felt the breeze move against her face, she listened to the clunk of stones below her; and at last, oh so slowly, she forced her eyes to open.

Looked only at her feet, where they stood firmly on hard dusty rock. There, that was good. Took a step sideways, with her hands still clinging and her back dragging along the rock. Better. Excellent, indeed. One step, and now another. And a third; and so on down the track, step by cautious step, she could have counted them all the way, she took such care about them.

At last the track turned, away from the wall of cliff on her left. For a moment she hesitated, reluctant to lose that hold she had: with her world so shrunken—cliff-face and path, her feet on the path and her eyes on her feet and nowhere else—it was a wrench to step away, to break out from what was so very secure. Besides, stepping away meant stepping into space, she knew that, it meant falling and falling . . .

But the path stepped away, and the path was not falling; *trust to the path*, some little whisper of sense in her head suggested. So she did. And no, did not fall, because there was no drop now, only good dry dusty ground on either side of the path; this was the valley floor, and she stood and walked upon it.

And lifted her head with a gasp, with a sigh; and saw

Elisande now, and saw what she was doing to make those noises, *knock knock* of stone on stone.

Remembered now, a picture plucked from last night's maze: a heap of stones not worked but gathered, and the path that ran from it lying silver in starlight, clear to be seen though nothing used it now, Elisande had said, stooping to brush with her fingers' tips at sand and dust. *This was a well*, she'd said, *and those who used it must have lived above, come, let's find what home they've left us . . .*

IT LOOKED MORE like a well now, or a little more: a dark narrow slit of a hole in the earth, with the stones set to make an awkward, jagged wall around it. Elisande's face shone with sweat beneath her turban as she laboured full in the sun's eye, lifting another stone and dropping it where it might almost fit, grinding it against its neighbours until it almost did.

"I'm no builder," she panted, straightening as she saw Julianne, "but this should hold a while. It'll serve to mark it out, at least; and make some windbreak, to hold the dust at bay."

"Do we need water?" Julianne asked, meaning, *do we need to spend our time and effort repairing wells when we're running, when we're hunted, when we have to be moving on?*

"Sharai manners," Elisande said, replying to what she had meant and not said. "Desert habits: you never break a well, nor leave one broken. Learn that, Julianne, it's important."

"More important than being caught and taken back? If they saw no water here, pursuers might give up for their horses' sake."

"Yes, more important," Elisande said flatly. "Water is life in the desert, life for all. You'll be grateful to your enemy and your family's enemies, every time you drink untainted water. That's how it has to be."

"This is not desert, and the Sharai are a long way from here."

"Even so."

"Well. Is there water, have you tried it?"

For answer, Elisande picked up a pebble and tossed it into the dark. A second later, a soft splash came back to them. The two friends gazed at each other, in contradiction but no hostility; then Julianne sighed, and sat down, and said, "Where will we find them, then, how far must we go?"

"Look." Elisande crouched at her side, swept the ground smooth with the flat of her hand and then drew quickly, one-fingered in the dust. "Here is Tallis, here is Elessi; these are the hills that border both, where we are now. East and south are the mountains, like a spine that divides Outremer from the desert and the Sharai. I don't think we could reach them, whichever route we chose. I can look like a Catari but you cannot, not with that hair and that skin of yours; and all those petty barons are so jealous of their land, they'll stop and question any stranger. Even if we did reach the mountains, I don't believe that I could take you through them. It's harder land than this, no wells and steeper climbs; the passes are higher than these hills." *Further to fall*, she was saying, and Julianne heard her.

"So we go north and east, we go around the mountains and come down to the desert. It'll take us weeks longer on foot, though we might find horses somewhere. That road is the Kingdom's border for a while, before it turns south towards Elessi. Out here they pay no taxes and offer no allegiance, though they don't make war either, they don't invite the attention of the Order. They're wild folk, nomads mostly, but they breed horses, they don't ask questions and they do like gold. We might even strike lucky. That raiding party that attacked the Roq—no, it was more than that, it was an army—but we might run into them and find ourselves an escort all the way. We can't go into the desert alone in any case, we'll need a guide . . ."

Was it lucky, to meet a Sharai war-party? Perhaps it was, now that her world had turned around, now that she was a reluctant fugitive in a land and a life that bewildered her. Imber was a golden vision trapped behind her eyes, as bright and hot as the sun; he must be held there, hidden and wrapped in a grief she had to keep private even from her friend.

Questions, though, she could surely ask questions; and now was the time to look for answers from Elisande.

"Rudel and that other man, Redmond," she said slowly. "Who are they? Truly?"

"You know who Redmond is," Elisande replied, smiling slightly. "He is two men, and you know about both. He is the prisoner from Surayon, who was being tortured in the cells at the Roq; and he is Redmond of Corbonne, who was known as the Red Earl."

Julianne nodded, as though there were nothing momentous in any of this. "And Rudel?"

"Rudel is also from Surayon."

"And not a jongleur?"

"Not only a jongleur, though perhaps he should have been. He has some skill in that direction."

"And you?"

"Oh, I too am also from Surayon. But you know that, don't you? You must have worked that out . . . ?"

"Yes, of course. I just wanted to hear you say it. I'm tired of secrets, Elisande." *Tell me your true heart's wishes, and I won't tell you mine. If you're lucky . . .*

"I know. I'm sorry. But I gave you hints enough, I thought. I couldn't actually say it in the castle. Words are birds, they fly upward and around and you never can tell quite where they'll settle . . ."

"Did some jongleur teach you that?"

"Rudel did." Said flatly, as though she resented the reminder or the fact itself, that something of his had become something of hers.

"Who is Rudel?"

"A man who thinks he has some authority over me."

"And does he?"

"No."

If the next question was obvious—*so who are you, Elisande?*—Julianne thought the answer was also; she thought she'd be told, *I'm a girl over whom Rudel has no authority.* Instead she said, "What will they do now, Rudel and Redmond? When we were discovered he said they'd turn back; but they wouldn't find it so easy to pass unnoticed a second time, not with all the guards alert and so much fuss . . ."

"I don't know what they'll do," Elisande said, losing the stubborn cast of her face all in a moment, looking fretful and concerned and suddenly very young. "There is a thing we can do, a talent we have to confuse men's minds so that they don't see what is in front of them, I suppose you'd call it magic. Not everything they teach about us Surayonnaise is false . . ."

Julianne saw another anxiety spring to life in her friend, and put an arm around her shoulder. "Not everyone in Outremer thinks that all magic is demons' work, Elisande. And I grew up in Marasson," *I have seen things done greater and worse.* "Is that what you did to Marron, when he came along the bank?"

"Yes. I didn't know who he was at first, and then I wasn't sure if he was safe to see us. That boy confuses me, I don't understand his loyalties. Rudel did the same to the Ransomers, only harder, he's stronger than I am and the need was great. And I again, later and lighter, to the men who watched the gully. But everything has its limits; we can only touch a few at a time, three or four at most, and it's a struggle if their minds are focused. Rudel might, he *might* have been able to maze the guards and lead Redmond away again, but I'm not sure. I think perhaps they'd just sit quiet and wait for another chance. But that's in his hands now, there's nothing we can do. We

have to look after ourselves, Julianne, and make our way
to the Sharai. That's all. Remember the djinni . . ."

"I haven't forgotten the djinni. Nor what it said. Must
we move on today?"

She'd tried to keep her voice even, *just another question, no more*, but by the look that Elisande gave her—
part sympathy and part frustration—she hadn't
succeeded. Probably it had sounded like a plea, perhaps a
child's whine.

"Better not, I think. We won't have left much of a trail
on this ground, but even so they may ride out this way.
We'd best hide up for the day, and move at night. That
cave's as good as anywhere. You can't see it from down
here, only the path, and we can brush that out at least a
little."

*Perhaps you shouldn't have built the well up, so that it
stands out so clearly man-made*; but Elisande had not
said what she might have said, *you're too exhausted to go
on, one night's march has worn you out, you have to rest
today*, so all Julianne said was, "Whose cave was this, do
you think? That's the God's sign they've cut into the rock
up there . . ."

"Oh, some hermit, some mad monk. The land was full
of them, after the King's armies claimed Outremer for
their God. Every desolate hill had its religious. The local
people brought them food and begged a prayer of them in
return, though like as not they only got a curse. But the
wild tribes raided here, sometimes the Sharai. The hermits were all killed, or driven off. With luck, your baron
will find so many caves he won't search out ours, or else
we'll be long gone before he does . . ."

Oh, her baron, searching for her: what must he think,
she had fled from him? Julianne gazed bleakly westward
and pushed herself to her feet, aching more in heart than
body though her body ached cruelly.

"Let's go up, then, they will have been early on the
road."

*   *   *

ELISANDE PRODUCED BREAD and oranges from her pack, and they sat in the light of the cave-mouth to eat, far enough back that Julianne could see the view but not the drop and didn't need to look at all, her hands so busy with tearing, peeling, segmenting.

"We've food for one more day, if we're sparing with it," Elisande said. "After that we must hunt, track down some people to beg from, or else go hungry," but she said it cheerfully enough. Julianne understood that going hungry was not a serious option; her friend was confident of her hunting ability, even with nothing more than a knife, or else she was sure of finding company in these drab and empty-seeming hills. Or else both, very likely both. She might have been walking for weeks or months already when Julianne met her, living off the land or its people; admittedly Less Arvon and most of Tallis were fatter lands than these, but they were probably less charitable also. There'd been feeling in her voice, when she spoke of the petty barons' jealousies . . .

"Why did you come to Roq de Rançon?" Julianne asked her. "It wasn't to rescue Redmond, he followed us."

"No, Redmond was — a coincidence, an inconvenience. Like that damned djinni. I don't *want* to go to the Sharai!" suddenly, vehemently. "Not now. Neither do you, do you? Of course you don't, except for your father. And the djinni could save him, if he needs saving; it could pick him up and bring him here in an eye-blink. But it wouldn't do that, of course, oh no. The djinn don't interfere with humankind, they're far too grand. Except when it pleases them, apparently, they just spin up out of the dust and send us off with no warning, and without even telling us *why* . . ."

"Elisande."

"Yes?"

"Why did you come to the Roq?"

"I came to collect something, if I could. If I could get at it. Something we need to have safe in Surayon, if only

to stop the fanatics, the Ransomers, men like Marshal
Fulke from putting their hands upon it. Or that Baron
Imber—not yours, the older one. Those men could destroy us; they have the means in their hands, if they only
knew it. I wanted to pick it up and walk off with it, and
leave them still not knowing; but I hadn't managed to get
to it, and then they brought Redmond in and I *know* him,
he's my friend, he was kind to me when I was a child,
when kindness was what I needed more than anything. So
I was—distracted; that's why I didn't want to leave, I
couldn't bear to leave him. And I hate not knowing
what's happened to him now, whether he got away or
not . . ."

"What about Rudel?"

"Rudel can look after himself."

"I mean, why did Rudel come to the castle?"

"Oh, the same as me, largely; he didn't trust me to take
care of this thing we wanted, so he came for it himself.
But actually it would be safer with me, that's why I came.
It was stupid of him to follow me. Stupid, and typical . . ."

"What is it, then? This thing?"

"Just something they shouldn't have, that we could
make good use of."

"A weapon?"

"Of a sort."

"Elisande, enough of secrets!"

"No. Not yet. Not till we're a lot further away from the
castle."

"Why, don't you trust me?"

"Of course I trust you. I have already, with my life;
I'm Surayonnaise, remember? A Surayonnaise witch,
they would burn me if they knew. But this is more important, and you're part of their world; if you dropped a
hint to your Baron Imber . . ."

"Elisande, I'm running away from my Baron Imber.
Remember?"

"Even so. This is not safe knowledge for you to have;

not yet, and maybe not later. We failed, Rudel and I; that thing is still there, and fatal to us. It may still be there in a month, in a season, in a year. Where will you be then? Perhaps in Elessi, back with your baron, if your father sends you there. Enough of secrets, you said; I won't give you this one, then, that you might have to keep from lord and husband and friends and all."

"You've given me enough of those already," Julianne said, but grumpily, giving in.

"Then rest, under the weight of them. Seriously," in response to a darting glance, "you should rest. We must walk the night away."

"What will you do?" Julianne asked, knowing only that *rest* was the one certainty, the one word she could be sure not to hear in response.

"Scout an hour, maybe two. There must be a village somewhere; those old mad hermits were not that mad, to live where no one would ever bring them bread or questions."

"Elisande, if they see you—"

"If they see me, I am a goat-boy strayed from my goats, and much in need of a whipping. But in this heat? They will be resting. Like you. I will be a shadow among their sheep-folds. Just to see what kind of people they are, which god they follow. Whether there are horses we can buy or steal. Or camels, we will need camels later, though horses would be better on this ground. Sleep, Julianne. Dream easy, and don't worry about me. If we're lucky, I'll bring a rabbit back."

WELL, SHE WOULDN'T worry, then. Why should she, anyway? Elisande was in her element out here. Skin like bark—smooth bark, smooth and soft and oiled—and sapwood muscles beneath, she could walk all night and carry her friend too, rebuild a well and scout and hunt under the sun's hammer while that same friend and all the world else was dozing . . .

Well. Every jewel has its setting. Julianne was competent too, in her own place, and sometimes as quietly assertive. She would not resent Elisande's competence here; indeed, she would doze, as she'd been told to. And wake stiffer than before, no doubt, gall to that resentment that she did of course not feel.

She crept into the cave's shadows, where the rock below her was cool though the still air was warm. Too warm for a blanket now; she lay atop both, for some padding against the rock. And closed her eyes, stretched herself into some semblance of a sleeping figure—*like a tomb*, she thought, *here lies Julianne, lost and alone where even the djinn could not find her*—and her mind spun her back to Marasson, to cool statues under high domes, and she lost the thread of even such foolish thoughts, and did sleep.

AND WOKE TO find that the sun had moved on so that its light slid across the cave-mouth without striking even a little way inside. She sat up in the dimness, remembered not to stand; thought about crawling to the mouth to see if there were any sign of Elisande's returning, remembered the long fall that waited for her out there and decided against.

No hope of sleeping more: her rested, restless body told her that. She wondered how the hermit had passed his time here; in prayer, presumably. That was not an option for her. She reached a hand out and traced his God-sign with a finger, running it along the loops, round and around again. Dust powdered down, and little flakes of rock; a sudden gleam of gold leaped out.

No, not gold. Golden light, looking bright only against the shadow of the wall; pale it was by the sun's measure, but rich none the less. The colour of gold dissolved in milk, she thought. And warm, warm against her finger's tip . . .

Puzzled, she bent close to look, while her finger went

on working. Dust and splinters fell away, the line of light stretched and ran; it flowed like milk, all through the crude-carved channel of the sign. And met itself and flowed on, round and around again as her finger had gone before it, though she'd snatched that back now. Warm enough before, too hot to touch the light looked suddenly. It was burning, almost too bright to look on; she squinnied her eyes, trying to see rock behind the light, and failing.

"Oh, the God's grief," she murmured huskily, wishing that Elisande was back. "What have I done . . . ?"

No answer from the wall, only that pulsing, flaring light running and running in its stony path; nor from any god either. This she had to deal with herself.

All right. There was a hermit—*a presumed hermit, but let's presume the hermit, please . . . ?*—who must have had some power, some magic, a contact with his God. This was what he did when he wasn't praying, he cut his God's sign into the rock and made it shine, an affirmation of his faith. And the power was not his but the God's, it survived him and lay latent in the rock, in the sign, until some other finger, her stupid ignorant finger was enough to wake it . . .

Yes. That made sense, if anything could be called sense in that fierce light, those pulsing shadows.

Of its own accord—no will, no choice of hers, surely—her hand rose again towards the light and the heat of it. Call it power, call it magic, call it living prayer: whatever it was, it had a wicked allure. She wanted to touch it now, in its glory, even at the cost of scorched fingers. Call it a girl's curiosity, call it her father's training, she needed to know how such a thing felt against her skin. Whether it really would burn her, or if the God had a care for even his most doubting subjects . . .

She touched: and no, even the flowing star of light—like a comet dragging its tail, she thought, and the light fading where it had burned and gone but never fading to darkness before here it came again—even that did not burn her. Her fingers tingled as it passed; she tried to cup it in her palm but it flowed on unregarding, seeming to pass through the flesh and bone of her.

Only a tingle and that pleasant warmth, she could get no touch of it else. Neither any touch of rock. Her fingers pressed further, deeper and a long way deeper than the sign had been chiselled; she could see rock still above her hand—though it was getting harder to see that, harder to see anything beyond the glow that spilt out of the blazing sign, poured out around her breaching hand—but she couldn't find it with her stretching fingers.

This was absurd, she must be dreaming; and yet she was not, she knew that with uttermost certainty. She pushed her hand slowly into the liquid light, without causing the least eddy in its run. The tingling feeling moved up to her elbow as gold washed over it, she lost sight of her hand altogether, and still her fingers clutched at nothing—

—until something clutched at them.

Julianne screamed.

Not a hand that held hers, nothing so human: more like a rope it felt, a hot rope. Or a snake, or a tendril of some grasping plant. Something flexible, that wrapped itself tightly around her hand and wrist. Her fingers clenched instinctively but couldn't grip it, couldn't get a purchase; they just seemed to sink into the thing as if it weren't there at all. When she tried to tug free, though, it clung like riverweed.

Sobbing for breath, sobbing for sheer terror, Julianne set her teeth and pulled. Slowly and steadily she drew her arm back from wherever it had gone, back through the glow and into the cave again.

Something else came with it.

She'd known it was coming, she'd been able to feel the weight of it, the resistance all the way. It was at least passive resistance, though, dead weight. Like pulling a pig of iron, she thought, rather than a living pig; at least it didn't pull back. Whatever it was, she'd rather this than the reverse, that it draw her through light and absent rock into its impossible place . . .

At first she saw it as a darkness, a shadow in the gold and a shadow on her skin, nothing more than that. Then, as her arm came free of the light's tingling touch, she saw it indeed as a rope, or a tendril, or a snake.

Just its tip was coiled around her hand and forearm, its thicker length went stretching back into the glare and back further, where she could not see; she only knew that there was more, much more of it than had hold of her.

She grabbed at it with her free hand, trying to peel it from her arm, but again her fingers found nothing solid to cling to. It was like clutching at smoke. Smoke that held its shape, but writhed and roiled within that intangible skin: beneath her panic Julianne's mind found a memory, another creature that fashioned itself with that same violence, by forces that she could not comprehend.

The djinni . . .

But no. Surely this was not the djinni, not any djinni: that creature's touch was lethal. She remembered the boy on the road, the man on the castle wall, both of them with their bodies ripped open to the bone. All she felt was pressure on her arm. Though she had heard that the djinn could shape themselves from anything, so why not from harmless smoke . . . ?

No. Still, not a djinni. She was sure. Something of the same world, though, something of spirit: and malignant with it, malevolent, she was sure of that also. It lay hot against and around her flesh, but her soul was chilled by its touch.

She scrambled awkwardly to her feet, gut-cramping fear keeping her crouched low below the roof as she backed slowly towards the cave-mouth. Her mouth was stone-dry, even breathing hurt; she couldn't have screamed again if screaming were guaranteed to bring rescue.

Every step she took away from the flaring wall, she had to drag against the weight of the thing that had roped itself to her arm. Its dark smoky shadow surged and seethed through the golden light, the gateway; and then suddenly it was a rope no more, its weight was gone from her, it was a great swirling mass that flowed and folded itself into a solid form at the back of the cave.

Julianne gasped; released, her stinging arm fell dead at her side. She clutched at it, drew it up and cradled it against her breast for a moment, then turned and plunged out into the sunlight.

Heedless of the fall so close at her side, conscious only of a far greater terror at her back, she leaped recklessly down the path, barely catching her weight on one foot before the other was stretching ahead. Stones skittered over the edge and her thoughts also teetered on an edge, on the very edge of a long, long fall; flight had released the pent-up panic in her bones, so that it was hard to think at all, hard to do anything that was not pure animal . . .

But animal she was not. She was daughter of the King's Shadow, and trained to do more, to do better than run. That training was a net which contained her even through that jarring, desperate descent, a net she could cling to, so that at the foot of the cliff she could halt, and did. She could straighten herself, and did; could even turn, to see what it was that she fled from.

And did.

And saw it coming after her, smoke no more; now it was something black and chitinous, a beetle perhaps though a beetle of grotesque size, balanced on too many sharp fast legs and with great claws extended, mouthparts moving behind them as though it chewed already on her flesh. And it had an idol's head above the insect mouth, red burning eyes and horns rising high: half-beetle and half-devil then, and either half inimical and deadly.

What did she have, to meet such a monster?

Knives. Two knives, and her arms and knives together too short by a distance to reach past those grasping, tearing claws . . .

Julianne turned to run again, all training useless to her;
but had gone no more than half a dozen stumbling paces
before she was aware suddenly of a figure rising from the
shadow of a rock ahead. She drew a sobbing breath to
scream her friend's name, to tell her to run also, to run the
other way, knives and courage were useless here; but
staggered to a halt again, seeing that this was not
Elisande who stood before her.

It was a man, a young man in Sharai robes of midnight-
blue, and he had a bow in his hands and an arrow nocked
already to the string.

He snapped something, a word she didn't know, but
his gesture was unmistakable: a jerk of his head, to the
side and down.

Julianne dived to the ground behind another rock, poor
protection if the creature came after her, but she had no
greater hope: neither knives nor speed would save her
now, only the young man and his arrows offered any
chance.

And the first of the young man's arrows had flown already as she dived, and his hands were busy with a second, notch and draw, aim and fire and pull another from
the rope that made the belt of his ragged robe. He had a
blade hung there also, a long curved scimitar, but he like
she must know that if this devil-beetle came to sword's
reach, the fight was over.

She followed the flight of the second arrow, saw it
strike the creature's gleaming black armoured body and
glance off, fall away. She could see no sign of the first,
and presumed that the same had happened. Well, that was
likely it, then. *The eyes, aim for the eyes*, but she thought
he was already; and if he could shoot no straighter than
this—and he had time for only one more arrow to prove
it, or the thing would be on them—then she might as
well decide to die now, and choose a god to pray to . . .

Briefly, she tried to be that cynical, that calm in the
face of catastrophe. Her body betrayed her, though, shuddering with dread; and if her mind was praying it was

only to the Sharai and not his god or any, *oh please, one more arrow, make it tell this time* . . .

He seemed to be praying too, holding that arrow in his hand and moving his lips above it while the creature scuttered ever closer. At last, though, he fitted it to his string and seemed not to aim at all, only to draw and release in a moment. Perhaps he had no hope and the arrow was only a gesture, as the prayer had been; or perhaps the thing loomed so large before him that he thought he could not miss.

And perhaps he was right, because he did not miss; neither did this arrow skitter off that unnatural chitin. It flew straight and true, and struck the creature not in either eye but between the two, below the bony black horns.

Julianne thought she saw sparks fly as it struck, sparks of gold.

The creature had no human mouth to bellow; but its jaws worked, and a shrill screeing sound hurt Julianne's ears. She clamped her hands over them, which helped not at all; then she saw the young man drop his bow, draw his scimitar and run forward. She opened her mouth to shout, *no, don't be a fool, stand back and use more arrows* . . .

But he'd never hear, above that scratching scream; and likely he wouldn't understand her anyway. So many tutors she'd had as a child, why had none of them ever taught her Catari?

Briefly, she thought she should draw her knives and go after him. But her short blades could add nothing to his sword, if that were not enough; and even it might not be needed. The creature was swaying, toppling already, its dreadful shriek fading to a moan; that single blessed arrow could be enough on its own account. For certainty's sake or for the pleasure of the kill, no more than that, the Sharai skipped lightly over a drooping claw and thrust his blade in through one of the creature's wide red eyes, thrust deep into its terrible skull. Julianne stood and watched as the fire died in that eye and the other, as the spindly legs collapsed, as the rounded body slumped and rolled. For a moment the head sprawled in the dust, those dead eyes seemed to stare directly at her in accusation, *you brought me through, to this*; then the gloss on the body clouded, what had seemed so strong and real turned back to smoke and held its shape only weakly. What little breeze there was stirred and broke it; the thing drifted like dust and was gone.

The young Sharai grunted, looked at his blade and seemed to find no blood, no mark, no sign at all. Even so he wiped it, he all but scrubbed it on his robe before he sheathed it, before he stooped to reclaim his more potent arrow from where it had fallen to the ground when the creature faded.

Slowly, on legs that she was determined not to allow to tremble, Julianne walked forward to join him. He glanced at her and she saw that he was younger even than she'd thought, younger perhaps than her own Imber, little more than a boy. He smiled effortfully, more shaken than he wanted to admit or her to know; murmured something soft and sibilant, gazed almost blankly at the rocky ground where his fallen enemy was not—

—and then turned abruptly back to her, his eyes widening. He said something more, sharp and demanding.

She shrugged, tried a difficult smile of her own and said, "I'm sorry, I don't understand you."

His hand touched the hilt of his sword, and she wondered if it would be her more earthly blood that next tainted his blade.

He held his hand, though; instead he scowled, seemed to fumble for words, at last said, "You are not Catari. Not a boy."

"No." No, and no again. "My name is Julianne. And thank you, you saved my life . . ."

He shrugged, and turned his face aside. "Cover your head. Woman."

Her head was covered already, by the turban that had helped to deceive him, hiding her long and lustrous hair.

She knew what he meant, though, and quickly unwound one end of it to wrap around as a makeshift veil. *There, is that better?* she wanted to say, sardonically, *does that distress you less?*

Instead, "Forgive me," she murmured placatingly. "I am new to your land, and your customs."

"You dress as a boy."

"I know. It was . . . necessary. But," with a sudden, unexpected shudder to say that she too was more shaken than she wanted to know or admit, not at all her father's daughter but only a girl too recently terrified out of her wits, "what *was* that thing?"

" 'Ifrit," he said shortly.

'Ifrit. Of course. Spirit like the djinn, but never neutral as the djinn were meant to be, always cruel, savage, terrible . . .

"It, it came out of the rock . . ." She wasn't going to say that she'd pulled it through, that it was her own curiosity that had so nearly brought disaster to them both.

He grunted and cast his eyes up the path towards the cave, as though he meant to climb it.

This time, Julianne did speak against his intent. "No," she said firmly. "There is no room up there to use your bow," *your magic arrow*, "and besides, there are no more." It had needed her arm, she thought, to make the breach, the gateway through that spinning light. Nor did she want the Sharai to see the light, the sign of an alien god alive and blazing. This was difficult enough already; stupid with aftershock—or so she told herself—she couldn't think how to talk to him, whether to hold him here or hope to see him go . . .

BLESSEDLY, SHE DIDN'T need to. There was a sudden scurry of footsteps behind them—deliberately loud, she thought, that girl could be as silent as a soaring hawk when she chose to—and the Sharai twisted round, his sword grating free of its scabbard in the same movement.

Julianne was slower, dangerously slow; Elisande could have died spitted before she'd even seen the stroke.

But Elisande was faster, in mind and body both. Her face was discreetly veiled already, as Julianne's was, with the tail of her turban; and she was standing quite still, quite unthreatening and more than a long sword's reach away.

Not a word to Julianne; she spoke to the Sharai, and in his own language.

He answered her, she spoke again, and suddenly there was a formality even in the way that he stood, almost a deference in the way that he listened.

No more that Julianne could do; she backed away until her legs came up against a rock, and then she sat on it. Her knees were trembling; aftershock for sure, she could think of nothing but the creature, the 'ifrit, how dark and terrible it had been. How close to death she'd come. She closed her eyes; that helped not at all, so she opened them again and watched the sere pale blue of the sky, wondering how long it would be before rain came to this forsaken country.

"JULIANNE?"

"Yes, Elisande?"

Rapidly, not to let him follow: "His name is Jemel. He was with the war-party that attacked the Roq, but he left them in anger, he would not so much as keep the horse that he was riding. He had a friend, a lover I think, who died on the wall; it may have been my knife that killed him. I have not told him that. He has agreed to guide us through the desert to Rhabat; my grandfather's name is worth that much at least. How did the 'ifrit come?"

Julianne blinked: so much information so quickly, and the question hard at its back. She recognised the technique, was not—quite—caught by it, but would not equivocate anyway.

"The God's sign, on the wall in the cave. I touched it,

and it glowed with light: light that I could push my hand into. The 'ifrit caught hold of me, and came through when I tried to pull free . . ."

"Ah. Well, he wants to go up. We must, I think; but we follow him, do you understand? We stand in his shadow now."

Yes, Julianne understood; that, and the chagrin in Elisande's voice. Her grandfather's name was not all-commanding, then.

She might have asked what that name was, but did not. She followed Elisande, who followed Jemel; and when they came to the cave there was no light running in the God's sign, no smoky shadows in the dimness, only rock and dust and their blankets and small goods strewn about.

Elisande reached to touch the gouged rock where the sign was, but held her hand a fraction short, before Julianne could call out to warn her.

"How could it . . . ?"

Julianne had no answer to offer her; nor did she seem to expect one. There was another brief, incomprehensible conversation between her and the Sharai, which Elisande translated. Jemel had agreed that they would not move on till nightfall; there might be other Sharai about, from other tribes than his. It would be better, safer, not to be seen by such. He would keep watch at the cave-mouth, and Elisande with him.

Julianne withdrew. Let them talk, let Elisande sate her curiosity, brandish her grandfather's name, come as close as she might or as close as she dared to that fierce, dangerous young man. Julianne would take the blankets and make a nest for herself in the cool at the back of the cave, as far as she could get from them and from the rough-hewn sign that drew her eyes, drew them and drew them until she screwed them tightly shut and turned her head away.

"JULIANNE?"

"Unh?"

"Julianne . . ."

"Yes, what is it?"

"Riders."

She hadn't meant to move. She hadn't moved for a while, not for a long time, and would have been just as glad never to have moved again. Now suddenly every muscle in her itched and twitched, she wanted to be up and running; already she was at the cave-mouth, crouched behind her friend.

"Who are they?" Elessans, brothers? Sharai, or some people other?

"I can't see, there's too much dust. But they're coming up the valley from the south."

Which meant that she didn't need to see, any more than Julianne. *From the south* meant *from the road*, meant men sent to chase them down and bring them back. Too late to do anything except sit exceedingly still and pray to pass unnoticed, in dun and dirty robes among these dun and dirty rocks.

And so she did, so did they all until,

"Dogs!"

"What?" Julianne's head jerked and her eyes stared, despite all resolutions.

"They've got dogs with them. See?"

Julianne lifted her hand to shade her dazzled eyes. She saw first the dust-cloud down on the valley floor, and never mind how high, how very high she sat, she had neither time nor temper to mind it now. Men and horses, yes, shadows in the dust; and little shadows to the fore making their own little trail of dust, and yes again, those were dogs.

"Sekari hounds," Elisande said, better used to the light and the habits of the country. "The Catari princes breed them, for hunting ground game . . ."

"I have seen Sekari." Tall lean dogs they were, with sharp noses and fine, beautiful silky coats of sand and white. All the fashion they'd been for a while among the Marasson nobility; her father had refused to let her have one as a pet. *They are hunting animals, not lap-dogs*, he'd said, and fetched her home a puppy suitable for a girl, a little wriggling, licking thing that had sat on her knee and slept on her pillow, claimed her love and never quite made up for her disappointment.

"If I'd known they had dogs with them . . ."

"You could have done nothing about it. I do not think you can confound the noses of a pack of dogs."

But she, oh, there was something she could do. She stood up, despite Elisande's hissed warning; she walked, no, she stormed down the narrow path with no thought at all for her weariness or for the long drop that had once so sucked at her mind and courage.

She stood beside the well, and waited. After a minute Elisande joined her, laden with their blanket-rolls and waterskins; Julianne spared her only the one brief glance. Jemel must be lurking still in the cave, and so farewell to their guide. She turned her gaze back to the building dust.

The dogs came first, baying their success, sniffing and circling restlessly around the girls, pressing close against them; Elisande stroked curious noses and tugged gently at long ears, made little fussing noises while Julianne stood stiff and unresponsive as rock, still waiting.

Then came the horses, with the men that rode them; one led the others by several lengths. That man reined in, jumped down and left his mount to his companions' care, striding forward through the scattering dogs. A shrill whistle called them away, but Julianne would not move her eyes to watch them.

The man—tall and young, lithe and strong—wore a scarf of silk wrapped around his nose and mouth, against the cloying dust. Julianne was vaguely conscious of the irony as she met him bare-faced, her turban torn away and left on the path not to give him any impression of disguise; she could find no pleasure in it.

He stood before her, and seemed to hesitate a moment before he unwound the scarf that veiled him. Blond hair and soft blond beard, hair and beard and skin all overlaid with grey now, with that creeping, insidious dust; when he spoke there was dust in his voice also, that coughing would not clear.

"My lady, I am glad to have found you . . ."

"Do you hunt me with dogs, my lord baron?" she cut him off, at last allowing her outrage its escape. "With *dogs*?"

And she lifted a hand and slapped him, hard and fast and furious, raising her own little cloud of dust that might have had her laughing another day, in another mood.

"Am I a hare or a deer,' she went on against his startled silence, against the rising murmur of his companions, "or a runaway slave, to be hounded down this way? Am I an animal?"

"You are a runaway girl," Imber said quietly, "in rebellion against a lawful contract and your father's will. If you were an Elessan yet, and in Elessi, you could be whipped for this. If my uncle were here and saw you strike me, you would be whipped regardless."

"I think not."

"You don't know my uncle," and there was a touch of a smile to his face and voice both, before he stilled it. "He may yet demand it, when he hears; but I can protect you from that, at least. If you ride back with me now."

"What if I refuse? Will you set your dogs on me again?"

Remarkably, he blushed; and ran a hand through his matted hair where dust and sweat together had made a glue, and said, "Julianne, I am sorry about the dogs; but they were the swiftest way to find you before my uncle could. I had meant them as a gift, to make you happy . . ."

There was something in him then that touched her, a yearning regret that laid wreck to her anger despite herself. Bereft, she said nothing, only gazed at him: at the marks her fingers had made on his cheek and at the lustrous eyes above that were green or grey or somehow both at once, fringed with lashes of gold . . .

"My lady," he said, formal again but still quiet, still

private, "is a marriage to me so terrible, that you must flee me after an hour's meeting? After you have come so far in obedience to your father?"

Yes, she thought, it must seem like that to him, that it was himself who had driven her away. What could she say to deny it? Nothing; and so she said nothing at all, only gazed in her sorrow at his own until he bowed and turned away, calling rapid orders to his men. He did not look at her again except the once, when he handed her his own scarf to veil her face, and his eyes were all grey now and turbulent with an understanding that was oh, so cruelly mistaken . . .

THEY SHARED A horse for the ride back, she and Elisande, while the man whose horse it was clung to another's stirrup and jogged beside. And sweated and gasped, and cursed with what little breath he had to spare, Julianne thought, cursed fey and fanciful girls in general and herself in particular; and those would be Elessan manners, she fancied, more common than his master's.

Though if not from the nephew, he might have learned them from the uncle; she was not looking forward to facing the elder Baron Imber. Being required to run away, being seen as an impetuous child who could not tolerate her father's plans for her, that had been sufficient humiliation, she'd thought. To be hunted down with dogs was worse, far worse; riding back with Imber's men packed close about her, their eyes scornful above their ill-concealing scarves, worse yet. The way everyone stood and stared as they came to camp, the very silence a contemptuous jeer, that was intolerable; and yet she tolerated it with her head high and her hands not even clenching on the horse's reins, not to startle the animal.

The uncle, though—she thought the uncle might be very bad indeed.

*   *   *

THERE WAS LITTLE left of the camp now, barely enough to merit the name. All the tents had been struck, bar one: that the tallest and the longest where the barons both had toasted her last night, together with a company from all parties, Elisande and Elessans, Knights Ransomers and Master Sharrol.

Men-at-arms were gathered in groups as before, but now their mess-fires were cold and their packs stowed in piles; their curiosity had turned sour, their nudges were sly and this time she was glad not to overhear what they muttered to each other as she passed. It must be as bad for Imber, too. If a girl would sooner flee than marry, what did that say about the man?

Squires came running to the horses' heads, gawping at her in her peasant's dress. Imber swung out of his saddle and came back to her, helping her down and then taking her arm to conduct her into the tent, a sop to her pride that only fanned the fires of her humiliation. Her jaw clenched behind the veil, as she walked stiffly at his side.

The canvas doors were tied back, to let some little air inside: not enough, she thought, walking into a stifling, stagnant wall of heat. It had been the same last night, an hour of desperate discomfort and not only because of the elder Baron Imber grunting and scowling, the impossibility of saying anything that mattered to the younger.

She thought this tent might be marked in her memory forever, as a place of distress of body, mind and spirit all at once. The elder baron was not there now, but that brought only momentary relief; he would surely come. And when he did, oh, when he did . . .

The tent was quite empty; even the long trestle table and the benches packed away, where the men would have eaten last night after she and Elisande had withdrawn. Women ate separately, it seemed, in Elessi. Only the frame and its cover were left standing: to give the nobles of the party some privacy, she thought, more than shelter from the sun. No one in their right minds would choose to sit in this suffocating air when a breeze was blowing outside, though it bore all the dusts of the desert.

Imber sent a boy running for a chair; she sat, and gladly. The same boy fetched fruit and juice; she was grateful, as much for something to do as for the refreshment. She peeled and segmented, ate and drank discreetly behind her veil while Imber politely turned his head away. And the silence was desperate between them, and both of them were only waiting; they had nothing to say to each other that they could say.

At last, too soon, there was a thunder of hooves and a cloud of dust and the storm broke all about them.

Imber's uncle came striding into the tent with a riding-whip in his hand, and the dark look of a man who meant to use it. Elisande's hands tightened on Julianne's shoulders, from where she stood behind the chair; actually — after one brief, shaming moment of quailing inside, of wanting to beg and plead, *don't beat me, don't hurt me* — Julianne thought her friend stood in greater danger than she did herself. Even the Baron Imber von und zu Karlheim, brother-heir to the Count of Elessi, would not whip the daughter of the King's Shadow. Certainly not before she was wed to his nephew, when she was only promised. A promise could be revoked by an angry father, and other trouble could follow. But *if you cannot whip the lady, whip the maid*; Elisande had no father to protect her, or none that she would lay claim to. Julianne was ready to beg, to plead if she must, though she thought it might do little good.

No need, though: Imber was ahead of her.

Ahead of his uncle's explosive temper, indeed; before the older man could do more than snort at the muggy heat and cast his riding-cloak aside, he said, "Uncle, thank the God; they are both safe, and back with us."

"Safe, is it? I would not say they were safe . . ."

"No, but I would."

"Oh, and would you? Making fools of us, leaving

moppets in their beds that cost me the life of a good man . . ."

Moppets? Julianne glanced up and back at Elisande, saw her shrug, then saw her startle behind the veil — she at least seemed to understand, though Julianne knew they had left nothing in their beds that might have looked like sleeping girls, they hadn't thought to do so.

Imber stepped forward, between Julianne and his glowering uncle; said, "I know you are angry, but this is not a time to be thinking about punishment. It was a girl's foolishness, no more, she won't try to run again . . ."

"She will not," the other rasped. "I'll be sure of that. Girl's folly, was it? Well, you'll make a woman of her, then, see if that engenders any sense in the creature. We ride for the Roq immediately, and you'll marry her tonight."

"BUT MY FATHER . . ."

Her own thought, or at least the one that had risen furthest from the jumbling chaos of all her thoughts; but not her voice, she hadn't recovered breath enough to say it.

It was Imber, either playing shield for her still or else voicing his own genuine concern, she wasn't sure; and it didn't matter, because she was grateful to him either way, and his protest was hopeless either way.

"Oh, you can have another ceremony at the palace later, with all the pomp and nonsense my brother wants. But she'll be married before the God this night, and we'll see if she's still so flighty when she belongs to you."

"My lord baron—"

"Not I, apparently; but he will be your lord, girl, and you'll go on with him as you ought, or bear the pains of it."

"My lord," she tried again, "I think my own father might have cause for complaint, if I am wed in privity and haste to the damage of my reputation, and he not there to see it done . . ."

"Girl, you have done your own reputation more damage than even a wedding may quickly undo." That was surely true; she blushed at her ineptness, to have gifted him so easy a score. "As to your father, he sent you to us to be wed; when and how we choose to do it is our own affair. He made his choice, not to accompany you."

"The King summoned him, sir."

The choleric baron only shrugged sourly. "We all hold our lands and honours in gift of the King, girl. If your father chooses to dance attendance upon him, that is his concern and none of ours."

That was so inaccurate and so unfair, she actually found herself gaping. Before she could respond, though, she felt Elisande's fingers dig deep in warning, heard her murmur, "Julianne, go where you are sent, and marry where you must."

Too loud a murmur; the baron said, "So. Listen to your attendant, girl. She may yet save both of you a whipping."

What more he might have said, and whether young Imber would have argued further in her defence or her father's, she was not to learn; they were interrupted by the sound of riders, then by another man's shadow in the doorway.

Imber's cousin Karel: he nodded to the elder baron and the younger, and bowed courteously to her.

"My lady, I am delighted to see you restored to us. We have been anxious for your welfare." Was he being sarcastic? She wasn't sure; his voice was graciousness itself, and the smile that backed it seemed honest. She decided to treat him in like manner.

"My lord, I am sorry to have been the cause of so much trouble." Neither he nor the elder baron had seen fit to ask why she had fled; they must be as certain as her own Imber, that it was only to escape marriage to him. Well, let them think so. *Go where you are sent, and marry where you must*: it had seemed so simple an instruction once, but its force had changed a second time. The djinni's warning would still send her to the Sharai, if she and Elisande could contrive it; but if she must marry Imber first, then so be it. Perhaps their guard would slacken, once the thing was done.

If she could only bring herself to leave her Imber, once the thing was done. It had been hard enough the first time; she doubted her own resolution. Perhaps he would treat her badly, so that she could remember the dogs, her outrage at being hunted, that would help . . .

"Enough of this. Karel, we ride immediately, back to the castle, before sundown. Alert the men."

HER OWN MEN brought up her palanquin to the tent's door. She was glad of that, not to have to face any more staring except for Blaise's, and he was more puzzled than vindictive. He told her that the other camp was broken already, that knights and brothers and traders all—the traders in complaint, he said; vociferous complaint, she understood—had headed back to the Roq, only he and his men remaining. Then he fought a silent war with young Imber, to hand her into the litter; remarkably, he won it, and in the brief time that he was close to her he murmured, "My lady, are you quite well?"

"Quite, thank you."

"I mean, well content, I mean . . . I could send a man, have him look for your father . . ."

"Blaise, thank you, but there's no need." *What, can one man find him and fetch him before tonight, before I'm wed, before I'm a baroness?* "I am content enough," she said; and there was a massive lie in that, because on her conscience she should be far from here and travelling blindly, going where she was sent. And another because the man she was to marry was being so stiff with her, was so visibly hurt, and her heart ached for his. And yet, and yet: if she must marry—and even the djinni had said that she must, had ordered her to do so—then this would be the man, the boy she chose. This was not how she would

choose to marry him, neither the place nor the style nor
the time; but still some part of her, some small and foolish voice was murmuring contentment to her bones.

THERE WAS SOMETHING between Blaise and her bearers
as they set out, some conspiracy of concern. The bearers
were wide-eyed, twitching and miserable; the sergeant
rode close beside the litter, as though to guard against
some risk that all the Elessan soldiery could not prevent.

The road took them back through the village, back
past the hut they'd not slept in—*moppets? Elisande had
understood that and she must remember to ask, but not
now*—and suddenly Blaise was sidling his horse closer
still, leaning it almost against the palanquin, and she
could see nothing past him until the horse reared suddenly, screaming, startling him and her and startling the
bearers too, stilling them for a moment in their nervous
trot.

Now she could see the hut itself through the panel of
gauze, her window onto a harsher world; and she could
see something nailed across the doorway. Briefly she
thought it was a man-sized moppet, until it moved and
she saw that it was a man.

The litter skittered beneath her as the bearers shied
like the horse, away from that dark figure whose mouth
could make no noise around its gag, whose eyes glittered
like a bird's eyes, unreadable, accusing.

Julianne couldn't swallow a sudden gasp, couldn't
hide its cause; Elisande peered past her, frankly curious.

"What is it, what's—? Oh. I see. Are you all right?"

Now she had to swallow, and do it a couple of times
before she could manage a reply. "Yes. Yes, I am. Why
would they, what had he . . . ?" Something that concerned
the two girls, obviously; no accident, that he should be
stretched out to die across their doorway.

" 'The life of a good man', the baron said . . . It must
have been him found the simulacra in our beds."

"What simulacra? The baron spoke of moppets, but we left nothing . . ."

"I think Rudel and Redmond took shelter there, when the cry went up. And they knew us gone, they could be sure someone would look to see if we were safe. There is a way we know to make a poppet that will stand and move and perhaps speak a little. That can muddle a man's mind."

"Is Surayon magic all about lies and deceit?" she asked, sharp with the vision of what that poppet's work had done.

"Not all. And it was not the magic that crucified the man. That was your husband's work," sharp in her turn, in defence of her people.

"Not him," *please, not him.* "His uncle."

"Little difference. The Ransomers torture my friend, the Elessans execute their own. Is it any wonder that we draw a veil between our land and theirs? Or that we lie, yes, and deceive, and hide, and kill in secret if we must, to keep ourselves protected and apart?"

"No, Elisande," only weary now, all passion fled and only wishing herself back in Marasson: not for the first time, and she was certain it would not be the last. "No wonder at all. Will you lie to me, too, when I am an Elessan?"

"Oh, I expect so," but her hands said not, drawing her friend close and holding her so as the litter swayed beneath them; they said she was lying already, which was the best comfort of that bad and bewildering day.

SHE DOZED THEN, and woke still in Elisande's arms, her body stiff and sore again when she sat up, or tried to. Oddly, her feet were higher than her head; she fell back, and the other girl caught her.

"Where are we?"

"Going up. Don't look," and Elisande's hands prevented her, holding her tightly.

"To the castle?"

"Yes."

Of course, to the castle. Where else? Her mind felt numb, stupid with more than sleep, with the loss of hope and an unexpected shadow growing. There was only one other question she could think to ask, and the answer was just as obvious.

"The djinni didn't come, then?"

"No, sweetheart, the djinni didn't come. Did you think it would?"

"Not really. It might have, though . . ."

"I told you, the djinn don't interfere. They're not concerned with the ways of men."

"But it has interfered, it saved my life. Twice, I think. And it told us to go to the Sharai, both of us, that's interference too. And we can't, we're prevented; and you said I owed it a debt, it would make me obey, and I *can't* . . ."

"I know. I don't understand it either. But it said you must marry, and the baron says so too; perhaps this is what it wants first. I don't know . . ."

AND SO ON, talking in circles while the litter was carried ever higher; then the light was taken from them as they passed through the castle gate, through the passage and the tunnel beyond. They came back to late sun in the stableyard, and were set down. Neither of them made any move, they only sat and listened to hurried voices beyond the curtains.

Eventually a hand reached to draw the curtain back, a hand with a black sleeve, a brother; she looked past him to see the preceptor himself gazing at her with some compassion, though little good that would do her.

"My lady. This is . . . unexpected."

"I know. Forgive me . . ."

"Child, you are as welcome as you were before. But Baron Imber has spoken to me, and there are matters we must discuss. Will you come to my rooms?"

"Your grace, again, forgive me. I am tired," exhausted, rather, and fretful as the child he named her. "May we not speak here?" There was little enough to say, after all; she had no choices left.

"Very well. Will you alight?"

She did so, glad of the silent brother's arm to help her out, and then of Elisande's slipping around her waist to keep her from falling.

"The baron has — ah, asked," *demanded* he meant, she understood him very well, "that you should be married to his nephew here, tonight. I am not enamoured of this haste; nor, I am convinced, would your father be. I understand that the circumstances are unusual, and I am prepared to allow it. Lacking your father's consent, though, I have insisted that I must be given yours. I would not see anyone forced into an unwilling marriage within my walls. So how say you, my lady? Shall I refuse the baron?"

Here was a chance from nowhere, a choice unlooked-for; but oh, she was so tired, and she couldn't bear to face the baron's anger a second time. "No," she said, despite Elisande's sudden tug, *say yes, say yes* . . . "My father sent me to be married; I think you can take that for his consent. It was my own foolishness that caused the baron's anger, and this haste. I will not resist him further."

"Very well, child. If that is your true desire."

"Thank you, it is. Your grace?"

"Yes?"

"Will you conduct the ceremony yourself? Please? My father would appreciate that, I think . . ."

He smiled, with more warmth than she had expected. "You flatter me, my lady. Perhaps I flatter myself, but I hope you may be right. I have known your father for many years now, and I admire both him and his daughter. None but I shall marry you, be assured of that, if you must be married here."

"I think I must, your grace. Again, I thank you."

"No need. Come, let me take you to your room; you need rest. And food, I think. I can see half through you, and that is more than weariness . . ."

HER ROOM FOR now, perhaps: for this brief time, and no longer. But she was glad to see it, gladder still to lie on the bed and shut her eyes, see nothing at all.

"Julianne, wait." Elisande touched her lightly on the shoulder, plucking at the coarse and dirty robe she wore. "Take this off."

"I don't care about their blankets," she muttered, throwing an arm across her closed eyes to shut out the light, the world the better.

Elisande laughed above her. "No more do I, but I care about you. Take this off and turn over, you'll rest the easier. I promise."

She grumbled, but she hadn't the will to resist; she was stripped quickly and firmly, then rolled onto her stomach.

"Now just relax." Cool fingers touched her head, on either side. Julianne remembered Marron in a daze, guards slumping unconscious into the gully; she jerked away, though it cost her a stab of pain in her neck.

"Is this more of your magic? I don't want it . . ."

"No, love, it is not. And don't say that so loudly, not here. Not anywhere, this side of the desert. Just lie still, and let me ease you."

She was rearranged, her head pillowed on her folded arms; then those fingers wove through her hair and worked her scalp lightly, soothingly. Moved down to massage her neck and then her shoulders, kneading, digging deeper with a wiry strength. She yelped; Elisande chuckled.

"It won't hurt for long. Don't fuss, trust me."

She muttered ungratefully, biting down on another yelp as Elisande's fingers seemed to sink right into her body, plucking on fibres stretched tight beyond bearing.

Gradually, though, she could feel her muscles relaxing, unwinding almost under that hard pressure; her mind also started to drift, tension falling away, anxieties lifting. Her thoughts lost their focus, only following the smooth, slow rhythms of Elisande's hands, gentler now, moving lightly down her back. She felt warm, comfortable, easy; weariness flowed through her body in waves, in irresistible pulses, there was nothing she could do but ride them, down and out and away . . .

WHEN SHE WOKE, the room was darker. A blanket covered her; she lifted her head to see Elisande moving around, lighting lamps.

"The preceptor has sent food," her friend said, smiling down at her.

"How long have I been asleep?"

"Not long, but long enough. Come, sit up and eat; we've time for that, but not for idleness."

Elisande glided across the floor towards her, making a deliberate show of it; Julianne said snappishly, "Why are you wearing my best dress?"

"I'm not, I'm wearing your second-best dress. You don't want me looking shabby at your wedding, do you? I chose that one for you," setting a tray down with a grin, and nodding towards the big chest in the corner. "Though I had to give it an almighty shaking, and I still haven't got all the creases out. I think I can guess how Redmond left the castle, and how he came back again, if they have come back."

Creased or not, the gown draped across the lid of the chest was one of Julianne's favourites, though Elisande couldn't have known that and it was something more than clever of her to have guessed. The gown was quite simply cut, not at all appropriate for high courtly occasions but absolutely right for a quiet marriage in a Ransomer castle, where luxury and immodesty both would have been out of place. Its deep-sea shades would bring out the

green that she loved in Imber's eyes, suppress the grey
and give a golden sheen to his hair; and had Elisande
thought of that also, how much did that girl see?

Like the preceptor, she saw the emptiness in Julianne's
belly, that much was certain; and the tray was heaped
high with temptation. Cold meats and candied fruits,
pickles and preserves, fresh fruit and fresh white
bread . . .

"Have you—?"

"Yes, I have. That's all yours. So eat it."

SO SHE DID; and when she and the tray were finished,
the latter as empty as she felt full, they shared the last of
the flask of *jereth* between them in a private toast, only
their eyes bespeaking what they drank to.

Then Elisande played servant girl, helping Julianne
into the gown and dressing her hair, persuading her into
a little discreet jewellery and finally arranging her veil so
that it conformed to custom, she said, but hid nothing of
her friend's great beauty.

There was no glass in the room—nor probably in the
castle—so that Julianne couldn't check the honesty of
her words; all she could do was blush and threaten
Elisande with a hairbrush, and tell her not to be so ridiculous.

"What's ridiculous? You might as well deny that you
have two legs, Julianne, or an impossible father, or a lov-
ing heart."

"My father's not impossible."

Elisande only looked at her, with just the slightest
quirk of her eyebrow.

Julianne had to swallow a giggle. "Well, anyway.
You're as pretty as I am."

Elisande seemed to consider that for a moment, before
allowing thoughtfully, "I make a very pretty boy."

That cracked clean through all Julianne's reserve. Her
laughter choked her; Elisande had to pound her back be-

fore she could catch her breath, and then put her dis-
arranged veil in order again, all the time scolding like an
old and privileged nanny, which only threatened to dissolve her once more.

"Stop it," she pleaded, wiping at wet eyes with her fingers because Elisande wouldn't let her use the veil.
"Enough. What time is it?"

"Time you were a-marrying that boy." Elisande took
her hands and drew her gently to her feet, linked arms
with her and stepped towards the curtained doorway.
"He's quite pretty too, mind," she added judiciously.
"Though you should take a razor to him. I don't like
beards much in any case, and as for that fluff of his . . ."

"Elisande, *stop* it . . . !"

THE TIMING HAD seemed casual, and was exact. As they
left the chamber the great bell above them struck the first
of its calling-strokes, to summon the brothers to sunset
prayer. They walked slowly—"Let everyone else hurry,"
Elisande murmured, "this is your day and your hour,
they'll wait for you"—down the stairs and across the
ward beyond, seeing black-clad figures scurry ahead of
them.

And so into the shadows of the castle proper as the
bell boomed again, and as its echoes died away there was
only the scurry of sandals to be heard in the passage, and
that fading also.

They came to the great door of the great hall just as
Brother Whisperer sounded its last single stroke; but this
time that door was not closed against them, nor did they
turn aside towards the stair up to the guests' gallery.

Elisande's hand squeezed her arm, just once, for
courage; Julianne stepped forward, and the two girls
walked into the main body of the hall.

Flambeaux burned in sconces on every pillar, to light
their path. Brothers knelt in dark ranks on either side,

rank after rank; beyond the black were two of white, the knights of the Order in their places.

Lifting her head, Julianne saw all the masters arrayed in line before the altar. In the centre of that line stood the preceptor; below him, on the lowest of the steps, two other men were waiting, watching her.

Karel, there to support his cousin, and of course that cousin himself: Imber, dressed in the best that he had brought, not wedding finery but soft green velvet that would enhance both his eyes and her gown. She thought she could see his eyes even at this distance, shining with hurt and with hope.

Told herself not to be foolish, this was no jongleur's romance; it was real life, rich with promises to be broken and dreams left brutally unfulfilled.

None the less she walked forward with an extra impetus, certainty added to pride, to claim this much at least of what was hers, at least for this little moment.

THEY STOOD SIDE by side on that bottom step, just a pace apart. On the other side, Elisande's hand was lightly linked with hers.

The preceptor lifted his arms and she heard a soft shuffling sound at her back, as all the knights and brothers rose to their feet. A movement snagged at the corner of her eye; stealing a quick glance, she saw people standing all along the walls also. Squires in white, servants in whatever were their finest dresses, traders in many-coloured clothes. She wondered vaguely if Marron were among the squires, if d'Escrivey had joined his confrères for once or if he kept a solitary vigil above, if indeed he'd come at all.

Less vaguely, she wondered if Rudel were here, and if so in what guise, as bright jongleur or hidden brother?

There must have been a signal given, by the preceptor or another master, but she didn't see it. All together, though, the Ransomers began to sing, and her bones thrilled to the sound of their massed voices.

It was the regular evening service, begun with a common prayer to the God; only that in honour to her or to the occasion, it was to be sung rather than spoken. Deep bass and rising tenor, the voices cut to the heart of her, and her hand tightened on Elisande's. Involuntarily her eyes moved the other way, to find Imber where he stood that short step away, his body in light and shadow. And caught him glancing at her: their gazes locked, and now her stomach too was churning, although she could not read his thoughts.

After the prayer, the responses: a single voice calling high and tuneful, a thundering reply. Tears pricked behind her eyes; she had to blink hard, and when her sight cleared she had lost Imber, he had turned his face forward and a guttering shadow hid even his profile from her.

So she too looked to the front, and then she understood the soft gasps she could hear from the sides of the hall. The sign of the God hung massively above the altar, and a cool blue liquid light was flowing through the endless double loop.

"BELOVED BRETHREN, WE all of us serve the God: those who bear arms in His service and those who may not, those who guard the Sanctuary Land and those who work or dwell or travel within it. Just as precious, to Him and to us, are the women: for without them, He would have no servants and we no children. It is always a blessing to see a marriage performed, doubly so when it is a wedding of two high houses, whose sons will be the leaders of men in their generation. I feel thrice blessed this night, that I may act in such a rite . . ."

The preceptor's voice was as mellow and musical as the singing; but where that had beaten brazenly in her blood, this lulled and gentled Julianne. She was happy to let the voice simply pour over her like warm honey, she felt no need to listen.

Her eyes were drawn back inexorably to the God's sign, to the light that flared there. *Like the light in the cave*, but this a light divided: two lights that chased and never met each other even where the two loops joined, two lights of different shades of blue that pulsed to different rhythms.

The preceptor's hands beckoned; she and Imber took one pace forward together, climbed another step. Elisande remained below, with Karel. Julianne missed the comfort of her friend's touch; she folded her hands demurely below her ribs, and lifted her head to watch those lights again.

It seemed to her that they ran more slowly now, but pulsed the brighter. She could feel her own pulse under her fingers; one of those lights was beating in time with her body, she could see the match and sense it also.

The other, it seemed to her, was beating a little faster. She glanced sidelong at Imber and locked her hands together, to be sure that neither one would reach out to take his wrist, to test him.

"THE GOD BLESSES all his children, but some He looks upon with especial favour. This His son Imber, heir to the County of Elessi; this His daughter Julianne, earthly daughter to the one known as the King's Shadow . . ."

Was she earthly? She didn't feel so, she felt luminous and unconfined. She felt she was that light, dancing in the God's grace; her eyes she thought must have turned to blazing blue, fiery pulsing blue, as Imber's also, surely.

"TAKE HANDS, CHILDREN."

She heard that but she didn't move, couldn't move, seemed not to have command of her body, so rapt she was, so caught by the spinning lights. Imber it was who reached across the gulf between them, who bridged it with his arm, whose slim hand claimed one of hers; his fingers lay lightly in her palm, forcing nothing, making no claim of strength. Her skin tingled at his touch; she thought of the cave again, and dared not grip tighter for fear of what lay deep in her, in him.

Now the lights ran together, still two but joined, two comets on the same fixed path. She felt his pulse and saw it, both at once; willed her own heart to beat more quickly to match his, and saw and felt it happen.

"STEP UP, AND give me your hands."

She did not want to do that, she wanted to still time and hold this moment forever, not to risk the loss of what was wonderful to her. Again it had to be Imber who moved first, who drew her up after him and gave her hand with his. She sighed softly as the preceptor broke the link between them, his soft skin against her fingers where she wanted only Imber's.

Above and behind him, the two lights stilled: one in each loop of the God's sign, both close to where the two loops joined. Beating, pulsing together, waiting.

"THESE RINGS I give you, as eternal witness that you are pledged, each to each and unto death. Wear them in faith, and trust in the God whose sign they make together, two become one."

A cool band of gold, slipped onto the smallest finger of her right hand; another onto Imber's left. The preceptor lifted both their hands high, then touched them together so that gold met gold.

The two lights blazed and melted, each into the other; and then there was only one that flowed and burned too bright to look upon, before it faded like a flower dead too soon. She felt its going like a silence falling, and was bereft.

*   *   *

"KISS HER, CHILD."

And he did; his dry lips brushed hers, and she saw no lights now except his eyes, and they were grey and doubtful.

NEVER MIND THE singing, never mind the lights nor what went on beneath them; this was still a normal evening service, there would and must be a sermon. After one more exultant prayer, she heard shuffling, rustling sounds behind her, and knew the congregation to be kneeling. Imber's hand reclaimed hers. She walked slowly backward in pace with him, back and down with Elisande's touch unexpectedly on her spine to guide her; at the foot of the steps they too knelt, and she tried one more sideways glance. Nothing, only his profile again, again in shadow. If he sensed her eyes on him, he didn't respond.

MARSHAL FULKE GAVE the sermon, another clarion call to arms, against the evils of Surayon. Julianne wondered how Elisande must feel, hearing herself and all her people condemned as heretics and witches. She schooled her face to stillness, and listened with only half an ear. She had other things on her mind this night: questions and anxieties that racked her, hopes and fears for herself and others and one great burning desire—entirely for herself, this, to quiet the trembling that ran bone-deep within her; except that it wasn't, it couldn't be, it had to be shared or it was nothing at all—that only served to confuse her further.

AFTER THE SERVICE, after the last great stone-shaking cry had dwindled to a single sobbing note, losing itself in its own faint echo and finally engulfed by silence, the masters came down the steps in two files to pass between

Imber and Karel, or else between her and Elisande. One or two, she noticed, drew up the skirts of their robes not to touch—not to be defiled by?—the gowns of either girl.

Only the preceptor remained above. Behind her she heard the congregation shuffling out, but she stayed as she was, on her knees and held by the hand. Because Imber did, because she didn't know what else to do.

It was Karel and Elisande who moved first, of the four of them: friends who stood and reached down, offered hands and help in rising.

With that assistance, she managed to stand up and not let go of Imber, nor look directly at him. His turn, if he would; she would not.

The preceptor came down the steps, his arms spread in pleasure.

"Excellently done, Imber, you will take a treasure home to Elessi. And you, my daughter: you have joined a famous name to a famous house. Only the best will come of this, the God will bless you both. Now come, Julianne," and he took her hands, both of them, denied her any touch or sight of Imber as he turned her gently, deftly away, "let your lord away to feast with his men; no doubt they will want to pledge your name and his. I myself will show you to your quarters."

Thank you, I know the way—but thankfully she recognised the futility of protest and held her tongue. Then, as he led her out through a side door, she realised that of course she did not know the way; all that was certain was that she would not sleep tonight in the room that she used to.

"My luggage, your grace . . . ?"

He smiled, and patted her hand. "Brothers have fetched it already, my dear, as they should also have prepared a bath by now. You have your woman to attend you"—and indeed Elisande was tailing them like a dog, a sour dog to judge by her sudden sniff—"and I will send some supper to you both. Be patient; the young baron's

men may seek to detain him, but I think he will come
soon."

Above all else she wanted one thing, one thought in
her head, *let him come when he will, why should I care
when he come or how, sober or drunk or reeling, vomit-
ing, stinking with drink?* And she could not manage so
much dishonesty, even in the privacy of her own mind,
and she could have wept with frustration: to be enslaved
to a boy — sold and seized and snared all three, by her father and his uncle and himself, and the last of those the
only one that mattered — when she had so much to think
about that was not Imber, so much on her mind that she
could not share, so far to go where she could neither take
him nor let him follow . . .

THE PRECEPTOR TOOK them out into the still, warm
night, across a ward and so indoors again; and those were
dried rushes that they walked on, that was a door she
knew and a stranger, an Elessan on guard alert beside it,
opening it, bowing them in when it should have been a
brother.

"Your grace," she said awkwardly, stammering almost, "these are your own apartments . . ."

"My gift to you," he said equably, and then with a wry
smile, "only for the night. It is no great sacrifice. The
elder baron is insistent that you must away tomorrow. So
I will sleep in the masters' tower as I used, and be very
comfortable there. My audience-chamber you know; the
bedchamber is here, and there is another room that con-
nects to them both, my study, where a bed is made up for
your companion," with a gentle nod to Elisande, pallia-
tive, almost conspiratorial.

"Your grace, it's very kind, but—"

"But not enough, I know. Alas, these are the most fit
quarters we can find, to entertain a baroness. And her
husband. I'll bid you a good night, my lady, and a blessed
wakening to follow."

Was that the suspicion of a wink, as he bowed to her? No, surely not. The Preceptor of Roq de Rançon was surely above and far above innuendo.

The Preceptor of Roq de Rançon, she reminded herself bitterly, was a man; and like all men of noble birth, no doubt he'd hunted as a youth, before he took his vows. Like all men, noble or otherwise, he was no doubt pleased to see another hunt successful, another woman caught and brought to heel, brought to bed . . .

BATHED AND FED, dressed in the most respectable nightwear that her baggage could produce, she sat in the bedchamber—on the bed itself, plain but comfortable and easily wide enough for two, though she was sure that it had never before entertained so many—and waited for Imber to come to her.

Elisande had played servant to the last, combing out Julianne's hair to a shining, glorious fall; playing along, Julianne had played mistress and dismissed her to her own makeshift bed, determined to wait out this time alone. She'd refused to talk, to plan, even to conjecture. Morning would come soon enough; tonight her thoughts seethed, she couldn't concentrate.

At last she heard footsteps, voices, two men talking; she heard quiet laughter—Karel's, that—and then a brusque goodnight, and a door firmly closed.

One man's booted feet; she watched the doorway and the hanging that closed it, and saw that slowly rise.

For a moment he stood there, tall and young and limned in light, his blond hair like a halo, bright, diffuse.

She rose to her feet as he stepped inside, and curtsied dutifully.

"My lord baron."

"My lady baroness." He raised her up with gentle hands, and touched her cheek; she gasped at the tingle, the thrill of his fingers on her skin.

He frowned, and stepped away. It was all she could do

to suppress a groan. She wanted to cling to him, and would not.

"My lady Julianne," he said slowly, effortfully, "I regret deeply the pain that this required marriage has brought to you."

"Imber, no . . ."

"We need not dissemble, with each other. Let us at least have honesty in private. You tried to flee; I wish I could be sorry that I found you. That I cannot, because truly I welcome this match. I am only sorry for the nature of it, my uncle's insistence that it be made so soon. I would have taken you to Elessi and given you time to accustom yourself to it, to learn I hope to love me.

"I will still hope for that. But I saw your reluctance in the ceremony, and I see what it costs you now, not to flinch from my touch. This much at least I am resolved upon, that I will not force my body on you while you are yet unwilling. My uncle need not know," and for a moment he was all boy beneath his careful formality, *please don't tell my uncle*, and her heart surged in sympathy, "but for tonight and for the future, until you are ready for me, let your companion sleep with you; I will take her bed."

"Imber . . ."

Imber, no, but she couldn't say it. Better if he did think her estranged, distressed, even disgusted by his closeness; he'd stay further off, give her more time and privacy with Elisande, perhaps give them another chance to get away. Better for the turmoil in her soul also: she had both yearned for and dreaded his body in this her bed, his body and hers tight as a fist. So closely tangled with him, she thought she might never break free . . .

So no, she said nothing but his name; and he took that for what it was not, apology and gratitude both. He bowed and left her, by the other door; moments later, Elisande came hurrying through.

The door closed quietly, firmly, irrevocably behind her.

* * *

JULIANNE WOULDN'T SPEAK; when Elisande tried to draw her out in whispers, "What happened? What did he say, what did he do?" she only shook her head in miserable refusal.

The two girls climbed into the bed, and when Elisande reached to hold her, to offer silent sympathy and comfort, again Julianne shook her head, and pushed her away.

And lay all night on the far edge of the mattress, as alone as she could be, touching her friend nowhere; and not till she was certain that Elisande was sleeping did Julianne dare to let her tears, the first of many tears, fall.

SEVEN

His Honour With His Clothes

MARRON HAD HAD a difficult day.

He'd never expected nor looked for an easy life; he'd genuinely tried to be a good and dutiful brother Ransomer, and felt that his failure there had not been his own fault; he wanted to make as honest a commitment to his new position. But if a squire had to work hard sometimes to please his master, having only one good arm made the work harder. It was harder still when his fellow squires treated him with contempt and derision; and when that same one-armed squire had dangerous secrets to keep hidden, when his loyalties tugged in opposite directions, what was already so hard became almost impossible.

The long ride back to the Roq had been weary enough. When at last they'd made the final climb up to the castle and through into the stable-yard, he'd wanted no more than to fall from his mule and find a pallet somewhere to sleep on. But a wide dark stain on the cobbles had made a cruel reminder that there were no stable-boys any more, to care for his mount or his master's.

He'd struggled through the crush alone, first with Sieur Anton's great destrier, and then with his own little mule. He'd found stalls for them both, and fetched them feed and water; he'd cleaned saddles and harness as best he could one-handed, and his wounded arm had ached brutally before he was done, for all that it was bound so tightly against his chest that he'd had no use of it.

Finished at last, he'd drawn one more bucket of water and thrust his head into it, had come up gasping from the cold refreshing bite of it. As he'd pushed his fingers through his dripping hair, he'd heard a jeering laugh behind him. "Oh look, little monkey's making himself pretty."

"All washed and clean and ready for the night," another voice had replied.

"The knight? Which knight?"

"Kind Sieur Anton, of course . . ."

Marron had stood up slowly, his fingers straying towards his belt, feeling for the hilt of his new knife; but he'd checked before they reached it, walked away without looking back. Didn't matter which lads it was that sneered at him, they were all one in this. And Sieur Anton would have been furious if he'd fought all or any one of them. Doubly furious if he'd died, no doubt. Which he would have, quite likely. One-handed and hurting, distracted and incensed, he'd have made easy meat for the skewer of another boy's blade. *Self-defence, my lord, your grace, Sieur Anton*, the other boys would have said, all in chorus. *Marron attacked him without cause, he was in peril of his life . . .*

So no, no fighting, only another scar on his soul and another derisive name they could call him, *scared little monkey*.

He'd made his way slowly through the castle's courts and passages, then taken an undutiful detour up onto the high walls, seeking answers where there were only views; he'd stood for a while gazing at the ancient stones of the Roq's hidden mystery, the Tower of the King's

Daughter—*the Tower of the Ghost Walker*, Mustar had
named it, and would not tell him why—and then he'd
recollected himself, and hurried to Sieur Anton's room.

Where he'd been roundly scolded for his delay, and for
his appearance, his tunic soaked and filthy: "The bell will
summon us to service any minute, and would you go before the God in such a state? On any night, let alone this
night, when the lady Julianne is to be married to Baron
Imber? Or had you forgotten that, in your dallying?"

He hadn't forgotten, because he hadn't known. He'd
offered no excuse, had only struggled awkwardly out of
his tunic when Sieur Anton threw a clean one at him. The
knight had relented then, seeing what he himself had
seemingly forgotten in his anger, Marron's injured arm in
its bindings; had helped him dress, even asked forgive-
ness where none was due or needed. The bell had interrupted them before Marron could answer, and they'd
hastened together down to the hall.

MARRON HAD STOOD by the wall with the other
squires, and even here before the God's altar their fingers
had poked at him and their eyes suggested, making a
lewdness of all that poking. More than anything Marron
had wanted to poke back, with his dagger in his hand; instead he'd sidled along the smooth plain plaster until he
stood more with the traders than the squires, and let people think what they would of his simple white against
their gaudery.

He'd been sorry for the lady Julianne, when he saw
her wed. She'd seemed so pale and reluctant, so stiff,
leaning on her friend as though she couldn't do the simple things, the walking and standing and kneeling, without support. That marriage must be a dire thing to her,
he'd thought, seeing how she fixed her stare on the God's
sign above the altar, wouldn't even look at her husband in
the making.

The God's sign was something to look at, he'd supposed, flaring with light chasing light. *Chased and caught*, he'd thought, and how bad could this wedding be, what reason did she have to dread it so much that she would run away, after having come so far in obedience? But the sign hadn't seemed so impressive to him tonight, only a trick; Rudel could do as much and more, and Rudel was a heretic. Did that mean that the light came not from the God, or did it mean that Rudel still stood in the God's grace regardless of the teachings of the Church, or Marshal Fulke?

Marron had no answers to such questions. Sieur Anton might know, but of course he couldn't ask him. Nor anyone, but especially not him. Sieur Anton was devout in a way that Marron had been, or at least had thought himself, when he first came to Outremer; but where Marshal Fulke's call for a great purifying holy war against Surayon only sickened Marron, even the words carrying the stench of slaughter with them, it seemed to inflame Sieur Anton as though he had never known carnage, had never said *these things happen here*, or else had said it with approval.

Wherever Rudel stood in the God's eyes — if God there were, and if the God were looking; both of which Marron was inclined to doubt, even here before His altar — the jongleur hadn't been standing there in the hall, unless he was still hidden among the dark ranks of the brothers. Even the traders' bird-bright clothes couldn't match Rudel's; if he'd been on the far side of the hall, in shadow and behind a pillar, Marron still couldn't have missed him.

Perhaps he and Redmond had after all slipped away in last night's rumpus, or else in the confusion of a breaking camp this morning. Perhaps they were far gone and luckier than the ladies, unsought-for, quite unmissed — though not for much longer, surely. How long could that poppet in the dungeon fool the guards? Or the questioners, next time they went to question? The girls had left others in their beds last night, it seemed, and cold daylight had shown them up for what they were, rags and rope and a man's death for believing in them . . .

If the Elessans would do that to one of their own, Marron had wondered just what they might have done to him, if their truth-speaker had actually forced him into telling true.

She'd been there in the hall, he'd seen her, easy to find with that face among the veils of the other women who rode in the Elessans' train: not whores, surely, in such a grim and righteous company, only servants. Cooks and launderers, if great lords travelled with such; he didn't know. Attendants to serve the lady Julianne, perhaps. She came of a great family, and travelled with none but Elisande, who was more friend than servant.

Come of one great family, she now belonged to another; he'd seen Baron Imber claim her with a ring, possess her with a kiss. Marron was half-surprised that she didn't faint, she looked so pale and shaken; it had taken Elisande as well as her new husband to keep her on her feet as they'd backed away down the altar steps.

MARSHAL FULKE HAD preached for an hour, and said nothing new throughout; all that was new or surprising or unusual had been to look along the kneeling row of knights and see Sieur Anton one among them.

He'd been simple to pick out, because his head was bare. Not that he'd been alone in that. Fulke himself had come to every service unhooded, since that first sermon. The preceptor had taken no action, against him or his increasing number of adherents; there were knights who routinely came to worship uncovered, there were squires and men-at-arms, there were brothers who dared the anger of their confessors by coming before the God bareheaded. Even some of those same confessors were at it now; tonight, for the first time, Marron had looked towards the back of the hall and seen Fra' Piet's shaven head shining in the torchlight. Fra' Piet and half his troop:

Marron couldn't be certain, but he thought he'd spotted Aldo's shock of brown hair among them.

WHEN THE SERVICE was over they'd all filed out in order, the squires almost last, as fitted their lowly station. The new-married baron and his lady had stayed behind, with their attendants and the preceptor; Marron had spared the lady Julianne one last glance as he left, trailing the other lads to avoid their jabbing fingers in his back. Brothers had been extinguishing torches, all down the hall; all he'd really seen of her was the gleaming hair and the line of one arm outstretched, one hand that Baron Imber had held imprisoned, *I have you now, I will not let you go.*

Marron had sent her a brief commiserating thought—an impertinent thought for sure from a squire to a lady, a new-made baroness; but she'd never know, and he did pity her—and then he'd turned to push his way through the mill of bodies outside the hall, looking for his master.

AFTER THE MARRIAGE, the marriage-feast: that was traditional, it was universal. Even here, in a castle of the grim religious that had been attacked and nearly taken three nights since, even after a match made in such haste and against such reluctance, there had to be a feast.

Not for the women, even had there been any women of rank present, besides the bride; that was not the custom of the house. The Order would welcome women guests because that was a duty laid upon it, so long as they kept decorously to their allotted quarters, where *here are the guests' rooms* meant *here are the women's rooms, safely in a tower apart*; it would shelter and feed, flatter where politic but it would not feast, it would not celebrate their being in the castle or the world.

Marron had expected nothing, then, like the marriage-feasts he'd known in long barn or village square: a riot of dancing and drunkenness, of fast feet and flashing skirts, fast hands and slapped faces; *licensed debauchery* the old priest used to call it, scowling momentously, though it was he who issued the licence and he who cried the musicians on, louder than any. One marriage in the endless summer of Marron's childhood had always seemed to lead to half a dozen more, and welcome so.

Here it must be different; he'd thought it would be dour, a required part of the wedding ritual and no more: the baron paying Master Cellarer as little as he might and then sitting sour and scowling with more intent and far more effect than the old priest ever had, turning the bread stale and the milk bad, driving the celebrants from table as soon as he could manage, later than he would like . . .

Well, no. Marron hadn't seriously thought they would be drinking milk. It would be the knights who feasted, after all, with perhaps a table also for the stranded traders, down at the foot of the hall. If the baron didn't supply them with wine enough, he'd thought they would send for their own.

He'd still thought it would be a dull affair, though. Elessans made famous fighters, but no one had ever woven a tale about their conviviality, their lightness of foot and touch or how quick they were to laugh, how slow to quarrel.

What Marron hadn't expected, who he had quite stopped looking for—hope triumphant over reason— was Rudel the jongleur.

MARRON HADN'T KNOWN there to be so many lewd songs in the canon; and yet he'd thought himself so wise, so experienced in the ways of wedding-feasts . . .

Rudel had wandered the hall at first—the lesser hall it was, knights' territory, neither brothers' nor the God's— drifting between the rowdy tables. He'd sung, he'd thrashed the strings of his mandora, he'd chivvied the young men into joining in where they knew the words,

humming along where they did not, when he could keep
them from exploding into raucous laughter that he had
himself provoked.

Like any squire Marron had served his master, antici-
pating no time to listen to the singing. Except that Sieur
Anton had eaten little—though the food was better and
more plentiful than Marron had expected—and drunk
less; so that after the first rush to see that the knight had
trencher and meat, goblet and wine within it when every
lad was fighting for the same and he had only the one
hand to fight with, in fact Marron had found himself with
time to stand behind his master's chair and indeed listen
to the singing.

He'd never thought to hear such bawdy stuff here.
Neither, apparently, had the Barons Imber. Elder and
younger, they'd both seemed startled when Rudel was
forced up onto a table and enough of a hush fell that the
whole hall could hear him. Marron's eyes had moved instinctively to the top table, to look for trouble before it
came; so he'd seen the new-wed baron's blush.

His uncle's face also had changed hue, darkened,
turned a livid shade of red all across his shaven scalp.
When Rudel had finished that one song and immediately
begun another, to a shouted chorus and a rhythm of
booted feet, the elder baron had had enough—but it had
been he who'd stamped out of the hall, with his own ret-
inue of friends and cronies following.

Sieur Anton had seemed to like the singing little more,
no more than he liked the food or the wine. He'd stayed,
though, so perforce Marron had stayed too. And had
watched Rudel as they all did, and listened with less attention than most, and thought that there was a private
message for him in this very public performance. *We're
still here*, he'd thought Rudel was saying, *and I'm still a
jongleur*. Which very likely meant that Redmond was
again a prisoner, the man taking the place of the poppet
and that whole escape brought to nothing. Undiscovered,

which was good; unavailing and undone, which was not good at all.

And there was a second message too that Marron had read, one that he'd heard before and saw now in how Rudel never glanced his way for a moment, ignoring him as he was ignoring every squire else. *Your task is finished*, Marron had thought he was being told, *lead your life, serve your master, forget about us. I know where and how; I've put him back alone, I can lead him out alone next time.*

RUDEL HAD SUNG on with gusto, what Marron most lacked. Soon his hand had found its own way onto the back of Sieur Anton's chair and he'd been leaning on it, only to hold himself upright. He'd snatched it away as soon as he'd realised, before his master could; but his legs had wobbled, his head had swum and he'd had to take a grip again to save shaming himself and Sieur Anton both.

Movement on the top table, ribald voices and laughter: he'd looked that way, focusing desperately against a sucking darkness, and had seen young Baron Imber on his feet. Blushing again, making his way out of the hall with a fixed expression on his face, followed by his grinning cousin Karel.

That was apparently what Sieur Anton had been staying for, his sense of duty not allowing him to leave before the guest of honour. As soon as the young men were gone, he'd pushed his chair back from the table.

And had felt the resistance of Marron's hand, jerked away too late; had glanced at his face and frowned, said, "Lad, you look terrible. Is that arm paining you again?"

"No, sieur," or *yes, sieur*, but no more than it had been half the day.

"I'm sorry," again, the second time tonight. "You need food, and rest. Bring that," with a gesture at the bread and meat he'd barely touched, "and follow me."

*   *   *

THEY'D COME TO Sieur Anton's room, where Marron had been told to sit on the bed and eat, without arguing. For once, he'd practised instant obedience; and when he'd eaten all there was to eat and had drunk a glass of his master's wine, Sieur Anton said, "Better?"

"Yes, sieur. Thank you . . ."

"Good. I keep forgetting, don't I?"

"Sieur . . ." *I keep failing you*, but he couldn't say that. Sieur Anton might ask how, and there was so much he daren't tell him, it was wiser far to curb his tongue and say nothing.

Knight sat beside his squire, laid a gentle hand on the back of his neck; said, "They'll be making their jokes about us now, as well as about the baron and his bride. I can't prevent that, I'm afraid. Do the other lads give you trouble?"

"No, sieur."

A little shake, from that strong hand. "Truly, Marron?"

"Only a little, sieur. It doesn't matter."

"Does it not? Boys can be cruel to each other. Worse than a bad master, sometimes."

Marron shook his head, before Sieur Anton could do it for him. "I'm used to it, sieur."

"Are you?"

Oh yes, that was true enough. His uncle's workers had made a great mock of him and Aldo, for years before they'd taken their vows and joined the Order; nor had their fellow novices been kinder. The squires' sharp tongues provoked more memories than distress, though those memories brought their own distress, a friend lost where he had thought the two of them immune, immutable, eternal.

"Why are you used to it, Marron?"

Marron just looked at him. He knew, he must know; and Marron didn't have the words in any case. Even Sieur Anton couldn't play his confessor, for this.

The knight's hand moved gently on his neck, squeezing, teasing, promising more.

"You're worn out, lad. I should let you sleep."

"No, sieur."

"No? Are you sure?"

"Yes, sieur."

"Your arm's bad, I don't want to hurt you . . ."

"You won't hurt me, sieur."

"Well. Just cry out, if I do."

He took his hand away and Marron wanted to cry out in protest, in hurt; but Sieur Anton only crossed his legs, seized his boot and wrenched it off, tossed it away across the room. Marron moved to help him with the other, but the hand came back for a moment, gripped his shoulder and, "No, you sit still. I am able to undress myself. And you."

And he did: stripping off his own clothes fast and carelessly and then helping Marron out of his, playing the squire almost, though a squire with impertinent, questing hands and a touch that made Marron alternately squirm and gasp.

Lastly, the bindings were unknotted and cast aside, so that the bandaged arm came free.

"Now, how shall we manage with this? We must put it out of the way. If you lie on the bed, thus, it should not trouble us. Good. Does that feel comfortable?"

"Yes, sieur. Do it again . . ."

That won him a chuckle, and a sharp slap. "I meant the arm, fool. Well, I won't mind it, then, if you don't. I have some oil here"—a flask of it, Marron knew, scented with thyme and rosemary—"which will ease things somewhat; but again, if I hurt you—"

"You won't hurt me, sieur."

"You seem very sure of that."

"Yes, sieur."

"Marron, my name is Anton. Only for tonight, while we're alone, do you think you might manage to use it? Or at least not to call me sieur in every sentence?"

"No, sieur. I like it . . ."

A slow sigh, with a smile hidden in it; and then no more talking, only those fingers slowly working on him and inside him, sometimes rough and sometimes tender; the scent of the oil rising as it warmed, only to mingle with and be lost in sharper, hotter smells; Sieur Anton's long, lean body against him and about him, within him, encompassing him absolutely.

"YOU ARE NOT quite stranger to a man's body, are you, Marron?"

"No, sieur." *Oh, Aldo . . .*

"Tell me."

And so Sieur Anton did play confessor after all; what had been unthinkable before was possible now, as he was held close and warm and weary while the candles guttered and died in the room around them, that seemed suddenly so far away. Slowly, haltingly, Marron told of his friend: childhood friend and friend of his youth, more than friend when they'd played boys' games together that had become much more than games.

"Only the one?"

"Yes, sieur." All that he'd wanted or needed or would ever need, he'd thought; and after they'd taken their vows they'd touched each other no more, despite what the other boys whispered. Their bodies given over with their souls to the God, they'd thought it would be a great sin. And there'd been no chance anyway, no possibility of succumbing to temptation in a novice's life or a brother's after.

"SIEUR?"

"Yes, Marron?"

"Forgive me, but—"

"Nothing to forgive. How could there be? I leave my pride, my honour with my clothes; it's only you who insist on bringing it to bed. Boy," caressingly. "Come, ask your question. If I know an answer, you'll have it."

"Sieur," as bold as he could manage, then, even lifting his head so as not to mumble into his master's chest, "you are the most devout man I know, more than any of the brothers, even. You say your prayers to the God, you serve the God, you gave your life to Him—and yet you do this too . . ."

"Ah. And do I leave my religion also with my clothes, you mean? I do not."

"Does the God not forbid this?"

"The Church forbids it. And the Order, too; there, yes, I break my vows. But the God? I do not know, Marron. I know this, though, that I have done worse things. And will do worse again, and soon, I think. Marshal Fulke will lead us against Surayon, as soon as they break that man in the cells. They say he is the Red Earl, Redmond of Corbonne. Master Ricard will know; they fought together, under the King. He has refused to go down, thus far; he says it is dishonourable to torture a man so, and he will have no part of it. I think he will yield soon, though, I think he must. The preceptor will order him, on his obedience. And when we are certain, then the man will be broken. No one can hold out forever, under question.

"And then he will tell us the secret, how to enter Surayon; then we will march, and the God will wreak a terrible vengeance against that damned land. And yes, I will be there; and I will kill, and I will burn heretics, men and women and children. I will do it; and against that, what can this matter? If I am to be condemned, I do not think it will be because I lie down with men. Or boys," and his calm, warm hands put an end to talking again.

For a while.

*   *   *

"SIEUR?"

"What, again? Go to sleep."

"Please?"

"Well. Once more, then. What is it this time?"

"Sieur, tell me what happened to your brother."

A long silence, a stillness in him that made Marron tremble; then, "I killed him."

"But how?"

Wrong question. "With my sword," coldly.

"*Why*, sieur? What had he done? He must have done something dreadful, you loved him . . ."

"You have been gossiping about me, if someone told you that. I dislike being the subject of my squire's gossip, Marron."

His throat was tight and dry, it was hard to speak; the words were gravel-sharp in his mouth. "I wanted to know . . ."

"I'm sure you did. Know this, then—but do *not* noise it around, boy, do you understand me? This is for your ears only, and only because I'd sooner you believed the truth than some chatterer's invention. Yes?"

"Yes, sieur."

"Very well. Yes, I loved my brother, and he me. Like me he was, as you say, devout; like the churchmen, like you, he thought it was a great sin for men to love each other with their bodies. There was talk about me, of course, then as now, but I suppose he shut it out, refused to listen. He never asked me for the truth of it.

"But he found me one day, in a field of maize, with another man. Charol carried Dard everywhere, I'd given it to him the month before, he was so proud of it; and I, I had Josette also, though why I can never remember, for a tryst in my own family's fields. The God orders these things, not us.

"Charol was mad, I think, with shock or anger. Disillusion, perhaps: he had admired me, worse, adored me. Worshipped me, almost. He drew his sword, and went to kill my friend; that man was older, he farmed on our land,

Charol must have blamed him, I imagine, for corrupting his perfect brother.

"I tripped Charol, and told him the truth as he lay at my feet there; I stood over him quite naked and said that it was I who had first seduced my friend, that I had done the same with other men, and always would.

"Charol scrambled up and swung his sword at me. Mine was the first blood Dard tasted: here," and his fingers guided Marron's to a thick seamed scar on his ribs. "He saw me bleeding, and turned away—sane again, I thought, for a moment. But then he went after my friend, and what could I do? He would have killed him. So I snatched up my sword and called him back, called him a coward to run after an unarmed man.

"He came, and we fought. I think his madness infected me—or perhaps I simply lost my temper. You know I have a temper," and this time his fingers touched the bandaged arm, and Marron remembered that long duel in sunlight, so long ago it seemed, the intense fury that had so nearly killed him; and the look on Sieur Anton's face that day as he'd flung his sword away, a look he understood now. *Not twice, not a second time . . .*

"I killed him," Sieur Anton said again, and yet again. "I killed him, and he died. And then I took his sword, because he had disgraced it, or I had, either one. In the end I came to the Order, I gave my life to the God to do what He would with it; and they sent me here. My father sent me money," bitterly, "to keep me from a brother's vows. He needn't have bothered. How could I ever be a brother again, anyone's, under any meaning? I can hardly bear to say the word . . ."

And then silence, painful and difficult: Marron lacked the insolence to break it. It was the great bell that did. Brother Whisperer's voice thudding into their bones. He stirred gratefully, tried to sit up, and was prevented; Sieur Anton's arm and his leg too held him down, comfortably pinioned between man and pallet and wall.

"I don't leave my religion with my clothes, Marron,

but I think this once we will say the prayers as we are. Call it an affirmation, if you like."

Some men, many men in this castle would call it sacrilege. Marron was far beyond knowing who was right and who wrong, beyond even trying to guess. He knew Sieur Anton's weight across his body, he knew the young knight's strength, he guessed what might happen if he resisted; and he knew how good it felt to lie constrained like this, though his arm ached sharply and every other part of him was numb and heavy with exhaustion.

"Yes, sieur," he said.

PRAYERS MUMBLED, ALMOST whispered like love-talk to each other, like those times when no matter what is said, it's the whispering that counts. These were prayers, though, and for his master's sake, for his piety Marron tried to focus on the words; but they drifted, they were a string he lost all grasp upon, grabbed for in the darkness, couldn't find.

He thought probably he fell asleep before the prescribed finish, though Sieur Anton did not wake him nor tell him next morning, and certainly he did not ask.

WHAT ROUSED HIM was the bell again, striking deep; anything less massive could not have done it, so little, far too little sleep he'd had.

This time no lying-in, no muttering of blessings with their minds and bodies too distracted. Up and kneeling, naked as they were; Sieur Anton's voice was clear and firm, which seemed unfair.

Then into his clothes, with the knight's help to bind his arm against his chest once more; and that aside it was clearly to be the normal routine this morning, and why not? Little enough had changed, except that what everyone suspected had finally come to pass. They were still squire and master, nothing had altered that.

So he ran for his master's breakfast, and his own; endured the taunts of other boys on the same errand, thinking how little they knew, and how foolish they sounded; went back to the room where he was happiest, saw Sieur Anton eat and drink, waited for permission to do the same.

All that time there was something stirring in his gut, though, where it had worked its way down overnight from his head, where he had heard it. This was what tore at him, this dual life he tried to lead, servant and traitor. He must betray one man, or betray the other; and it wasn't really any choice at all, because one betrayal had the stink of inevitable death upon it, one death soon and many more to come. The other, who could tell? Not he. Only that it might forestall some people's dying . . .

SO WHEN SIEUR Anton dismissed him—"I want some swordplay, and not with you; I won't risk any more damage to that arm, and neither will you. You're to rest, Marron, do you hear me? Go sit in the sun and sleep an hour"—he used that licence to search for Rudel.

The castle had never seemed so crowded; there were men everywhere, and none of them the man he sought. The stable-yard was hectic with traders' wagons and their grumbling owners. None had seen the jongleur, nor had any patience with Marron's questions; Baron Imber had decreed that he and his party would leave that afternoon, and any traders who wanted their protection on the road must be ready. Which they would be, but resentfully: their animals needed rest after the long haul back yesterday, they themselves would have appreciated a day or two to recover from the wedding-feast, and why was this boy bothering them . . . ?

He tried the great hall and the lesser hall, the kitchens and the dormitories, even the latrines, and had no joy. At last, thinking that Rudel must have left the castle altogether—with Redmond, perhaps, finding another way to smuggle the prisoner to freedom?—Marron went up high onto the walls, careful to keep some distance from the brothers who stood guard. Perhaps he would practise a little obedience after all, find some warm seclusion and let sleep wash over him.

But his feet took him almost without permission to the place where he had stood before, where he could overlook the tower that had no doors, the Tower of the King's Daughter; and there, when he had quite given up on his search, there he found Rudel.

Found Rudel standing as he had himself, gazing down on the squat and secretive tower; said, "Sir?" and saw the man startle, saw him turn sharply, warily, and only slowly relax with a huff of breath and a hand scratching at his beard.

"Marron. What are you doing here?"

People were always asking him that, as if he had no right, no place in their mysteries. He stifled his first response, *and what are you? Sir?*, and said only, "I was looking for you."

"Why so? What you have done, I am grateful for; but you shouldn't—"

"Sir, I have to tell you. Did the Earl go back into his cell?"

"Yes, he did. He insisted, but he was right in any case. A simulacrum has a short life, only a day or two at most; it was wiser that the real man replace it for a time. A little longer, he can bear that. I have strengthened him, as much as I am able . . ."

"Forgive me, sir, but it won't be enough. My master tells me"—*and I betray his trust by telling you*—"that Master Ricard can name Redmond."

"We've always known that, Marron. Ricard has his own honour, though, he won't—"

"Sieur Anton says that he will now, he can't hold out any longer against Marshal Fulke and the preceptor. And when he does—it may be today, even, as soon as the Elessans have gone," that was his own embroidery on

what his master had said, but it was true enough, it might
be today, tomorrow, any day, but soon, "when he does,
they will put fresh questions to the Earl," use other of
those machines, no doubt, "and he won't be able to resist
them then, my master says . . ."

"Your master is very probably right. Redmond is
wiry, wily and tough; but they have been holding back
somewhat, I think, in case his accuser was simply mistaken. One old man can look pretty much like another,
and it has been forty years. Once they're certain, though,
they'll be implacable. And no, not even Redmond could
resist them then. He would deny that, but every man
breaks at last. Very well, this changes things. You were
right to tell me, Marron, and thank you; we are in your
debt again."

"What will you do?"

"I'll take him out immediately, today. During midday
prayers, I think; the brothers are more watchful now, but
there'll still be many fewer eyes to see."

"How will you escape the castle, though? You can't go
disguised as brothers, not during prayers, the guards on
the gate would stop you . . ."

"And they're too many for me to confound, I know
that. But there is another way out of this place. I had
hoped not to take Redmond that way, it's a dangerous
path, especially for a wounded man. Necessity forces my
hand, though. Redmond must endure the risk."

"Another way, sir?" There was famously only one gate
into and out of the Roq.

"A secret way, Marron, every castle has its private
exit; and no, I will not tell you. We are in your debt, but
what I said before still holds. You have your life, your
own path to follow, and here it separates from ours. Take
our gratitude, and be content with that."

"Sir, I don't want—"

"It doesn't matter what you want. This is how it must
be. Outremer is a land divided, and we find ourselves on
opposite sides of that divide. How it will be resolved, I

cannot see; as it stands now, we must pray that we never meet again. If we do, it will probably be on a battlefield. Go on, lad, leave me now. I need to prepare . . ."

He turned his back; Marron hesitated a moment, then left him.

OBEDIENCE HAD BEEN drilled into Marron all his life; rebellion was a new condition, difficult to sustain. Doubly difficult, after last night. But last night had been a blade with two edges, each of them biting deep. He felt both bound and cut free, terribly torn; he also felt desperately curious, and determined not to be set aside so casually, to be granted no place in this story's ending.

Rudel might have rejected him, but he still had one way to turn. Obedient to no one, making his own choices at last, he went towards his master's room but not so far. Went instead into the buttery, where the knights' little luxuries were kept; put a bottle of good wine and a pair of goblets onto a tray and carried that awkwardly one-handed through the castle to the preceptor's own quarters, where gossip said the new Baroness Julianne had slept the night with her lord.

There was an Elessan guard at the door, to confirm the rumour. He frowned at Marron, and said, "What's this?"

"A gift, from my master to your lady," trying to sound like a squire on a tedious errand of courtesy, no more. "He cannot come himself to bid her farewell, but he sends wine in token. May I go in?' For all the world as if he didn't care, he'd be just as glad if he were turned away.

The guard shrugged. "Aye, boy, do."

He even opened the door, to pass him through; Marron nodded his thanks, and went inside.

Julianne was there, with Elisande at her side. As soon as the door was closed, she lifted an eyebrow above her veil and said, "Marron?"

"My lady, forgive me—but do you still want to leave?" *To run away* he meant but was too embarrassed to say, face to face with two young women, ladies of rank and one of them high rank, new-married, whom he was inviting to flee her husband. "If you do, there may be a way . . ."

EIGHT

A Door and a Daughter

HE COULDN'T HAVE meant that, could he? What she'd just heard him say?

She stared at him and he'd never seemed younger, never more of a boy: his hair awry and his face flushed with nervousness above a worn and grubby squire's tunic that didn't fit, one sleeve hanging loose and empty while his injured arm made an unsightly bulge beneath. Almost her fingers reached out to tuck the sleeve into his belt, to smooth his hair and make him neater, while her mind reeled.

She couldn't answer him. She didn't know the answer.

Elisande it was who reached to touch him, but not to tidy him into some more fitting semblance of a knight's squire; she seized his arm, his one arm, and spoke sharply.

"What way?"

He only shook his head mutely, still gazing at Julianne and seeming to wait for her word. Elisande gave his shoulder a wrench that nearly spilled the wine from the tray he carried, forcing him to turn to her.

"What way?" again, more urgently.

"I don't know, my lady," he said, looking around apparently, absurdly, for somewhere to set the tray down. Julianne recovered just enough of her wits to take it from him, and then stood as she had before, befuddled, only listening.

"You don't *know*?"

"No. But Rudel does. You know Rudel, and, and his friend," in a mutter, with a quick glance towards the closed door and the man beyond who guarded it. "You met them in the gully, you know who they are, don't you?"

"Yes, we know. Explain."

"Rudel is taking him, his friend, away. Today, during midday prayers. He says he knows another way, a secret way, out of the castle. He didn't tell me how. But you could go with them, perhaps. He said it would be dangerous, but I thought, if it was important to you, my lady," his eyes coming back to Julianne, "if you wanted to . . ."

"What do you want, Marron?" she asked, again putting off his question, to which she could still find no answer.

"To see them safe, my lady."

"For yourself, I meant."

"I don't know, my lady . . ."

Well, there were two of them in that case, then. Not three: it was blazingly clear what Elisande wanted.

"I know what he means to try," she said. "We must go with him, Julianne. We *must*."

"There is a guard on the door," Julianne said, equivocating pointlessly.

"One guard. He is nothing. If we meet others I can maze them, or you can play the haughty baroness, you do that well. But we have to go. Remember your father, remember the djinni . . ."

This all felt increasingly familiar to Julianne: Elisande

mysterious and insistent, Marron useless and herself so
muddled and confused when all her life she'd been accustomed to knowing her own will and making her own
choices, right or wrong but always certain.

If she slipped away again, if she even tried to, and was
caught — she thought her new Uncle Imber would take
her back to Elessi in chains. For sure she'd be disgraced,
humiliated beyond recovery, mewed up for a lifetime and
powerless in the land, which would destroy any point as
well as any pleasure in this marriage her father had made
for her.

If she stayed, if she held to Imber's hand and Imber's
fortune, then her father would die. The djinni had said so;
the djinn did not, could not lie.

Had it said so? Perhaps not. Great danger it had said,
though; and her father was more important to Outremer
than she was, baroness or no. For the land's sake, she
should save him if she could.

Was her father more important to her than Imber?
There again she felt her mind shy away from the question. She couldn't do that, she couldn't balance one
against the other and see which weighed the more.

Which brought her back to reason and sound argument, and she was glad of that. She took a breath and said
firmly, "We'll go." Good. That was a decision made, and
never mind the consequences. "What should we take with
us?"

"Money, jewels, knives. Nothing more. We can't be
seen walking through the castle with blankets and packs."

"My lady, I could . . ."

"No, not even you, Marron." He sighed softly; Julianne thought that perhaps he regretted the loss of an excuse, a reason to come that little further with them.
Elisande read it otherwise, though. "This time we daren't
take risks, there's too much at stake." *More than our
lives*, she seemed to be implying. Well, Rudel's and Redmond's lives, for certain; but beyond that . . . ? "What we
need, we can find on the road. Wherever that may lead

us." Again there was more in her voice than her words allowed; again Julianne bit back a challenge. They were putting themselves into Elisande's hands here, and it was poor policy not to trust your guide.

Still, "Where are you taking us?" One was entitled to ask, after all.

"Truly, Julianne, I do not know."

"You said . . ."

"Oh, I know where the road begins, I know how Rudel hopes to get away from the castle."

"And how is that?"

"By, unh, a hidden gateway. I can't tell you more than that, I don't know much more. I know where to find it, but I don't know how it works."

I couldn't make it work would seem to be the truth of that, or so it sounded. Julianne thought that this must be why Elisande had come to the Roq, to find and work that gateway; there was so much chagrin in her voice, in her face. Rudel could make it work, where she could not. Or thought he could, at least; and she must hope that he was right, as they all must if they were to get away. A bitter draught, clearly, for Elisande.

"WHAT TIME IS it?"

Elisande went to the window—narrow and tall, an arrow-slit knocked out, but not too far: the preceptor's suite of rooms was in one of the older parts of the castle, which had needs made its own defence—and twisted her head awkwardly sideways to see the sky, try to see the sun.

Just as she did so, Marron displayed a sweet sense of timing, saying, "It's rising noon now, my lady. Half an hour, maybe; not more."

"We'll be expected to go to service," she said, over Elisande's snort of irritation. "If we wait here, my Imber"—she could do that now, she could say *my Imber* in public that way, and let them all think she did it only

to draw the distinction—"will come to escort us." With
the grinning Karel, no doubt, and numerous others; not
she thought with the louring uncle. He wouldn't dance attendance on her, not now she was married. Part of the
family, submissive, safe. Why should he bother?

"Then we'd best go immediately, before we can't go at
all."

"Yes. My way, though, Elisande. At least we'll try it
my way." She hadn't forgotten the sight of that man crucified across a doorway, set to dwell in the house of his
own pain until he died; she wanted no more men pun-
ished for seeing where she was not, or for not seeing her
where she was.

Quickly they collected up weapons and what small
valuables they could—"water would be better than half
of this," Elisande grumbled, "but we've no skins to carry
it, so we must just want for water"—and then Marron
opened the door, and Julianne swept out.

When the guard moved to bar her way, she lifted one
caustic eyebrow and gave him the full benefit of her
glare.

"We go to holy service, man. Would you prevent us?"

"I have orders, my lady . . ."

"Indeed? To keep us prisoner?"

"Not to let you wander without an escort. The castle is
a confusing place," he seemed to be reciting rather than
speaking his own thoughts, "and you might lose your
way."

"But we have an escort," with a waft of her hand at
Marron. "This squire is a resident here, he knows every
stair and every turning. There is no danger of our becom-
ing lost. And I want some period of quiet contemplation
at the God's altar, before the Order assembles for general
service. You may be dismissed to rejoin your troop for
prayers; there is no purpose in your standing guard over
empty quarters. Is there?"

"Er, no, my lady. Thank you, my lady . . ."

He bowed and hurried away, ahead of them, even; so

keen he seemed to be gone, she wondered if Elisande had after all leaned on his mind a little, to urge him into compliance. She didn't know if the girl could do that, and decided not to ask. The man might have to face his lord's anger, but she had reason to hope not, if he'd reported his orders accurately. A knight's squire ought to make an acceptable escort, to the military mind; Elessans were not famous for their imagination.

ELISANDE LED THEM a way Julianne did not know, that took them nowhere near the great hall, but further into the dark and ancient heart of the castle. Walls climbed high on either side of them, the sky was a slender band of blue above; they met no one coming or going, heard only the silence of old stone and the whisper of wind against it, the rustle of their own clothes, their own soft footfalls and tight breaths.

They came into a small ward of cracked uneven flagstones, where the body of the castle made two sides of the court and a wall the other two. That was unmanned, a simple wall with no walkway on its height. In the furthest corner stood a tower, squat and square; after a moment's puzzled gazing, she realised that its age-blackened stones held no visible door or window.

Behind her, she heard Marron suck in his breath, more understanding than surprise.

"The Tower of the King's Daughter," Elisande said, her voice little more than a whisper. "This is where he will bring Redmond, this is his route out. And ours."

"The Sharai call it the Tower of the Ghost Walker," Marron murmured.

"Do they?" Elisande laughed shortly. "They would."

There were currents here, tugging at both, that Julianne could not read. She said simply, "How do we get inside?"

"Well, that's the question. I don't know. I thought I did, but I was wrong. We must hope that Rudel is not."

They lingered in the mouth of the narrow way, not venturing out into the clear space of the ward; Julianne peered up at small windows in massive walls, and said, "Can they see us down here?"

"Those are the knights' rooms above, my lady," Marron told her. "There might be men and their servants up there now, changing for prayers; we should keep out of their sight. When the bell sounds, they will leave." But his face changed even as he said that; he went on, "Except for one. Sieur Anton will pray alone, in his chamber. He won't be looking out of the window, though. Er, will you excuse me? Just for a minute?"

Having politely asked permission, he didn't wait for it, but turned and ran off regardless.

"Where's he going?" Elisande demanded.

"I don't know . . ."

"Maybe he needs the latrines in a hurry?"

"Don't joke, Elisande."

"I'm not. I could half use a pot myself, I'm nervous."

"Of what's in there? Marron said it could be dangerous . . ."

"More than he guesses. It could be fatal. But no, what I'm really nervous about is just what Rudel is going to say, when he finds us here waiting for him."

Again it sounded like a joke; again, Julianne thought, it was not.

They waited in silence then. Shortly they heard light footsteps running towards them, and both girls stiffened; but it was only Marron returning, fumbling to buckle a sword one-handed to his belt as he ran. The scabbard gleamed, white and silver as sudden sunlight drove the shadows back.

"Marron?"

"My lady?"

"Is that your own sword? It seems very fine."

"Yes, my lady," though he flushed as he said it, and not she thought at her implication that it was not his, that it was too fine for a humble squire. "Sieur Anton gave it me. He wasn't there," *not quite*, his panting breath suggested, "and Lady Elisande said we should go armed . . ."

"So we should; though blades will do us little good in the tower. Did anyone else see you?"

"Oh yes, my lady." Julianne smiled, seeing how he struggled not to say *what of it?* with voice or gesture. He was right, though. A squire running in and out of his master's room, fetch and carry, in empty-handed and out with a sword: it was hardly remarkable.

Elisande acknowledged as much with a nod, a fraction late; then she said, "I suppose you couldn't possibly call me by my name? Formal manners make me uncomfortable at any time; very soon now, they're going to sound ridiculous."

Not in the tower, she quite clearly meant, but in the face of Rudel's anger. Marron smiled at her distantly, as though he were thinking of something entirely other; then he confirmed it by flinching visibly away from whatever stray thought or memory it was had caused that smile.

Elisande received no more answer than that. Just then the great bell beat out its first summons. Although no window overlooked them here in this narrow passageway, although they were so far hidden by thick stone that they couldn't hear the rush of sandalled or booted feet that would be sweeping like a breeze through every other part of the castle, still they pressed back warily against the wall, trying to squeeze themselves out of the sun that beat down almost vertically now to find them.

"Won't we be missed?" Elisande murmured, under a sudden doubt.

"Perhaps. Imber will have come to escort us, found us gone; but his place in hall is on the floor with the Ransomers, he did his year's service among the knights, all those Elessans do that. Didn't you see the badges on their clothing? Even if he looks, it's hard to see who's in the gallery from down below. I don't think we'll be missed. If he has doubts, what's he going to do? Stop the service, to send out search parties?"

"His uncle would."

"His uncle won't even know to miss us, until afterwards." *I hope.* "And by then . . ."

By then Rudel and Redmond should have come, and they should all be inside the tower. She hoped.

The Tower of the King's Daughter, they'd called it; also the Tower of the Ghost Walker, which had made Elisande laugh as though it wasn't funny at all.

Perhaps they were both of them joke names. After all, one thing that was certain — one of the few certainties about that particular man — was that the King had no daughter . . .

"Why does the tower have those titles?" she asked.

"Can I tell you when we're inside? Please?"

Meaning that if they didn't get inside, it was safer or wiser or better if she still didn't know. Meaning that trust went only so far, even between friends who took such risks together.

Meaning that she could strangle the girl, actually. But she didn't, she only turned her head the other way to watch for Rudel's coming.

AT LAST HE came, they both came: Rudel in jongleur-garb and with a pack slung over his shoulder, his slow-shuffling companion once more in the black habit of a brother, probably not for disguise so much as necessity, the choice that or prisoner's rags, which meant that or nothing.

Surely, surely Elisande would not work her mind-tricks on this man, these two men, even if she could. Did magic work on magicians? Julianne didn't know; but Rudel must have been confident of not being followed or challenged, at this time and in these hidden alleys. His sword-arm gave his friend support, their heads were bent close together, Rudel watched Redmond's feet and neither one of them noticed the three who waited in the bare fall of shadow.

Not until Elisande spoke.

"Rudel, you won't go through the tower without me."

She'd kept her voice deliberately soft, not to startle them, though her words were challenge enough and typical of the girl. Neither man did startle; for a long moment neither one so much as spoke, they only looked. Redmond looked, at least. Rudel glared.

His eyes moved from Elisande to Marron and back again, as though he couldn't decide which of the two of them more deserved a beating. If he'd had his hands free, Julianne thought, perhaps they might both have received one, justice swift and severe.

When he did speak, it was to her; he said, "These two may make a game of what is deadly, but I am disappointed in you, Baroness."

That stung; she hoped her face did not show how deeply, but was very afraid that it had.

Her voice was steady enough, though. "No game, sir. Not for any one of us. I think we all wish to see you safe—"

"Then go back. You endanger us all, simply by being here. Do you not know how they will search for you?"

"We all wish to see you safe," she said again, calm and even, as though she'd never been interrupted, "and we also each of us have our own reasons for going with you, if you can truly show us a way out of this castle unobserved."

"Lady," and in his mouth that was no title of respect, not now, "you clearly have no idea, no concept of what you are asking. I am looking to slip quietly away from here, with a day's grace before they realise that either one of us is gone. You will have the whole garrison turned out at our tail within an hour. That's assuming we survive the tower. Bad enough to go in there with one wise and crippled old man; with a gaggle of foolish children clinging to my belt—and one of those hiding a fresh wound beneath his tunic—I wouldn't put money on any one of us coming out of it whole."

"You misunderstand me, Rudel," Julianne replied. "I am not asking anything from you. Except that you open some way into the tower, which you intend to do anyway. We will follow you through, wherever it may lead us; and once through, we will leave you and go our own way. I do not think you can prevent us, except by abandoning your own intentions. Again."

"Oh, can I not?"

His eyes grew wide and bright suddenly, hawk-sharp and staring; and then his face was fuzzy and all her thoughts were blurred, her legs were uncertain beneath her, she couldn't quite remember where she was or who was with her, but she did very much want to sit down . . .

But there was a slap that sounded in her ears, and her mind cleared in a moment, although it was not she who had been slapped. Rudel's face was piebald, red and white: white fingermarks on his cheek and all red else, and Elisande looked much like him, her bones showing pale while her skin flushed in her fury.

"How dare you, how *dare* you? Trying to maze my friend? I should—"

"You should stop this. All of you." That was Redmond, unexpectedly throwing his hood back and glowering around him. His voice was thin and drained, but sharp enough to silence Elisande. "We haven't time for dispute. Rudel, there may be advantage in their coming with us. We don't know what we may meet, in the tower or afterwards; extra hands could be useful."

"Of course we will be useful." That was Elisande again, not crushed for long. "You *know* that I should carry the Daughter, it's only sense . . ."

It sounded like nonsense to Julianne. Whoever or whatever the Daughter might be—the way she'd said the word, it definitely had a capital letter to its name—Elisande was the smallest of them all, the least likely porter. But after a moment Rudel nodded briefly, reluctance and anger and acceptance all contained within that one small gesture as he turned to walk without further argument across the small court towards the tower.

Marron and Elisande followed; Julianne delayed to offer her arm to Redmond, but he shook his head and smiled gently.

"Thank you, but I have taken enough strength from Rudel; this much I can manage."

Even so she stayed at his side, matching his slow pace. It was perhaps an opportunity to ask questions—*what is the Daughter, how do we gain access to the tower, how will it lead us out of the castle?*—but she was tired of being given misleading answers. Time would reveal all.

Or not. When they caught up with the others, Rudel was already frowning at the blank wall of the tower, frustration showing on his face and in his hands where he had laid them against the stone, as if he were trying to push his way inside.

"I *tried* that," Elisande said, only poorly hiding her satisfaction.

"Then we must try something more."

Julianne was still watching his hands; she saw them clench for a moment, fists to batter the wall or possibly Elisande, before unfolding again to trace invisible patterns on the age-worn stones.

He muttered a few words and phrases, each by the sound of them in a different tongue, each incomprehensible and each to no effect. No effect on the wall, at least; there was some noticeable deterioration in his temper, which was not improved by Elisande's steady, repetitive murmur, "Tried that."

"Elisande." Julianne beckoned her over, and was a little surprised when she came; had to think fast, and said, "Just how much magic do you people have?"

"This isn't magic," was the quick reply, "it's power."

"There's a difference?"

"Well. Perhaps not; but it's not our magic. The power's in the wall, in the tower; say the right words and a door will open. Anyone could do it. You could, if you knew the words."

As in the cave, when my finger was plenty, anyone's finger would have been enough . . . But she didn't want to think about the cave. "And do I take it that neither of you two does know the words?"

"Ah. We thought we did." The insouciance in her voice was belied by an anxious glance at the sky, at the relentless sun; they were running out of time.

Rudel stepped away from the wall, shaking his head. "My father said . . ."

"Your father," Elisande rejoined instantly, "does not know everything."

That won her a glance, but no words; after a moment, he went back to the wall.

"Who is his father?" Julianne asked quietly.

"A sweet old man. You'd like him."

Julianne reminded herself again not to ask questions.

Redmond shuffled slowly forward, to join Rudel. He laid his hands above the younger man's, and said, "Together, now."

They spoke slow words in chorus, and had a response at last: the wall seemed to groan, so deeply that Julianne didn't so much hear it as feel it in her ribs; she thought she saw flakes of light fall like cinders about the men.

Redmond breathed deeply, and wiped sweat from his face. "There is a block."

"I know that. If there were no block, we would be inside by now."

"I mean a resistance, something works against us. The words are right. Elisande, stop your mocking and give us some help."

Perhaps because it was he and not Rudel who asked— commanded, rather—or else because the urgency of their need overrode even her bitter tongue, Elisande stepped up immediately. She stood between the two men, and added her hands and her voice to theirs.

This time the groan was palpable, bone-shaking; the

wall faded for a moment, and light shone between or perhaps through the stones. Julianne saw it touch Marron's face, turning his skin a strange, sickly colour.

He gasped, as the light died. She moved quickly to his side, and reached to touch his wrist; it was chill, and slick with sweat.

"Don't be afraid," she murmured, trying valiantly to suppress her own heart's rapid beating. "Mystery is always unnerving, but only because it's unknown." She was quoting her father, for her own comfort as much as the squire's; she added, "They know what this is," and only hoped that it was true.

"I'm not afraid," Marron answered, thin-lipped. "My arm hurts, that's all."

Typical boy, hiding his fear behind a confession that didn't hurt his pride. She nodded easily, patted his shoulder and let him be.

"Once more," Redmond said. "Be confident. It has to comply; that is laid into its foundation."

Again the same words, not shouted but spoken with force, three voices joined in determination. Julianne knew the syllables now, if not the sense; she could chant along with them, and would if it were necessary, if it would help.

No need, though. This time the stones seemed to cry their own word in response, and that light—it had a colour, but none she'd ever seen before, she didn't know how to call it—blazed out across the ward, from a doorway too bright to look upon.

No, not a doorway. A door. Redmond laid a hand against it, and maybe it was only because she was squinting but she thought she saw the light shine through his flesh, showing his twisted bones beneath; certainly she saw how his hand was stopped by it, how his fingers spread and pressed, how solid it was to him. She also heard the soft hiss of his breath, as a gauge of how much the contact hurt him.

"Not you," Rudel said, grabbing his shoulder, pulling him away.

"Why not? It'll be no easier inside. If I can't bear it, better to learn now."

"Don't play with me. You can bear anything, old man."

"Well, then?"

"Well, be careful, then. It may be more than blocked, it may be guarded."

"Yes."

If Redmond did take any more care after the warning than before, Julianne couldn't see it. He only placed both hands on that door of light, and pushed. Not hard, he didn't have the bodily strength, but with determination, with strength of mind.

And as he pushed, so the door retreated. It didn't swing open, it wasn't hinged; but it drew slowly back from him and coloured smoke seethed around its edges, unless it was mist, unless it was light gone to liquid, like inks dropped into water.

Every step he took, it was as though Redmond stepped on and into pain, stronger and deeper, further than the step before. He hissed, gasped, cried aloud and kept on walking. The smoke, mist, whatever it was wreathed itself around him; Rudel fidgeted, suddenly snapped, "Come, then," and followed.

Elisande was only a pace, half a pace behind Rudel and hurrying to catch up, not to follow him.

Julianne felt briefly forgotten, almost abandoned: those three had overriding interests of their own in there. She glanced sideways at Marron, ready to give him a wry smile and a polite arm, to make nearly a joke of this; but he looked dreadful, his eyes glassy and all his skin shining with sweat although the whole ward was chilly now, despite the high bright sun. She reached for his hand instead, gripped trembling fingers and squeezed encouragingly. She must look like this, she thought, those times, those few and dreadful times she stood of necessity on a high place and gazed down: pale and feverish, shaking, terrified.

"They're leaving us behind," she said, trying to sound cheerful and sounding only false to her own ears, an adult jollying a nervous child.

It was true, though, they were being left. That vivid door was only an opalescent glow now, lost behind clouds of colour; their companions were shadows within its frame, and fading.

She walked forward determinedly and Marron came with her, his hand locked painfully tight about hers. Tendrils of misty light seemed to reach towards them, wrapping around their legs and bodies, arms and faces, fogging her eyes so that she didn't notice when they passed through the tower's wall.

It was her feet that felt the change, from hard-edged broken stones to something softer and more resilient: like walking on water, she thought, startled, looking down instinctively and seeing nothing but roiling mist.

She dragged her eyes up again, with an effort; whatever it was that she stood on, it bore her weight and Marron's, they weren't sinking. And the others had come this way: there they stood, three murky figures off to her right, beside the shining panel of that strange door.

And here came Rudel's voice, speaking snappishly to her, "Hurry, we need to let this close . . ."

She tugged at Marron's hand and felt him come stumblingly after her, breathing in short hard gasps. Dizzy with fear she thought he was, totally dependent.

Close to, the figures resolved into Elisande and the two men, their faces only a little blurred by drifting mist. Redmond stood stiffly, leaning on her friend's shoulder, as though the effort of opening the door had exhausted him despite the help he'd had. It was Rudel who reached a hand out to touch the door, fiercely bright again at this little distance, who murmured other words to release it.

It had taken three to force it open; one was enough to undo that. Julianne expected to see it spring forward, to fit again into the wall before it vanished, but the light seemed simply to fray into the swirling fog. It dissipated in moments, and was gone. When she looked behind her, she could see no way back, no sign of the sunlit ward.

The fog carried its own light, though, or else was itself made of light, if these sad, unearthly colours could be lights. A floating veil that was neither blue nor green draped itself across Elisande's face; Julianne could still see her friend's features through it, though sickly shaded. As she watched, the veil stretched and curled itself into a rope, and twined around Elisande's throat and Redmond's, both at once. She thought she saw it tighten, and moved to snatch; but the rope parted before her fingers reached it, and was no more than threads of shifting colour among great wafts of the same.

"Where are we?" she whispered.

"In the Tower of the King's Daughter," Elisande said, valiantly chuckling. Pity was, that the valour was so evident.

"Perhaps; but—"

"You stand on a bridge, Julianne." Rudel's voice was pitched soft but not gentle, low and rumbling and forceful. "A bridge between worlds, the one you know and another like it and yet quite unlike. I am sorry to have led you this way, because that other world is deadly; but mortals can walk within it, and we must. Follow me, and do not stray. All of you—and I mean you particularly, Elisande—mind what I say, and do as I tell you, and we may survive. But remember, one false step, one false word may be fatal. Now come. You two girls, help Redmond and Marron; they have been hurt, and this place is not easy for them."

She could see the truth of that, though she did not understand it. Redmond stood cramped and awkward, head low, while the mists eddied around him, seeming to probe like clutching fingers beneath his robe; when she glanced at Marron she saw a skein wrapped all about him, pulsing to the ragged beat of his blood that she could feel against her fingers where he still clasped her hand.

She tugged at him and he followed slowly, dumbly. Elisande had put her arm round Redmond's waist and was murmuring to him softly as she led him forward; he moved like a man in terrible pain, and she thought Elisande wasted her words, she didn't think he was hearing anything outside himself

The floor they walked on — smooth and yielding still, *smoke made solid* she thought, and then didn't want to think about that any more, for fear that it might be only faith or ignorance that kept it so — rose underfoot much like the arch of a bridge, though Rudel surely hadn't meant it so literally. A long bridge, a high bridge: unless this was all magic, all deceit, they couldn't possibly be still within the walls of that squat tower. There simply wasn't the space.

The higher they climbed, the harder it was on Marron; and on Redmond too. She could see him stumbling at every step, almost, needing all Elisande's strength to keep him upright and moving. Julianne was doing something of the same service for Marron, though that boy had a stubbornness to him that was helping also. She'd changed from leading to dragging and from dragging to hauling, her shoulder under his for extra support. He breathed raspingly in her ear, set his jaw and swallowed any noise else, though she could read so much into his sudden pauses and hard silences, he might as well have cried aloud each time the searing pain ran through him.

She'd been wrong before; it wasn't fear doing this to him, to both men, working on them so savagely. *They have been hurt*, Rudel had said, and that was surely true of Redmond. But Marron only had a cut on his arm, albeit a bad one and slow to heal; he'd been running round the castle an hour since, and now he couldn't walk without assistance, could barely breathe without pain . . .

"Elisande," she called ahead at last, "what's *wrong* with them?"

"It's the Daughter," the reply came back. "It's not a safe thing, not for men, even when they're healthy. When they're not—well, you can see. Coming this close costs them greatly."

"What is the Daughter?"

"It's what I came here for," and she was still being oblique, and Julianne was not going to accept that any more.

"I know that. But why, what *is* it?"

"To us, to Surayon it's a terrible danger. It could be the weapon that destroys us all. That's why I came, to take it, to keep it safe where Marshal Fulke and his kind couldn't find it . . ."

She'd heard all that before. Foolish to expect any straighter answer, or any answer at all if she went on asking straight; so she tried a little subtlety. "Why is it called the Daughter, the King's Daughter?"

"Because the King thought it a great joke. I guess he thought it was funny to leave it here, too, where Fulke or someone like him could lay their hands on it. That's why—"

"That's why you disobeyed your father and your grandfather, to come here," Rudel's voice joined in suddenly, from the mists ahead. "It wasn't likely that Fulke would ever have found his way in here, though. That door needed more than knowledge: it needed more than a woman's strength, but it needed a woman's voice. Which is as good a lock as any, in a Ransomer castle. Nor would Fulke have known what he had, even if he'd laid hands on the Daughter."

"Redmond would have told him, in the end. Wouldn't you?"

"I might have tried to show him, what he had. I'd have enjoyed that. Where is it?"

"Here," Rudel said.

*   *   *

VERY LIKE A bridge, the slope they climbed had levelled at last; if it weren't a bridge it might as well be a hill. Artificial or otherwise, the top of it flattened by man or god, she couldn't see the ground to guess and wasn't going to stoop and feel with her fingers. She truly didn't want to touch that resilience her feet still reported, another state of smoke. She thought it was a construct, a spell-made thing woven from art and charm and little more, and she was glad the bright colours of the air hid it from her.

The drifting banks and swirls of coloured fog were less vivid up here, or more diffuse, as though they'd climbed above the thick of it. There was nothing but darkening, purpling shadow above their heads, there was still only the fog's own luminescence to see by and she still couldn't—thankfully—see her feet; but she could see further ahead than before.

She could see past Redmond and Elisande, where they had stopped walking and stood still, only looking now; she could see Rudel standing beside some kind of plinth, the first solid matter she had seen since they'd walked through what had previously seemed so very solid, the old weathered wall of the tower.

A plinth, a pedestal—it might have been a broken pillar if it weren't so neatly cut off at what was chest height to a big man like Rudel, what would be near enough chin height to Elisande. It was angular and a little tapered, but still easily broad enough at the top to have been a pillar, to have taken some massive load entirely alone.

Like the air she breathed—and felt in her lungs, damp and heavy, so different from the clean dry breezes in the castle or the hot dusty air of the road—like everything that belonged in this place it had a colour, its own colour that she couldn't give a name to. Somewhere between blue and grey, she thought vaguely; only as soon as she thought either "blue" or "grey" it didn't shift but her perspective did, whatever label she gave it she knew instantly that she was wrong, so it must be the other colour, only that it never was.

It was a colour she'd know again, though, if ever she saw it in that other world they'd come from; and the shape of the thing she would know also, if ever she saw something similarly cut. She wondered what artist had figured this so finely, its angles so perfect, and from what rock, if rock it was . . . ?

The plinth was more impressive than what lay upon it. That seemed to be a ball, a hard and chitinous ball of red ochre, about the size of a man's head. She frowned: something strange there. Even having so little to make a judgement on she was sure that there was a judgement to be made, and that it mattered.

It took a moment for her own thoughts to catch up with her; but of course, again it was the colour. Whatever it might be, this thing had a colour she could see and name outright; which meant that it had no right of place here, it was a thing of her own world that had been set where it was for some deliberate reason. As a safeguard, she would have guessed, even if she'd known no more.

"Here it is," Rudel said, and he reached to pick it up—

—and stopped, at Elisande's uninhibited shriek.

"Don't *touch* it!"

He stilled, turned his head to look at her with his hands still half-cupped, ready for their burden, poised a finger's length away on either side.

"Why should I not touch it, Elisande?"

"You know why, don't be so stupid! It isn't safe for you . . ."

"It isn't safe for any of us."

"For me it is. Of course it is, why not?"

"I will carry it, if it must be carried."

Julianne startled, they all stared: that was Marron making the offer, and the surprise was only partly at his speaking at all when he'd been so silent for so long, turned in on himself. It was his voice that was shocking, thin and racked, desolate almost, as though he felt so lost already that no further danger could touch him.

"*No!*" Elisande again, a moment ahead of Rudel's own

refusal. "Haven't you been listening? No man can touch it safely, and you least of all. You shouldn't even have come this close, neither you nor Redmond. This is my task, it's why I'm *here* . . ."

"And I'm here to prevent you," Rudel said flatly. "You're too young to handle this. You betray yourself, even by thinking that it's safe for you to take it. The Daughter is subtle, where you are not. You deceive yourself, it will deceive you, and that is peril for us all."

"Age does not equate to wisdom," she spat back. "Are you so sure of yourself, Rudel? You have no scratch on your body, you won't so much as prick your finger on a thorn between here and Surayon?"

They glared at each other across the plinth; Rudel did draw his hands back, but then he moved deliberately to place his body between Elisande and the object they were both so wary of.

Julianne disentangled her fingers from Marron's, and walked slowly forward to see it more clearly. Its skin was textured, smooth in places and elsewhere oddly ridged, with crevices so deep she thought she could force a finger into them. It seemed to have sunk a little into the glossy surface of the plinth—not stone after all, she thought, but some substance as strange as its colour was strange to her—as though it were monstrously heavier than it looked.

Her veil hung around her neck, long since pulled free of her face. A formal length of silk, intended to satisfy the strictest brother, hanging almost to her waist: she slipped it off, held it a moment in her hands, then reached to wrap it around the red ball on the plinth.

It was Redmond who noticed first, who whispered a warning to the others, "Watch, she has it . . . !"

Too late by then: she had already lifted the veiled thing in her hands, and was hugging it against her. Not heavy at all, oddly light it felt, for something so momentous; she had to grip tightly to feel sure of it, as she watched the little dimple in the plinth's surface rise and vanish.

"Julianne, don't . . ."

"Why not?" she challenged Elisande, all of them. "Someone has to, or we'll stand here bickering till the world ends. If it's safe for you, it's safe for me also; if not, let me run the risk of it."

"You don't know its dangers."

"So I'll be all the more careful. It might carry dangers that you don't know, that you wouldn't think of," that was what Rudel had meant, she was sure, "so better if I have it, because I'll never be complacent."

She wanted to show Rudel that she could be subtle in her thinking; he didn't look happy, but he nodded slowly.

"You carry it, then. For the moment. That may be the best solution; I need my eye on the path we take from here, and having the Daughter in my arms would distract me. Redmond, come; we've lingered too long already. I'll help you. Julianne, behind me, but not too closely, for his sake; Elisande, you bring Marron."

With his dispositions made he led them on past the plinth, though the decision in his voice was belied by his constant glances back. Julianne nursed the Daughter in her arms and followed; at her back she could hear Elisande cursing under her breath.

Like a bridge, like a hill the floor she walked on fell away from its summit, smoothly but uncomfortably steep. It was hard to keep her balance, when she had both arms wrapped around the Daughter—what *was* it, this thing that her companions were so mysterious about, that felt both hard-shelled and hollow, like the blown egg of some monstrous bird, only not so securely shelled?—and the billowing mists played constant tricks on her eyes.

She leaned back against the tempting drag of the slope and kept her head down, focusing on the burden she carried; and so almost walked into Redmond's back, was only alerted by his sudden gasp of pain. She jerked to a halt and scuttled to the side, remembering Rudel's warning, not to come too close to the ailing man. Only then did she lift her head, to see what had brought the men to such an unexpected stop. Rudel was confronting a great wall of shadow, a darkness that loomed through the fog, rising far above them and stretching away both left and right, barring their way absolutely.

"What is it?" she asked at last, after Rudel had stood silent for a full minute.

"I do not know," he answered her.

A futile question, but she asked it anyway: "You don't have any words, like before, that could pass us through?"

"No. I was expecting a gateway, into that other world I spoke of; and for that, yes, I have the words. But this is something entirely other, and I will not waste my breath on it. Some power has closed this way to us."

"The same that blocked the door before," Redmond whispered, "though that was only an echo of this. That we could force; this, not."

One more question, then, and again she was sure that she knew the answer already. Someone had to ask it, though. "What must we do?"

"I am afraid," Rudel said, "I am very afraid that we must go back."

Back over this mystical bridge, and back into the castle, escape denied a second time; back to where she was undoubtedly being sought by now, to where their small party could not hope to avoid discovery, however cautiously they slipped from shadow to shadow.

"What of the Daughter?" Elisande's voice came from behind her, oddly tight and anxious. "Should we leave it where it was?"

"We dare not, now. If they take us, we could not hide the truth."

That was certain; Julianne knew that she at least could not withstand the Order's questioners. She lacked Redmond's courage.

"What, then?"

"I am afraid," he said again, and this time he did indeed sound frightened, "that we must use it."

"Rudel, no!"

"How else?" he demanded, and Elisande could find no answer.

NINE

The Devil Runner

MARRON STEPPED—OR shuffled, rather—into the courtyard, Elisande his prop and motive, her springy body compelling his. There was nothing more he could do, nothing he wanted except perhaps to stop, to lie down and never move again; but he was so drained he lacked the will even to do that much, that little, while her arm and shoulder and purpose nudged him forward.

She gasped, as they passed from gauzy mists to clear air; he felt her sudden rigidity, saw how her head turned to look back, to look up. He couldn't manage so much curiosity, but his head moved none the less in echo of hers, all his body tuned to imitation.

Behind him he saw the pale lights and twisted colours of that place they had come from, of which he had only dim and confusing memories—his companions' voices and a few of the words they'd said, pain and sucking and being passed from one girl to the other for a reason he could not now remember—and he saw those lights not fade but disappear. First they shone, and then there was a

wall like a curtain, through which they shone; and then
the wall was stone, and lights won't shine through stone
so of course they didn't, and Marron stood in darkness.

Near darkness. Above him stars, and starlight all there
was to see by; and slow he might be, in this as in everything, but he understood Elisande's startlement now. It
had been midday when they'd entered the tower. That
was when his blurring nightmare had begun, and he had
little sense of the passage of any time at all during that
period of reeling dizzy horror, but even he was puzzled.
They'd gone in and not gone through as they had meant
to do, and so had turned and come back—bearing something with them, a trophy, they called it the Daughter and
Julianne carried it, which was why Elisande was all but
carrying him—and so brief a foray, it could surely not
have taken half a day?

Half a day and half the night to follow, he thought,
seeing how the sky glowed a little silver above one black-
shadowed wall; the moon had passed that way already.

Not only he was puzzled. Julianne and Rudel were
murmuring together, a few paces off. Odd that Elisande
hadn't abandoned him to join them, so strident she was
with her opinions: he glanced down, and saw her finger-
ing his tunic, scowling.

"I didn't notice in there," she said, "with all those
lights and strangeness, nothing looked right or felt right
either—but this is soaked, I saw it before the light went,
all this side looked black. It's blood, isn't it? Your arm's
been bleeding, ever since we went in there . . ."

"Has it?" It had been hurting, worse than ever it had
hurt before, pain run rampant; he hadn't thought about
bleeding. She was right, though, now that he reached
with the other hand to feel. His tunic was saturated. He
lifted his damp hand towards his face, and his nostrils
filled with the warm copper tang of fresh-drawn blood.

"Take it off," Elisande ordered. Then he glanced aside
at the others, "Whatever's happened, whatever they
choose to do, it can wait a minute. All those windows up

there are shuttered, no one's overlooking us; and if we've lost so much time already, a little more can't matter. If you've lost so much blood already, a little more might matter a lot. Take the tunic off, and let me see."

He tried, but couldn't do it. His belt came off easily one-handed, but the tunic was wet and heavy, clinging to his skin; and his one good arm, that felt heavy also, too much so to lift above his shoulder. The effort only made his head swim and the ground buck unsteadily beneath him.

Elisande helped in the end, undoing the ties and then tugging the tunic over his head. While he was in that deeper darkness, he heard her voice, snappishly, "He's hurt. *Look* . . ."

The tunic fell free of him, and now he saw how it was that the others might look: a little ball, a star of golden light hung in the air above them, softly shining. By that light he could look too, and see how not only the bindings that held his arm but all his ribs and stomach were sheeted with blood.

While Elisande fought with wet knots, Rudel said, "Take your time, and see to him properly. Things have changed, and my first thought is not perhaps the wisest route to follow."

"I *told* you that . . ."

"Things have *changed*, Elisande! Somehow we've lost touch with time, in that tower. Even assuming that this is the same day, or the night that follows that day, the situation is completely different now."

"How so?"

"Foolish of me, I know—but I wish you would think sometimes, before you speak. Julianne will have been missed, immediately after the midday office. The castle will have been searched thoroughly, and she not found; so they must have assumed that she had slipped away somehow, past the guards on the gate. They will have been scouring the country, and perhaps they are still. The gates may be open, parties coming and going; if we can

get to the stables unnoticed, then five more riding out in
brothers' robes might not be stopped or questioned."

"Ifs and maybes," Elisande said, but she said it with
more relief than criticism.

"Quite so. But we may be lucky; and the alternative—"

"No. There *is* no alternative. You mustn't."

"I may have to."

"*No!* Think of your father . . ."

He sighed, and said, "See to Marron, Elisande. And
pray that we'll be lucky."

After a moment, she nodded; her fingers went back to
picking at knots.

At last, the bindings came loose. She slid Marron's
arm free, and glanced at him anxiously. "Does it hurt?"

"No," he told her, truthfully; it felt nothing but numb
now, no part of him, only a stiff and useless weight joined
somehow to his shoulder.

She looked disbelieving, but turned her attention to
the bandage on his arm. That needed her knife slipped beneath, to cut it away; she threw the sodden linen to the
ground and probed gently at the wound, which had burst
open around its stitching.

"It's a terrible mess, but it's not bleeding much, not
any more. I can bind it up with these," the wet lengths of
bandage that had bound it to his chest before, "only then
there'll be no way to support it . . ."

"It doesn't matter," he said, speaking true again, albeit
with an effort. It was hard somehow to care. "I can't feel
it anyway."

Elisande sighed, nodded reluctantly, and began.

HE WAS JUST dressed again, with the dull dead weight of
his arm tucked under his belt, the best they could manage, when the sudden call of Frater Susurrus startled
them all. Three slow strokes, that brought a brief smile to
Rudel's voice.

"Midnight. We may be lucky after all. We'll wait ten minutes, let the brothers go to pray . . ."

Not all would go, that was understood; but those left on guard should be looking outward, a lesson learned at cost. At least the way to the stables ought to be clear.

At the second sounding of the bell, Marron's gaze drifted upward, looking for one darkened window among many. Sieur Anton should be in his room by now, if he wasn't out hunting a runaway bride . . .

One window among many was suddenly aglow, softly shining around a man's shadow as the shutters were thrown back. Marron stared, and felt his stare returned.

"Elisande," a tight whisper, not his own, "the light . . . !"

The little star vanished, plunging them into darkness, too late.

"We'll go," Rudel said sharply. "Now."

And they did. But they went first without Marron, who stood staring up at that window even after the figure it framed had wheeled away and was gone; stood staring until Elisande came to pluck at his elbow, to hook her arm through his and drag him away, hissing in his ear, "Do you *want* to face the questioners, and betray us all? Come *on* . . ."

THEY HURRIED THROUGH the darkness, or tried to. Marron struggled against his exhaustion and his distraction both, but Sieur Anton filled his thoughts, overriding even his companions' urgency. What had the knight seen, what was he doing now? Saying his prayers and letting them go? Or snatching up his sword and running, crying the alert, racing to intercept them . . . ?

Marron couldn't answer the questions, nor escape them. He wasn't even sure what answers he wanted. His feet stumbled on broken flags, and he thought that was a sign: he was consumed by temptation, he wanted to push Elisande away and stay, abandon the others, just wait for his master to find him.

It was only his indecision that kept him moving, that and Elisande's tugging hands. Even at his awkward pace, they caught up soon; there was a glimmer of gold ahead, another little ball of witchlight, and it showed them Redmond shuffling along with one arm against the wall for support, while the other two waited at a corner further on.

As they all came together, the older man wheezed, "I can't rush, I'm sorry. You could go on, and leave me . . ."

"Not alive," Rudel countered grimly. "And I haven't gone through all this to kill you now, old friend. We'd be wise to tread slowly, in any case: slow, and without light, once we get into the open wards where the guards might look down and see us. Take my arm, we'll go at your speed. If any of you believes in prayer, pray to be lucky . . ."

THEY'D BEEN LUCKY once, to have emerged from the tower at such a time, with night blanketing the castle and the bulk of the Order going to prayer; perhaps that luck had been outmatched by Sieur Anton's opening his shutters just then. The God's path ran through light and darkness both, and Marron had been taught that men's lives reflected that path. If there were any truth in that teaching, he couldn't say. He only followed Rudel as they all did, prayed not at all nor hoped neither; escape or capture, he saw no real hope for himself in either one and was simply too weary and too distressed to gift his share of hope with his companions.

Luck or the God or something else, pure chance perhaps brought them all the way through the main body of the castle unchallenged. No stray brothers, no sight or sound of the knight's rousing the guard; down the long passage to the stable-yard they came, and though he had none himself Marron could hear the dawn of hope in the way Elisande breathed at his side, he could feel it in her fingers where they lay more lightly on his arm now, urging but no longer compelling him on.

Out into the open they came, and a light breeze touched them as they crossed the cobbles, like a promise of freedom. Elisande, he thought, believed it; he saw her head lift, her eyes shine in the starlight. No doubt she smelled the horses, saw herself and all her friends saddling, riding, down to the gate and away.

All he smelled was his own blood, and all he saw was darkness.

"No torches," Rudel murmured, echoing his own thought. "If there is a search, it's long gone from here and they don't expect it back this hour. Still, the gates may be open, against its return; or if not, the three of us can perhaps maze the guards, between us . . ."

Three of them? Three Surayonnaise, but only if Redmond were fit to work magic, and if that magic worked. If not, there were only two fit to fight, and one of them a girl. He didn't count the lady Julianne; stubborn and determined she might be, but she was trained to a court life, a lady's life, she couldn't be a fighter. Besides, she had that thing they called the Daughter, that most precious thing, and no other weapon visible. The Daughter was a weapon, he remembered, someone had said that, but she wouldn't have the skill to use it even if she knew how.

Elisande at least had a blade, and a sharp one; he thought she could probably fight. He thought she was very little of a lady under her fine dress, and that was Julianne's.

He thought he himself would be less use than the ladies, and Redmond the same. If the gates weren't open or the guards not susceptible to magic, he thought they were doomed, dead, death by burning it would be in the end; and by report, by inference a whole land would burn and be dead beside them, if the Daughter were the key to Surayon.

Best hope or pray, then, and he could do neither . . .

*   *   *

NEITHER HOPE NOR prayer would have saved him anyway, he thought later: hope had always been his undoing,
and it was prayer—other people's prayer—that betrayed
him now.

Rudel stepped lightly through one of the high arched
doorways into the great stable complex—*room for a
thousand mounts* was the boast, and Marron believed
it—and beckoned them in after. He swung the great
doors closed at their backs and then lit another ball of
witchlight, so that they needn't fumble in darkness for
harness and horse.

And there by its shine, a warm fire that burned nothing, Marron and all of them saw men: a troop of men rising from their knees in an empty stall. Where they must
have been saying the midnight office silently, or else had
fallen silent when they heard footsteps in the yard, because they might have been praying but they were still on
guard. And they had their swords ready at their sides, and
there were too many of them already; and forth from the
midst of them strode Fra' Piet with his shaved head
gleaming like a hairless skull and his polished axe-head
glinting at his side, and he was too many on his own.

Behind him, none of the brothers was hooded any
more than he was, although they must have been at
prayer; among the boys and men who crowded at his
back, Marron saw Aldo and Aldo and no one else but
Aldo.

RUDEL DREW HIS sword, and stepped forward. Marron
reached for Dard as Elisande left him, but stayed with his
hand on the hilt. What was the point? There were two
dozen men confronting them; they couldn't make a fight
of this, it was hopeless. Rudel must know that too . . .

And perhaps he did, perhaps he only had surrender on
his mind, some hope of protecting the ladies at whatever
cost to himself and his people. But Fra' Piet scowled,
shielded his eyes from the wickedness of the witchlight

that shone down on them all, made the sign of the God with his finger and lifted his axe; cried, "Heresy! For your souls' sake, lads, be at them . . . !"

And leaped at Rudel with his axe swinging.

Blade met haft, with a shock that resounded through the stables. Rudel grunted, heaved, sent Fra' Piet reeling back; and as he staggered the sword's point sliced across his face, opening a gash from nose to ear.

Blood ran. Fra' Piet roared and came back, axe-head scything, glinting in the light; and his men came boiling after.

The first to reach Redmond overlooked Elisande at the old man's side, and felt her knife in his ribs before his slashing sword could bite home. He slumped and fell, and those behind him checked. A moment bought, no more: just time enough for Marron to hear Julianne's gasp, to see her glancing desperately about her, her arms still wrapped around the veiled Daughter.

Here was something he could do, at least, for what little good it might be worth. He lurched towards her, reached and snatched one-handed. With that thing taken from her, he thought she could run, she could escape this madness and survive.

He groaned to see her reach instead into her gown and pull out a knife, a pair of knives. With his one arm clutching the Daughter against his chest, he wrenched his dead other from his belt and tried to stretch it out, to bar her way to the fight—

—and felt it come to burning, agonising life just as his other arm burned to match it. Crying out, staring down, he saw brief flame flow like liquid spilt across the thing he carried; and where it ran it left flakes of ash that had been the dense silk veil.

Pale grey ash, dark red beneath—and what was red was stirring, shifting, opening . . .

It could be the weapon that destroys us all, he remembered that, someone had said it when they were inside the tower. If ever they had been, if that place could exist within those walls.

Whatever it was, this Daughter, it was surely destroying him. His right arm was singed and flinching, twitching as the thing grew hotter, as cracks in its shell split wide; but his other, his left arm was beating blood again, throbbing to an alien pulse and every pulse was pain.

Well. If it was a weapon, let it bite on others, not on him. He lifted his head and twisted his body, cocked his arm as best he could, ready to throw as far as he could manage. It was very light, but oh, he was hurting; he didn't expect to toss it any distance.

Didn't need to. There was stillness all about him, the swarming brothers had fallen back; even Fra' Piet and Rudel had stepped away from each other, snared first by his cry and now by what he held, what he was doing with it. Only one brother was moving, plunging right at him, and Marron tried to hurl the Daughter full into his face.

Tried, and failed. It uncurled in his hand even as he threw it, and though his fingers burned on the skin of it, somehow it still felt less solid than it had, as if that hard shell were dissolving; and inside it was nothing but smoke, red smoke that hung in the air and suggested something living, an animal, an insect, a monstrous breeding of the two.

Beyond it, the black-robed brother stood as still as any of them now, only staring.

It twisted in the air like smoke in a breeze, although there was none; it turned and changed, drifted back to Marron, wrapped itself around his dripping arm and seemed not to vanish but to slip through the sodden fabric of its bandaging, seek out his running wound and pour through into his body, against the current of his flowing blood.

Or so it seemed to Marron. He felt it as an alien heat, a wave; but as a creature too, mindless but sensate, a stranger making a habitation of his body. Its rhythms jarred with his as it hammered through his flesh, followed the paths of his bones, licked and learned him from his toes' ends to the inside of his skull. It curled around his heart, he thought, and for a moment, for an eyeblink it seemed to rest, almost to sleep.

Then it was living and moving again, stretching to all the limits of his skin; but this time pulsing to the beat of his own heart, strange still but no alien now, melded with him.

He gazed at the world with hot eyes and saw it smoky, shaded red.

And saw Aldo right there, the brother before him, stilled no longer; saw him raise his sword and swing it with a scream of disgust and horror and ultimate betrayal.

Too late to draw Dard, if he could even have managed to grip the hilt with his burned and blistering fingers, if he could have wielded the blade against a lifelong friend gone so suddenly to foe.

Really Marron wanted simply to stand and wait for the blow to fall; he had a moment to make his choice and that was it, to die here and now at Aldo's hand. It didn't seem so bad. Worse for Aldo, who must survive this and dwell on it later, have Marron's lingering ghost infest his soul, whispers of a bonding broken for such petty reasons . . .

But that was his mind's choice, and not his body's. Instinct flung his arm up against the blade, no more than that: a gesture that should have proved useless, a moment of further life bought with a scream.

He flung his arm up, and it was his left, his bandaged, blood-soaked arm; and from the dark dank mass of bandage came a thread, a wisp of crimson smoke that frayed and fell like a veil between him and the shining blade in its death-stroke.

Gossamer-thin it was, but he felt it like his own skin, almost, a new and further limit to his body. He felt when and where the sword met it; and there was no jar, no shock of contact—why would there be, when steel meets smoke?—but neither did the blade hew through to find and hack his own flesh. The haze sparkled and spat, Aldo

shrieked and dropped the hilt of his sword, which clat-
tered and spun on the floor between them; its blade was
gone, shattered, and Aldo's face was a horror, glinting
grey where a thousand splinters had pierced his skin.

Marron stared, saw the grey turn to red as blood began
to ooze, saw Aldo lift trembling hands to his blinded
eyes; and was almost relieved when that veil of smoke
moved to swathe his once-friend's head, seeming to
thicken as it went, making a mask that hid the sight from
him.

Almost relieved, he was, and only for a moment.

He couldn't see it, but he heard Aldo's choke, and had
a sudden dreadful picture of what might be happening
within the wreathing smoke, how it might be pouring
down Aldo's throat and filtering through all those tiny
punctures in his skin; for a heart's beat he thought he felt
Aldo's racing heart beating against his, all out of time
and desperate.

Then there was a soft implosive sound, and Aldo's
black habit ripped itself to rags and what had been inside
it, what had been Aldo was a dark wet mess, a spill of
blood and shreds of flesh flecked white with shards of
bone.

Marron sobbed, once, a deep tug of loss and guilt and
love betrayed that tugged at his gut but was only a gasp
in his throat, he had no voice to sound it; and then the
madness took him.

THE DAUGHTER, THE wraith of smoke that killed, hung
in the air before him; all around, people were stiff and
gaping. Perhaps predictably, Rudel recovered first. He
took one swift step forward, made one swift thrust, withdrew his sword cleanly. Blood followed the blade, and
Fra' Piet fell.

Blood was the token. Aldo's blood hung heavy in the
air, was rank in Marron's nostrils, a spray across his face;
he closed his eyes, took one hard breath, and howled.

His own blood surged like rampant fire in his veins. He burned, all weakness seared from him; he opened his eyes again, saw the brother nearest to Elisande —*Jubal*, his mind supplied the name and an image, a memory, Jubal on horseback with a mace, slaying and slaying— and he flung up his hand to point, to pick his target out.

The Daughter needed no such gesture; it was moving already, flying to engulf the hapless man. Jubal saw it coming, had just time enough to start a scream: a scream that was cut off suddenly, horribly, as the red skein cloaked him.

Again that quiet sound, again the slumping catastrophe of ruined flesh. Marron's eyes were already moving on, finding another face he knew, a name and some history his mind could supply; but his thoughts were all on death, and destruction followed his gaze.

VAGUELY HE WAS aware of sobs and pleading, of brothers on their knees hurling their swords away, of his own companions shouting his own name; but nothing reached him, nothing could touch him now. Blood was all he sought, and blood he found. The floor ran with it, soaking his boots and overflowing the drains and still there was not enough, there could never be enough blood to drown Aldo's voice or wash his face away.

IT WAS ELISANDE who halted him at the last, who seized his shoulders, shook him, slapped his face.

"Marron, enough! Stop this, *stop* it, you've done too much already . . ."

He stared at her and felt the Daughter come, knew how it loomed behind him. She must have seen it; there was terror in her eyes, but she said his name again though her voice trembled against her control, said, "Marron, it's finished now, the fight is over. Do you hear?"

Over? He didn't understand. There were still two,

three brothers living, penned in a stall there, he had names for them all; Rudel stood before them with his sword drawn, but it was Marron he was facing, his back turned to the black-robed men, and he added his own voice now.

"Marron, call it back. It is no longer needed. Take it into your body again, your blood will draw it."

Slowly, slowly he lifted his bleeding arm—no pain now and the muscles were his own again, but still the blood dripped endlessly from his fingers—and there was a swirl of hot red mist around it, a diminishing eddy to his eyes and a fierce flood within him, a doubled pulse that was all to the same beat, all one.

He watched his fingers, saw when the blood stopped coming.

"NO HORSES. THIS whole block is empty."

That was Redmond, stating what must have been obvious to anyone who could remember why they had come here. Horses would have been maddened by so much blood, kicking and screaming, filling the night with their terror.

Rudel looked round from where he knelt, tying the brothers throat to ankle, using their own girdles to do it. "There must be parties out looking for us; be glad they took all their mounts from here. These brothers will have been left to watch, I suppose, and tend the horses when they returned. We'll try another stable. Though it'll need the three of us," *us Surayonnaise* he must have meant, "to settle them, with the stink of this work on us all. Julianne, can you bring Marron?"

"I don't want to—"

"You must; above all, we can't leave him after this. Be easy, girl, he'll not harm you. Look at him, he couldn't even harm himself just now, which is something new for that boy. Follow us, but don't let him near the horses."

Marron needed no girl's arm to support him, all his

body throbbed with power and his mind was racing; but there was a gulf somehow, a broken bridge between the two, his will was missing. His ears followed the talk, but his eyes were still fixed on his fingers and what had dyed them; he carried Aldo and half the troop else on his skin, and their killer inside it. The Daughter, himself, no difference . . .

So it did after all take Julianne's tentative touch on his elbow to make him move, her hoarse and tear-stained whisper, "Marron, will you come?" to draw him to the doorway; where they found the others not gone ahead but strangely waiting, Rudel standing to one side, Redmond and Elisande the other.

THE REASON STOOD in the yard there, alone and deadly: Sieur Anton, sword in hand.

Rudel had snuffed out his witchlight before he opened the door, but the stars were enough to mark the knight, to name him. For Marron, one star would have been enough.

Julianne's fingers clenched on his arm, but no need. Whatever happened, he would not call the Daughter forth again, not this time. Not for this.

No more had Sieur Anton called the guard. If he knew what had happened in the stable, he gave no sign of it. He said only, "Forgive me, my lady, but I cannot allow you to leave. With my squire, or without him. Marron, come to me."

A moment of bitter hesitation, again a sense of irredeemable loss; then two soft words, the final disobedience. "No, sieur."

"Well. So be it. You, sir," and the sword picked out Rudel, who still carried his own weapon drawn, "will you lay down that blade?"

"I will not."

"Then I must take it from you."

"You must try, of course."

"May I know your name, before we begin?"

"You know it already, Sieur Anton. My name is Rudel."

"Truly?"

"Indeed. Shall we . . . ?"

Those polite manners hid the truth of it, but this would be a fight to the death. Marron thought someone should cry a warning, but there was only him to do it and he didn't know which man to warn. Both, he knew, could be lethal; the death of either one would be unbearable. He supposed he should hope for Rudel's victory, for the others' safety if not his own, but that must mean the knight's life and he could not, could not wish for that . . .

Neither did he have to. The two men approached each other cautiously, touched swords—and Sieur Anton swayed where he stood, lowered his point, lifted a hand to his head and fell without a sound beyond his sword's clattering on the cobbles.

Marron wanted to cry foul, to rush over and tend to his master, mourn his master if that were all that remained; but his body was still only tentatively his own, and when he made choices he made mistakes, people died. All he did was call weakly, "What have you done?"

"Not I, lad," Rudel answered. "Him," with a nod toward Redmond.

"Dishonourable, wasn't it?" the older man confessed, with the suspicion of a smile in his voice. "But we couldn't afford a duel, out here in the yard. There are guards on those walls, they'd have heard it and come running. Oh, don't worry, he's not dead. Not hurt, even. I could take him unawares, with his focus all on Rudel; he's little more than sleeping, though his dreams will be a sore puzzle to him."

"Enough now. Leave the knight; we need horses, and we need to be gone. Marron, you stay with Julianne, and keep out of sight; Elisande, Redmond, with me. You two, wait for my whistle."

*   *   *

THEY WAITED, HE and Julianne, standing against the
wall's darkness; he saw how she would not meet his eyes,
how her own moved incessantly, irresistibly back to the
black arch beyond which he'd practised his black art,
slaying and slaying for Aldo's sake, all of Aldo's brethren
to give him company before the God.

"Please," he whispered, "don't be afraid of me."

"Of you? I'm not. I'm afraid of *that*," with a nod towards and through the arch, meaning the Daughter. The
same thing, Marron thought, only she didn't think so, or
else she didn't understand. "So should you be."

Oh, I am, he thought, though it wasn't really true; how
could he fear something that beat to the rhythm of his
own heart, that shared his skin and his intent? He drew
breath to say so anyway, *oh, I am*, just to comfort her, but
she forestalled him.

"No, I'm wrong," she said flatly, "I am afraid of you.
Ignorance is always frightening, ignorance married to
power is terrifying; and you don't know what it is any
more than I do. Do you? You don't know what it can do,
or what you can do with it . . ."

No, of course he didn't. He had a stranger in his veins,
a clamorous, calamitous stranger; and there was nothing
he could say to comfort her, he thought perhaps there was
no comfort left in the world.

THEY WAITED, AND no one came. The guards must all
have been watching the shadows on the plains, listening
to the wind, the castle a surety at their back and the only
danger outside the walls.

They waited, silent now, no more to be said; and at last
they heard a soft, summoning whistle, and moved obediently at its command.

Another archway, with the faintest glimmer of witchlight within to guide them; they went through into another stable, this one warm with the presence, the smells
and sounds of horses.

There was the usual double rank of stalls, with a wide aisle between. In the aisle Rudel stood with two horses ready, saddled and harnessed. He had a hand hooked into each bridle and was murmuring quietly, soothingly as the big animals stirred and stamped. Behind him, Elisande and Redmond had charge of one horse each.

"There are five of us," Julianne said slowly.

"Marron cannot ride," Rudel told her.

"Yes, he can. I've seen him . . ." There was almost a smile in her voice as she said it, but puzzlement too, *of course he can ride, why not?*

"Not now. No horse would carry him."

Marron didn't understand any more than she did, but he saw how both Rudel's horses shifted, shying away from him even at this distance. He stepped back automatically into one of the empty stalls, to leave a clear path for them out of the stable; behind him, someone screamed.

He twisted round, startled, and saw a tiny creature cowering atop the wooden division of the stall, at the very extremity of its leash. Only a monkey, the trader's monkey that had loved him so much before: he chirruped at it, and it screamed the louder.

"It must be the smell of blood on you," Julianne said uncertainly.

"No," a voice came from the deeper shadows at the back of the stall. A woman's voice, thickly accented; straw rustled as she stood, and he recognised Baron Imber's truth-speaker as the light fell on her appalling face. "He is the Ghost Walker. I knew."

"What does that mean?" It was Julianne again who asked.

"It means fear and wonder, it means he is blessed and cursed; animals see it as I do, but they only see the cursing." She shuffled forward and touched his hand, straw in her hair and her eyes wide and white. "I knew," she said again.

Marron nodded. At his back he heard the passage of horses, and then Rudel's voice.

"Come, we must hurry. Julianne, I think we have landed lucky; this should be your own palfrey, by the harness we found with her."

"She is."

"Lead her, then, and follow me. I have mazed her, just a touch; the skill is effective on horses also. Marron, you must go in front. Woman, return to your dreams; you have not woken tonight, do you understand me?"

She snorted. "I am the baron's truth; me he believes." She turned and went back to her concealing shadows, pausing to touch the monkey into shivering stillness, its eyes dark pools still fixed on Marron. He sighed for another loss, and slipped away.

DOWN TOWARDS THE gate they went, down the slope of the tunnel and the steps beyond. Rudel would allow no lights here, for fear of shadows flying ahead to warn any watchers at the gate; Marron had to grope along the wall in darkness, his only guide the rag-muffled sound of hooves behind him growing louder to say when he was going too slowly.

The steps were easier; there was at least a slit of sky above him, a hint of starlight. He found then that he could see better than he'd expected to; perhaps it was only the change from utter black, but it seemed to him that there was a red cast to the world, as if the Daughter were lending him better eyes than his own.

A gentle hiss stilled him, on the bottom step. The gate lay just ahead, around a corner; he heard the horses halt, and Rudel joined him.

"This is your task, I regret, if the gates are closed," the man murmured in his ear. "We will mount now, and follow you. If they are open, then just run through; if not, you must break them down. Try not to kill, but unleash the Daughter."

"I don't know how . . ."

"I do. Give me your arm."

Your left arm, he meant. Rudel gripped it, pushed back the blood-soaked sleeve and cut the bindings away to expose sodden leather stitches and raw flesh. "I am sorry, Marron," he said, "I never meant that this should happen to you, but there is no escaping it now. I have you; I must use you."

And with that he unpicked the stitches with the point of his knife and slid the edge of it into and across the wound, not deeply, just enough to make it bleed again. There was no pain.

Smoke seethed up around the blade; Rudel squeezed Marron's shoulder, and pushed him lightly on.

HIS GOOD HAND gripping stone, the Daughter fogging the air in the corner of his eye—and the world gone darker, that red light lost to him—Marron peered around the corner. He saw torches and shifting shadows on the wall above the gate, and moving figures, men on guard; light also in the window of the gatehouse.

The gates were closed.

He took a breath and stepped out, glad at last of so much stain on his white tunic, making him only a small dark figure against a deeper darkness. He gazed at the gates, attacked them with his eyes, thinking nothing of their great weight or the massive bar that held them.

Where his eyes and his will went, there went the Daughter. He saw that thin smoke flow forward, felt the contact when it laid itself against wood and iron; flinched from the sudden cracking, snapping noises and the shooting sparks, and then stood gaping foolishly at the absence where the gates had been, the clear road beyond.

*   *   *

CRIES OF SHOCK, of fear; men running to and fro along the wall, all of them staring outward still, looking for danger where there was none.

At his back the rush of hooves; Rudel rounding the corner, his mount shying and screaming, almost throwing its rider as it backed in terror from Marron.

"Run, Marron! Run on . . . !"

And Marron ran. He plunged through the gate, just as a lone iron hinge fell with a crash from its shattered post; he sprinted down the hill, fearful of an arrow in the back, but none came. Only he thought he heard a voice cry his name, "Marron . . . !" and at the bend he chanced one glance over his shoulder, thought he saw a man in white standing solitary on the wall, staring after him.

Marron ran.

At first he ran alone; but soon the Daughter caught him, flowed back into his arm, filled his body with its strength and fire, gave its light to his eyes. Then he ran like a demon, he thought, faster than any horse would dare on this winding, perilous slope.

He had run like this with Mustar, wildly behind their cart, and ended in disaster. But Mustar was dead and Marron had become a thing that boy had feared, a devil perhaps; for sure he had a devil's luck tonight. His every footfall was firm and certain, he tasted the breeze and outran it; at the foot of the hill he waited, but he could have run on till dawn and after. He was all flame and smoke, he had forgotten what weariness was.

HE WAITED, AND eventually horses came: four horses, he saw and counted them from his distance as they followed the twists of the road above him. They came with more caution than speed, one led by another rider, Julianne he thought by Elisande; too slowly for his liking but fast enough, he couldn't see any pursuit yet however high he looked.

"Well done!" Rudel called, drawing his horse up some

little way away. Marron made no move to come closer. "Now we must ride. North and east. Can you run?"

Marron ran.

DAYLIGHT FOUND THEM resting in a gully below a cliff, where the horses had sniffed out water: a muddy pool fed by a spring hidden deep in the rock, where it could escape the season's drought.

Marron stood by the cleft that had given them entrance, gazing out over the baked land. He needed no rest, nor the warmth of their little fire; neither the warmth of their company.

He could hear their talk, though, his ears as sharp suddenly as his eyes were sharper; and he listened, because they were speaking about him.

". . . Why are his eyes red?"

No answer. She knew the answer. They were not his eyes.

"What is the Daughter?" Julianne again, this time in a different voice: exhausted but determined she sounded, demanding true and clear answers.

"The Daughter is a key, and a door." It was Redmond who replied, his voice faint but his spirit renewed by flight. "It leads to that same other world to which the tower holds a bridge. The bridge may be barred, but nothing can bar the Daughter."

"But, it destroys things, it killed all those men . . ."

"Used properly, used fully, it will tear open a doorway from world to world; used only partially or in ignorance, it simply tears where it touches. Marron knows nothing."

"That's why you called it a weapon?"

"No. Used properly, used fully, it could bring a thousand, ten thousand men marching into Surayon. *That's* why we call it a weapon; that's why we dared not leave it where it was. There are voices all across the Kingdom, crying war on Surayon. Fulke is response, not cause; but how if Fulke had found it?"

"Is it alive?"

"Not truly, or not alone. It has some mockery of life; but it enters a man and melds with him, and then, yes, it has his life and purpose, as he has its strength and powers. Which is why we dare not let the Order have Marron now, why we must take him out of Outremer altogether. The King called it his daughter because it marries itself to a man, and he meant to make that marriage. A bad joke, but a good marriage: it cannot be broken until the man is dead. The Sharai call him the Ghost Walker; traditionally, he is very hard to kill."

"We were going to the Sharai," Elisande, muttering.

"As Marron must, I think," Rudel, "to learn what it is that he has now, what he has become. I cannot teach him. Why were you going to the Sharai, Elisande?"

"Because the djinni sent us."

"What? What djinni?"

"Wait." Julianne again, interrupting sharply. "We will tell you, but I want to know one more thing first. Who *are* you? Both of you? Not your names, I believe your names, but I am tired of your secrets."

"Very well, then," Rudel answered her softly, just as Marron spotted a blur of dust at the limit of his sight and a dark shadow within it, someone coming this way, a single man afoot. "I am the son of the Princip of Surayon."

Marron could even hear Julianne's gasp, so acute his hearing was.

She recovered quickly, though. "And you, Elisande?"

"I? Oh, I am the granddaughter of the Princip of Surayon. I told you, he's a lovely man, you must meet—"

"Stop. Wait. You the granddaughter, he the son? What are you two to each other?"

"He's my father," said coldly, and with such bitterness to it.